The BAREFOOT SERENADE

the WAVE TAMER

-Book 2-

BRANDON OSWALD

Publish Authority

For Devin

"I live at the edge of the universe, like everybody else. "

   - Bill Manhire

Editor: Janie Mills
Cover Design Lead: Raeghan Rebstock
Interior Design: Teresa Evans

ISBN 978-1-967213–08-5 (Paperback)
ISBN 978-1–967213-09-2 (eBook)

Published 2025 by Publish Authority,
300 Colonial Center Parkway, Suite 100
Roswell, GA, USA
PublishAuthority.com

Printed in the United States of America

onin Blue awoke early in his *fale* on an already sweltering morning. Sunbeams streamed through the blinds, projecting dust and sand, and even spilled through the mosquito net, warming his mostly naked body. He sat up, hoping to escape the scintillating, sunrays and called out for his Samoan girlfriend, Aumua Tuputala. Signs that she had moved in with him for the past several months were evident throughout the *fale*: there were new furnishings, such as a small dresser and a chest, a few mats, a clothesline with a couple of dresses, *lavalavas,* and T-shirts hanging from it, a large *siapo*, which actually added some color to the place, and a crucifix that hung on a pole facing his mattress. The crucifix made Blue uncomfortable, particularly when he was making love with Aumua. He often moved it to another pole in the *fale*, but it always found its way back to its original place. He wondered if the crucifix's movement was some kind of divine intervention because he never witnessed Aumua moving it back to the pole near their bed.

Blue quickly wrapped a *lavalava* around his waist and went to a washbowl on the dresser where he washed his face and brushed his teeth. After this, he picked up the bowl and tossed the water outside. Although it was difficult to see through the village, he got a feeling that something was happening at the Tuputala *fale*.

He then donned a tattered T-shirt that was cool and comfortable (that clashed with his *lavalava*), packed his computer in his backpack, and zoomed out of the *fale* into the sun's death rays. As it was still the rainy season, he hoped a shower would come sooner than later to cool off the earth and himself.

Along the road to the Tuputala's residence, Blue's dogs came springing by him, greeting him a good morning before vaulting each other towards the beach to see what the morning fishermen had left behind. Since Aumua had moved into the *fale*, the dogs, sadly, had to move out. But Blue was able to negotiate a compromise that if it was storming, the dogs would be able to take shelter in the *fale*. To Blue, however, a drop of rain constituted a storm, and the hounds often merrily made themselves at home.

Blue stopped at the Tuputala's, where he saw Aumua lying on a specially made mat and Maeva sitting next to her. Aumua was in the process of finishing her *malu*, or tattoo, that would cover the upper thigh to her lower knee. Traditionally, only the daughter of the high chief received the *malu*. This beauty enhancement opportunity was quite rare, given to only a select few women who ranked high enough. Nowadays, however, it was much more common is questionable. I hate to say it, but it looks like you went native just like Miles Coach. I warned you not to go native."

"What does that mean?"

"It means that they will use you until you have nothing left. Then, like Miles Coach, you will run naked into the bush."

"Who are they? Using what?"

"Take my advice, Mr. Blue, return home as soon as possible. Good day."

Lola moved to the door as Fiame re-entered.

"We'll be in touch," Lola said to Fiame and left the room.

Blue, who was a little embarrassed at the situation, couldn't look at the principal. However, he was inclined to speak first.

"I'm sorry, Fiame. I shoulda spoke up months ago. I guess I didn't think it was all that important to force reading English on the students."

"Tell me, Mr. Blue, do you think of this village as your home?"

"It's my home away from home."

"Do you consider yourself like one of the villagers?"

Blue quickly grew tired of the questions, so he threw it back at Fiame.

"Does the village think of me as one of their own?"

"We always try to make the most out of our volunteers. Sometimes, we feel like they stay too long. It's hard to be away from family and friends and live in a strange place you're not accustomed to."

Blue looked at her. He knew that she didn't answer the question.

"Like Miles Coach?"

and there were more and more women of all ages getting it done.

The design of the *malu* upon Aumua's thigh was in tradition with her family. Indeed, the word *malu* would translate to mean protect, shelter, or security. The *tatau* was a representation of her matriarchal ancestors, symbolizing the strength and resilience of the woman, while paying tribute to her mother and grandmother. Her body was being used as a canvas where ancestral knowledge was being passed down to the next generation. It was a special moment for Aumua, who would now be expected to perform key ceremony tasks and represent her village during ceremonial occasions. The *malu* also carried more duties and more expectations to serve the family and village.

It took a few people to create the *tataus*. The village traditional healer, Taaiti, was making the dyes by burning candlenuts over a fire and then collecting the soot in a coconut shell. Once she collected the desired amount of soot, she mixed it with sugar water. Taaiti's two sons were the *tafugas*, or tattoo artists. They used traditional tools to poke, stamp, and pierce Aumua's thigh.

Although Aumua was in some pain, it was a proud discomfort full of *mana*. With each tap and poke of the skin, she felt the strength and spirit of her ancestors.

Blue winced at the sight of the blotted blood. But he also knew that a ceremony like this would bring forth a feast, which would probably take place tomorrow. He already anticipated the smell of the *umu*.

"You're next, Mr. Ronin," Maeva said in Samoan. "We start with your tongue."

Everyone laughed. Even Aumua cracked a smile at her best friend's joke.

"Show me a man with a tattoo, and I'll show you a man with an interesting past," Blue quoted in English. "Uh... Jack London."

"She's a woman," Maeva reminded Blue in Samoan. She never liked speaking English to Blue. Thus, Blue would respond as best he could in Samoan for the rest of the conversation.

"Right."

"Does she not have an interesting past?"

"It's just a quote. Man or woman—it's understood."

Actually, Blue had no idea what Aumua's past was like, but he wished he never said anything.

"What kind of tattoo would you get, Mr. Ronin?" Maeva asked. "Shark teeth?"

Everyone laughed.

"Leave him alone," Aumua said, defending her man.

"I don't think I'm Samoan enough to get a tattoo," Blue responded in broken Samoan.

"Only when you talk like a two-year-old," Maeva playfully said.

Everyone laughed.

Blue quickly grew tired of Maeva's sass. Her remark stung him because he believed that his Samoan was getting much better. But whenever Maeva got a chance to ridicule him, she never wasted the opportunity. Her jibes got even worse when she enrolled at the University of South Pacific, Apia's campus, earlier in the year, and she had to make up for lost opportunities to make fun of Blue because she was away at school. Blue appreciated that she wasn't with

Aumua as often as she used to be, and he rather liked the respite from her facetiousness and derisive tone. Plus, when Maeva was away at university, it meant that she wasn't hanging around his *fale*.

If Maeva's brazenness wasn't enough for Blue now, Lance Lafau then appeared out of the shadows of the *fale*, walked to Aumua, and stood over her. He stared at Blue with a smirk.

Blue hadn't forgotten about the beating he suffered from Lance and his thugs in an Apia alley. He returned a vengeful glare like a boxer who endured a cheap shot.

"Haven't you seen you in a while, Lance?" Blue said in English.

"I didn't want to miss Aumua's ceremony." Lance would never speak Samoan to Blue.

"Where's your bandana-head buddy from Apia?"

"I don't know what you're talking about."

"You know the dude you pick people's pockets with like some street rat."

Lance moved aggressively forward to the edge of the *fale*.

"A *palagi* would never understand what I do," Lance sneered.

"Hey, Al Capone just called, and he wants his goons back."

Nobody laughed.

"What are you talking about?" Lance asked.

"I mean, you just look guilty, dude," Blue exclaimed.

"And look at you. You look like you sleep with dogs," Lance said venomously in Samoan and spat at the volunteer.

Everyone laughed except Aumua, who leaned forward and signaled the artist to stop his tattooing.

"Pardon me, but I have been sleeping with Aumua," Blue rebutted in Samoan.

An uncomfortable hush came over the crowd. Aumua was embarrassed. Maeva was appalled. Lance was stung.

Blue couldn't believe he blurted that out. But by everyone's reaction, he was pleased that he said it in perfect Samoan.

"You know, it's not customary for a *palagi* to be here during this time of tattoo," Lance stated. Blue wondered if he made that up.

"You should go to school, or you'll be late," Aumua told Blue, turning her head away from him. Blue hated her tone, which sounded as if she agreed with Lance.

However, the tattoo would take the rest of the day to complete. Despite the comment of a *palagi* being around, it also seemed obvious to Blue that she didn't want him watching her grimace and gasp in pain with each stinging jab of the tapping stick.

Blue kissed Aumua on the top of her head. He could hear Lance growl.

"I'll see you later."

"She'll have to stay here tonight," Lance said.

"You won't, Ronin," Aumua said, agreeing once again with Lance. "I'll see you at the ceremony tomorrow."

Blue stared at the two for a beat. He questioned whether Aumua was upset with him or was happy that Lance had returned to the village. Either way, he felt as if he was being pushed aside.

"Not all the monsters have fangs," Blue blurted, looking at Lance and Maeva. "Also, London."

As Blue turned away, he could hear Maeva asking the

others in Samoan what Blue was talking about, but he didn't care. They could gossip about him all they wanted. He was glad that he got the last word in.

Walking away, he saw Father Krimple and Iris heading towards the *fale*. The priest was carrying a mat, while Togi's woman, Iris, had her youngest son, Keanu, in one arm and two plates of food in the other. The two plates held fruit- mostly papaya, mango, and banana- and the other plate was piled high with *panikeke*, which were golden brown balls and known for being Samoan-style pancakes. A satchel was also slung across Iris' shoulder that probably contained the different jams to serve with the pancakes.

"Ronin. How's your girlfriend doing?" Father Krimple asked.

The word "girlfriend" caught Blue by surprise. They never really used that term in the village, and perhaps throughout Samoa. To Blue, the term seemed very Western. But since it was a Canadian asking an American, Blue let it slide.

"She's a trooper, Father K. I don't think I could handle that much pain."

"Ah, Samoan women have a high tolerance for pain. It's quite exemplary."

"We can give birth in a *fale*," Iris added.

"I got queasy just watching them," Blue admitted.

"Go on, it's a big occasion. You should be proud of her."

Blue found the priest's enthusiasm a bit odd. He knew that the missionaries tried to stamp out the art of the *tatau* throughout the Pacific Islands, particularly because of the partying or ceremonies that were associated with someone getting a tattoo. Many missionaries simply considered the art as a savage and heathen practice. On the other hand, the Catholic priests who arrived in Samoa in 1845 believed the practice of tattooing wasn't religious and, thus, didn't think it was much of a threat to their teachings.

Nevertheless, it was chiefs and individuals who encouraged the villagers to continue the practice through living the *Fa'a Samoa* way. They believed that tattoos were a way to advertise or emphasize one's identity and allow certain privileges for the one getting the tattoo. As the Samoans generally adopted Christianity, they were able to hold on to their *tatau* practice. Nowadays, it was typically a priest or preacher who initiated the tattooing process by approving and consecrating the place where it would happen.

"What do you have there?" Blue asked, pointing to the mat under Father Krimple's arm.

"I made this mat for Aumua."

Blue was impressed that the priest knew how to make a mat. He remembered how important gifts were, especially during these kinds of occasions, and felt guilty that he didn't have anything to give Aumua.

"I'm sure she'll sleep on it tonight," Blue added with a little spite in his tone.

"You know, Ronin, you should come to Mass with Aumua now that... you know, that you're together."

Blue rolled his eyes. This was another attempt by the priest to convince him to attend church. In fact, Blue had been trying to avoid running into the priest the past couple of months in fear of hearing a lecture about living together with Aumua without being married. He knew that the priest would like to see more marriages and less traditional marriages take place in the village. Ironically, Iris and Togi hadn't yet married in the church, and Blue wondered if Father Krimple was trying to moralize both of his current companions.

"Oh, yeah, maybe…"

"After all, Aumua's there every Sunday," the priest said.

"She sings beautifully with the choir," Iris expressed.

The only way I'm going to church is if a giant wave carries me in.

"I better get to school. I'm late as it is," Blue said in Samoan.

"Go on."

Blue knew that Iris made the best *panikeke* in the village, and he took advantage of Iris's hands being full and took a couple of the pancakes off the plate.

"Oh! Mr. Ronin, those aren't for you."

"*Faafetai lava*, Iris."

Blue also grabbed a couple of pieces of the papaya before rushing off to the school. Iris watched him leave with some disgust.

"What kind of manners was that?" Iris asked Father Krimple. "He's spending too much time with Togi."

Blue's classroom was much different from when he arrived. The cobwebs and the windows were cleaned. The boxes and the broken student desks were removed, which then provided enough space for a few functioning student desks. The crucifix was straightened, and the calendar was replaced with one of the current year. Even a small wooden desk was placed in the room for him. Although the ceiling fan still did not work, Blue had bought a standing fan while in Apia and lugged it home on the bus.

After a year, students refrained from coming into his room for reading lessons. They still didn't come at the start of a new term. But the room wasn't devoid of students every day. On the contrary, his room was used quite frequently by girls looking for a place to practice dancing or boys playing restricted gambling and card games away from prying teachers' eyes. Both boys and girls would use the space to make cultural items and arts and crafts for school. Sometimes, teachers, such as Vaveao Suisala, would come in to hang out and complain about their spouses or spill the gossip of the day. Blue never minded these interruptions, particularly when he was writing his book and was stuck on a scene or passage.

When Blue arrived, he went through his morning ritual of turning on the fan and opening the windows to get as much air flowing as possible. He placed the *panikeke* and the papaya on his desk and opened his backpack to take out his computer. He sat down and anticipated a good day's worth of writing. He felt good that he would get a lot done today.

The feeling was short-lived as Togi burst through the door.

"Bro, let's go practice the *Manu Siva Tau*," Togi said with enthusiasm. "The rugby match is tomorrow."

"Dude, it's too hot for that. Besides, I really don't want to play rugby."

It wasn't long before Togi had sniffed out the food on Blue's desk and helped himself.

"You got the chant down?"

"Yeah. *Samoa! Tatou e tau le taua! Tau e matua tau!...* Hey, don't eat my breakfast."

"Did Iris make these?"

"Yeah."

"Why didn't she give me any?"

"I don't know. She brought them for your sister, who's getting a *tatau*."

"Right. There'll be a ceremony tomorrow. More food, bro."

"Before or after the rugby match?"

"After. The match is at 1 p.m."

Togi sat on top of a desk. Blue winced at the thought of his friend's massive frame squashing the desk like a shoe flattening a bug.

"Are you sure *palagis* are even allowed to play?"

"*Ioe*, bro. Father K plays every year. You'll be on his team. That's why you gotta learn the *Siva Tau* because he knows it really well."

Togi took out a rolled cigarette and lit it. Blue knew instantly that it was a joint. Togi puffed and exhaled.

"Dude, smoke that shit at your house."

"No way, bro, you know Iris would kill me," Togi stated. "You wanna hit?"

"No. This is a Catholic school, dude. All right, just one punch."

Togi smiled and handed the joint to the volunteer. Blue sucked it and coughed.

"Whoa, that's strong stuff."

Blue took another hit. He felt like a high school kid smoking in the boy's toilet.

A knock at the door came loud and strong. Blue quickly handed the joint to Togi and stood up. Togi hopped off the desk and didn't know what to do with the joint. He put it out on the desk and then tossed it out the window as the door to the room opened. The two flapped their arms, trying to help dissipate the odor.

The school's principal, Fiame, entered with the Helping Hands Volunteer Organization administrator, Lola, who was, once again, pregnant. The scent of marijuana hit them both. It didn't seem to bother Fiame, but Lola sure smelled something off and gave a quick glance around the room to see if she could find the source. When she didn't see anything, she turned her attention back to the volunteer.

"*Talofa*, Mr. Blue," Lola said, scrutinizing Blue's appearance.

"Mr. *Lanu Moana*," Blue answered. "That's what the kids call me."

"Oh. Well, it's time for your Helping Hands annual review. I apologize for being a few months late."

"I didn't even know there was an annual review."

"Yes... I can see."

"We can meet in my office," Fiame said, holding the door open.

"I was leaving. You can stay here," Togi said in Samoan. As he left the room, he patted Blue on the back, which felt like a bear's claw smacking him.

"Is that weed I smell?" Lola asked.

"Oh, uh, I think it's some kind of plant outside. I know, it smells like pot to me, too," Blue lied.

Damn it, Togi.

Blue was hoping that Lola would simply leave it at that, but she didn't.

"Oh, I've been living here for the past seven years, and I never heard of a plant like that in Samoa before."

Blue knew better than to ask a woman if she were

pregnant, but he was desperate to change the subject and had no other choice.

"Wait a minute. Is that the same baby as when I first met you?"

Lola laughed.

"Heavens no. I met you over a year ago. This is a new baby."

"No way. How many does that make now?

"This will be my fourth."

Fiame grew a little impatient. After all, she had a school to run.

"Have a seat, Mr. Ronin," Fiame softly commanded.

Blue sat at his desk as Fiame leaned against one of the student desks. Lola preferred to remain standing. She also acted as if she didn't want to stay long …

"Mr. Blue, recent reading scores from this school are quite alarming."

"Reading scores?"

Lola pulled out a folder of papers from her tote. It was the same bottomless bag that she used when Blue first met her that seemed to have everything she needed, including a kitchen sink. Lola plopped the papers on the desk in front of him.

"Yes, we typically assess the students annually," Fiame stated.

"In every category," Lola added.

"Category?"

"I'll be blunt, Mr. Blue. We're concerned that the children here are not getting the reading instruction that is required for adequate assessment marks," Lola said. "As your program director, I've been given the task of investigating your curriculum. You ticked a lot of boxes."

"What boxes?"

"On our evaluation form."

"Tell me, Mr. Ronin, what are your teaching methods?" Fiame asked.

"We, uh... we follow the program book..."

"Did you know that new books were issued at the beginning of the year?" Lola interrupted. "We sent you an email to come get them. You never picked them up."

Damn me.

"I... I didn't know."

"Have you been teaching reading in this school, Mr. Blue?" Lola sternly asked.

Blue took a deep breath. He decided that it wasn't worth pretending any longer.

"The children never came, and if they did, it wasn't to read."

"What have you been doing for a year and a half?"

"He has been a big help around the school and church," Fiame interjected.

Blue thought that it was a nice gesture for Fiame to speak for him. Blue felt that Lola's objective, however, was already decided before she came to Vaimasina.

"I'm sorry, Mr. Blue, our contract stated that you were accepted into our program to teach reading, which you obviously have failed to do. Thus, the Helping Hands organization has no choice but to release you from your contract. You may return home at your earliest convenience. If you need it, we can arrange your air transport."

"That won't be necessary."

The atmosphere in the room suddenly grew more intense, and the heat started to rise. Blue could feel sweat beginning to form on several areas of his body.

"Typically, we are instructed to escort a volunteer to the airport in the event of a work termination."

"I told you. It won't be necessary," Blue reiterated.

Blue couldn't believe that he got fired from a volunteer job. But it was the disappointment in Fiame's eyes that truly crushed the volunteer. She tried again to rectify the situation.

"I feel this was my fault for not supervising more closely. Couldn't we start again with an entirely new program?"

"I'm afraid the organization is currently looking for a replacement."

It was at this time that a strange man opened the door and poked his head into the room. Everyone looked at him. He squinted at the group. Blue thought the man looked familiar, but couldn't place him. Nonetheless, the small distraction was perfect timing to calm the brewing storm in the classroom.

"Can I help you?" Fiame asked the man in Samoan.

"*Fa'amagalo mai a'u,*" the man answered. "Pardon me." He closed the door.

"I will see who he is," Fiame said and left the room.

Lola packed the folder of papers in her bag.

"Well, I must head back to the office. I'm sorry, Mr. Blue, that we have to part ways like this."

"I'm sure I'm not the first one to get let go."

"Actually, you are."

"Oh."

"You ticked a lot of boxes, Mr. Blue. Even your demeanor

"Miles was on drugs that he brought with him. Add unrequited love with one of the village girls, and he couldn't make good decisions. It was a real shame. We liked Miles."

"Sounds like a F. Scott Fitzgerald story."

"Do you think you've stayed too long?"

"Fiame, it was a question of my work integrity with Helping Hands, not if I like living here. I love Vaimasina."

Blue wondered if that was true, especially the way he was treated at the Tuputala's *fale* earlier by Aumua, Maeva, and Lance.

"I'm glad to hear that. By the way, that man who was just here is Saitele, a piano fixer from Apia. I told him where he could find the piano in the church."

"Oh, right! Can you do me a favor? Can I bring him to *Sa* tonight? I promised him food as part payment for helping with the piano."

"Yes, of course."

"*Faafatei.*"

Blue was relieved to use Saitele's arrival to leave the room in a rush as if the piano tuner was on the top of his "things to do" list.

As he left, Blue knew it would be just a matter of time before the entire village knew of his sacking. The villagers wouldn't care that much about Blue losing the school job. Most of them hardly had paying jobs themselves anyway. But without a doubt, they would question and start rumors about how long the volunteer would remain in the village.

Blue found Saitele in the balcony of the church, already at work on the piano. A black bag of tools sat on the piano bench. The piano tuner wore a *lavalava*, a flower-printed collared shirt, and sandals. His *lavalava* hardly fit his skinny frame, and he often had to pause his work to adjust it.

"You finally made it," Blue said in Samoan.

Only six months later.

"I busy," Saitele answered in English.

"Busy tuning pianos?"

"*Ioe*, and playing."

"Are there that many pianos in Apia that need tuning?"

"*Leai*, but all churches on Upolu have pianos. They need tuning and playing."

Blue thought how true this was. In fact, Christianity, which arrived in the Samoan islands in 1830, would boast of having approximately 97 percent of the population who identified themselves as being in one of Samoa's Christian denominations. There seemed to be a church or two in every village and on every corner of Apia. Indeed, religion was sacred. On Sundays, everything was closed, and the day was considered as a day of rest and worship. Unless an *aiga* in the village had a *toonai*, Sundays were calm and quiet writing days for Blue.

Saitele stopped to shift his *lavalava*.

"Three hundred forty-five *tala* to do job."

"I thought we agreed on three hundred."

"*Leai*. Old piano. Very difficult. Three hundred and forty-five."

Before Blue could rebut the price, Saitele had crawled head and shoulders first into the top of the piano like a hobo looking for his lunch in a trash bin. A muffled voice came from inside the piano.

"What?" Blue asked.

The muffled voice spoke again.

"I'm sorry. What?"

Saitele lifted his head partially out of the piano.

"Three hundred and forty-five and a meal."

That evening, Blue returned to his *fale* from Fiame's dinner earlier than usual. His stomach wasn't feeling right, and he wondered if it was something he ate, or the heat, or both. Typically, it was both. He brought his dogs some leftovers, which they consumed gleefully without any complaints. Blue then lay down on his cushioned mat, hoping that sleep would comfort and ease the fire that was infusing in his belly. Unfortunately, the sleep never helped, and he wondered which end his dinner would eventually exit.

As he tried to sleep, he felt queasy thinking about the mounds of food that Saitele ate at Fiame's dinner. It was extraordinary. Where was he putting all that food? He thought that the piano tuner had two hollow legs or something. The man ate plate after plate, finishing off every item by licking his fingers. It grossed Blue out. In fact, that was one of the customary things that Blue could never do— eat with his hands. It always unsettled him watching others eat with their fingers. But watching Saitele manhandle his food and stuff his face to the point where juices ran down the sides of his chin was too overwhelming. He wanted so badly to hand the piano tuner a napkin. When Blue bid his farewells for the evening to Fiame and other members of the *aiga* (not Lance), Saitele even tried to buy Blue's leftovers for the dogs.

A swiftly moving rainstorm pushed the heat of the night away and dragged in the humidity. But it wasn't long until the rain traveled to the ocean and the heat lugged itself back to join the humidity. Together, they made an impressive yet oppressive team that Blue hated to face. He turned his fan on high—a temporary reprieve. The overbearing atmospheric team was patient and waited just beyond the airflow of the fan.

Blue also tossed and turned, asking himself whether to stay or leave Samoa. Had his time on the island run its course? He didn't feel like returning to his home in San Diego County, plus he wasn't even halfway done with his novel. But what would he do here? Could he leave Aumua? His mind addled with the pros and cons of going home. Besides missing his Aunt Ophelia and air-conditioning, he really didn't have anything waiting for him there—well, except, perhaps, his girlfriend or fiancé, Harper.

Blue then pondered a little about Harper, who should be moving along in her law degree and getting closer to finishing. Would she actually wait for him? Could he truly marry her? No. He was in love with Aumua now. Harper's emails to him had died down over the past several months, and he wondered if she had started seeing someone else. Blue chuckled, which hurt his tummy. He knew that Harper never really needed to go out of her way to "see anyone," as they typically attached themselves to her like flies on fruit.

Perhaps it was a fever dream that made him doze on and off throughout the night. He dreamt of all kinds of weird and fleeting vignettes that made little sense. Although most of these bizarre scenes moved rapidly to the next, there was one odd snippet that seemed to linger: Blue was racing naked with Miles Coach along the grassy field, and he was hoping to reach Aumua at a finish line first, just beyond the *fale tele*. A small group of villagers were dancing the *Siva*

Tau. As he was nearing Aumua at the finish line, Miles Coach swerved and headed for the jungle, never to be seen again. Blue made it to Aumua and fretted about being disqualified because he was naked. It was Harper, however, who was holding up tattoo tools and teasing the volunteer that the first tattoo would be completed upon his penis.

Blue awoke in a sweat and turned on his side.

The pain in his stomach was still percolating. He had experienced these kinds of nights a few times since his arrival to Samoa, and each one never ended well. He farted, which gave him quick relief.

He had a hard time falling back asleep. The thought of Harper crept back into his muddled thoughts, and he wondered if another reason why he came to Samoa was to get away from her.

Blue couldn't help but recall the night when he told Harper that he was leaving for Samoa. It was a chilly December night at a kitschy, insipid, and overpriced beachfront restaurant in Encinitas, where the ersatz and trendy wannabes hunkered at tables underneath patio heating lamps. It was called The Galley, and Blue didn't want to be there. However, it was Harper's favorite restaurant where she liked to hang out with friends on the patio and watch surfers, tourists, and other passersby strolling along the beach. It never ceased to amaze Blue how she would know at least a half dozen of these sand dwellers who would come immediately when she called their names.

On this particular night, Harper's two best friends, Myna and Cherry, were dining with them, which made the evening even more unbearable for Blue. Cherry was as much of a talker as Harper, and Myna simply agreed with everything they said. When the three were together, they seemed to talk about the most asinine topics. Blue couldn't help but call the trio the gorgons.

"The cute barista wrote my name wrong on the cup," Cherry said excitedly. "He wrote, Sherry, not Cherry. Do I look like a Sherry?"

"Not even," Myna answered.

"I was, like, so livid. I told him my name is Cherry. He apologized."

"He apologized," Myna repeated.

"I'm, like, so sick and tired of them messing up my name. I think we should make up Starbuck names," Harper said.

"For sure, Starbuck names," Myna added.

"Get this. I told the cute barista that the next time I wasn't going to use a name and instead I would give him my number," Cherry divulged.

"You didn't?! Harper stated with a gasp.

"Your number. Cool," Myna replied.

"What did he say?" Harper asked impatiently.

"Yeah, what did he say?" Myna repeated.

Cherry leaned closer to the others.

"Okay, so, he was, like—well, why don't you give it to me now, and I'll memorize it for the next time, and he handed me a cup!"

Harper and Myna screeched.

Blue sighed.

Damn me.

"Cherry, you're a maniac!" Harper exclaimed.

"A maniac, for sure," Myna replied.

"That's so hot," Harper added.

"So hot," Myna agreed.

"So, did you write your number on the cup?" Harper asked.

"Hell, yeah, I did and surrounded it with hearts!"

They all screeched.

Oh my God.

"Wait. Wait. My Charlie Brown wanted to tell me something special," Harper stated, hoping it would be as good as Cherry's story. "That's why we're here tonight."

Cherry and Myna practically forgot that Blue was sitting with them. They turned to stare at him, which made him feel uncomfortable.

"I, uh, it can wait for another time," Blue stammered. He naively thought that Harper and he would be alone at dinner, and he would break the news of his leaving for Samoa to her. He should've known better because being alone with her rarely happened.

"He wants to ask you to marry him!" Cherry blurted.

The girls screeched.

"I accept my wishy-washy Brownie," Harper teased. "I finally have a fiancé."

The girls laughed. Blue still thought that Harper's snort was endearing.

"Wait. Does he even have a job?" Cherry asked.

"He's a writer. He's working on a novel. Tell 'em what your novel's about."

"Oh, uh ... it's an adventure story about forsaken lovers who meet amid a disaster on a boat."

"Like *Titanic*!" Cherry uttered.

"I love that movie," Harper said.

"I love Leo DiCaprio. He has dreamy eyes," Cherry stated.

"So dreamy," Myna repeated.

"It's so cool being a writer. Easier than being in law school," Harper expressed. "I should've been a writer. My short stories got better grades than his when we had a fiction class together."

They all laughed. Blue's face blushed with embarrassment. Perhaps now would be a good time, after all, to tell Harper the special news.

"I'm going to Samoa," Blue called out.

"Where?" Cherry asked in a confused tone.

"To do what?" Harper asked.

"Whatever they need me to do," Blue answered.

"Whose they?"

"The Helping Hands Volunteer Organization."

"What's a Samoa?" Myna questioned.

"It's an island in the South Pacific," Blue responded.

"Samoa," Harper thought, "Oh, there's a surfer from Carlsbad whose name is Samoa."

"That's right!" Cherry exclaimed. "He's a total dweeb from, like, Texas who thinks he can surf."

"Total dweeb," Myna added.

"I didn't know his name was an actual place," Harper said.

"So lame," Cherry declared.

"Totally lame," Myna agreed.

"You know all that sun is, like, bad for you," Cherry stated to Blue.

"Yeah, bad for your complexion," Myna concurred.

Blue glared at Cherry. He thought that for someone who fried her skin in a tanning salon three times a week and looked like a discolored raccoon, he couldn't believe her audacity.

"How long will you be gone?" Harper asked.

"Two years."

"That's a long time."

"They need volunteers."

"Eww, I hate volunteering," Cherry said. "Everyone's so needy."

"So needy," Myna added.

There was an awkward pause.

"Well, looks like my Charlie Brown is an Indiana Jones," Harper said with a desultory smile. "Who knew?"

"Indian Jones is way cooler than Charlie Brown," Cherry said.

"Way cooler," Myna repeated.

"I'll miss my wishy-washy fiancé," Harper teased. "We'll have to spend every moment together from now until you leave."

"Are you two really engaged?" Cherry asked.

"We should be. Right, Charlie Brown?"

Harper kissed Blue on the lips, which excited him very much. As a heterosexual young man with a very attractive girlfriend, he was hoping that his forthcoming absence would ignite at least one, or maybe two, passionate moments that would lead to sex with her.

But it didn't happen.

After the night at the restaurant, Harper turned her attention to finals week in her first semester of law school.

Then, she flew to Cabo with her family, where they spent Christmas and most of her winter break. By the time she returned, he had left for Samoa.

Blue awoke late in the morning and rushed out of his *fale* to the outhouse. The bad case of diarrhea proved to be a momentary relief for the pain that was brewing in his stomach all night. When he returned to his *fale*, he guzzled a bottle of water that went right through him, and he ended up rushing back to the outhouse.

He dozed on and off but awoke when he heard drumming coming from the *fale tele*. He knew it was for Aumua and wished he could be there for her ceremony. He hated that he would be missing Aumua dancing the *taualuga*, which was a graceful solo dance that would not only display her *malu*, but it would also serve as a showpiece to honor and celebrate her father. Indeed, the *taualuga* was considered the zenith of Samoan performance art form and the centerpiece Samoan culture. It was often performed as the grand finale at significant ceremonies. Aumua had been practicing her dance for many months before she received her *malu*, and there was no doubt that she would be called upon to perform it during future events.

When the drumming stopped, Blue fell asleep for another couple of hours, only to be awoken by Togi, who was wearing a blue Manu Samoa rugby jersey. Blue groggily opened his eyes and looked at his blurry friend. Before Togi could say anything, the volunteer quickly stood and flew out of the *fale* towards the outhouse.

Togi followed Blue and leaned against the outhouse, waiting for his friend to emerge. He was holding an older rugby shirt. After a few minutes listening to Blue moan, Togi impatiently banged his head against the outhouse.

"Bro, it's game time," Togi said.

"I can't play, man. My stomach's like a burning cauldron."

"You gotta play."

"It's a crucible," Blue moaned.

"Team Krimple needs you," Togi added

"Surely you can find someone else to take my place."

"Nobody will take *palagi*'s place, bro. The game is for you."

"Shit."

Blue emerged from the outhouse looking a little green.

"Bro, you look pale as death."

"I'll never make it to the field."

"Here—my old jersey. Give you good luck," Toga said with a smile and tossed him the jersey, which landed on Blue's head. He pulled it off with a cringe in his face.

"Oh God. When's the last time you washed this?"

"No wash. Good luck."

The annual rugby match took place on the grassy field. It was an appreciation match that pitted a coed team composed of the two largest *aigas*, the Tuputalas and the Lafaus, versus a team made up of villagers, volunteers, and visitors captained by Father Krimple. If a villager wasn't playing, then he or she was a spectator. Children, particularly the boys, loved to watch the game, and they dreamed of someday being old enough to be able to play. A feast for the entire village would always follow the match in and near the *fale tele*, thus nobody ever left early.

Togi helped Blue to the grassy field, where it seemed that the entire village was waiting. The two teams were already on the field warming up, and Togi brought Blue to Father Krimple.

"Ah, Ronin, you look like you got the devil in you. Go on. That's what we need."

Blue pathetically held his thumb up.

Team *Aiga* began their *Siva Tau* chanting and gesticulating with fierce facial expressions. Blue was impressed how in unison they were despite having never ever seen them practice together. He also noticed that the team was composed of not only Togi, but it also included Aumua, Lance, and a few other fit villagers that looked like they had played the game often. He then looked at his team and noticed that it consisted of a smaller group, such as Father Krimple, Savea, and Maeva. He instantly thought that his team was going to get pummeled. Fortunately, he saw the bulky Lemanu standing by himself behind the priest and mentally preparing for the match. He looked as intense and intimidating as any member of their opponent, and Blue was relieved to believe that Lemanu could win the match all on his own.

When Father Krimple's team began the *Siva Tau*, they weren't as fluid as Team *Aigas*. Although Blue practiced the movements and the chant, he had a hard time keeping up with the rest of his teammates, mostly due to the pains in his stomach. It was difficult for him to concentrate. He could hear many of the spectators laughing in good jest, especially whenever Blue or a teammate made a mistake. Father

Krimple, who performed the dance impeccably, didn't like the blunders that his teammates made. Nevertheless, he smiled and clapped when hearing the applause after they finished.

As everyone went into position for the kickoff, Blue stood still and looked at the large crowd that had gathered around the field. The match, in fact, had a reputation in the region that attracted many people from other villages to watch and then join in the feast afterward.

Blue observed that the crowd consisted of a kind of who's who. He saw that Chief Joseph was sitting underneath a pitched tent with several other *matais* like Fiame, and even other chiefs from nearby villages. Blue also noticed that Misi had made the journey to watch the match. He wondered if the *fa'afaline* would provide the halftime entertainment. Perhaps the oddest fan that Blue noticed was Saitele, who was standing and eating a banana. He had thought that the piano tuner had gone back to Apia, but then realized that Saitele must have caught wind of the impending feast and decided to postpone his journey back to the capital.

"Do you even know how to play the game?" Maeva asked Blue in Samoan with a bit of repugnance in her tone.

"Yeah. Just put the ball in the goal over there," Blue lied. The only thing he knew about the sport was watching the village boys playing, which they did almost three times a day. "Now, why don't you create a path for us with that scary face of yours."

Maeva scoffed and ran into position.

The match kicked off, and right from the start, Father Krimple was barking orders to his team, which Blue didn't understand. It was rough with tackles. Arguments from both teams quickly ensued over alleged fouls, knock-ons, and offsides. During one of the game's pauses because of a disagreement, Blue looked at Aumua and Lance, who stood staring at him like a couple of lions that spotted their lunch. Blue pathetically smiled at the two. He sweated over his gurgling stomach, and he looked to see how far he was from the outhouse. It was far. He decided that he couldn't hold back a fermenting fart, and he uncontrollably let it rip. Although Blue was a little embarrassed by emitting gas, Aumua and Lance were appalled and treated the gesture as if Blue was taunting, or trash-talking, them. Blue wished he were anywhere else than on the field.

For the first ten minutes, the match was a stalemate with both teams turning over the ball. On those moments when it looked like Team *Aigas* was just about to make a breakthrough, Lemanu single-handedly made sure to stop their progress with a brilliant tackle or steal.

Blue managed to mostly stay out of harm's way by keeping a distance from the action. His stomach pains grew worse under the heat of the sun, and he was ready to tell Father Krimple that he couldn't continue. Then, the momentum quickly turned as Savea ran with the ball and zigzagged across the field towards Blue. Before he was tackled, he dished the ball behind him to Blue, who caught it. Blue only knew one thing to do, and that was to run forward. He felt alone, like a fox being hunted by dogs, and he looked to find a teammate that he could toss the ball to. Before he could find anyone, Aumua came out of nowhere and slammed into him, driving him hard to the ground and forcing him to fumble the ball. The hit was so violent that

Blue lost his bowels, and diarrhea exploded in his shorts. He could hear the gasping groans of the crowd and the teams when he hit the ground.

Blue's girlfriend had literally knocked the shit out of him.

The game paused as players checked to see if Blue was all right. Blue remained on the ground, stunned by the hit, but he was even more humiliated by the fact that he made it in his shorts. Looking up, he could see many faces staring down at him, their bobbing heads periodically blocking out the sun. He saw Lance holding his nose, and somebody said that he smelled like a pig pen.

It was Togi who helped the volunteer sit up.

"You okay, bro?"

"I think a freightliner hit me."

"It was just my sister."

"I think you better hit the shower, my friend," Father Krimple said.

"Yeah," Blue agreed.

Blue tried to stand but couldn't.

"Bro, take your time."

"Yeah."

As Blue tried to gain his sense of equilibrium, he heard Father Krimple pontificating about the roughness of the sport. Blue also noticed how Lance and Maeva were trying to hold in their laughter. Aumua, who became disgusted with the indifference and shallowness of her two friends, went over to Blue and, with her brother, helped lift him to his feet. Together, they walked Blue towards the shower. A round of applause came from the crowd that thankfully signified that Blue was going to be fine.

Along the way, Blue's hounds came bounding about and got excited after sniffing his bottom. Aumua and Togi swooshed the dogs away with their legs. But they were persistent. Blue, of course, didn't mind. After all, the dogs were the only ones who appreciated his stench.

After a shower, Aumua and Togi helped Blue change into clean clothes and laid him down on his mat in his *fale*. Aumua sat next to him. Togi kept looking towards the direction of the grassy field when he heard the crowd cheering a good play. Blue felt guilty that his friend was missing the match.

"Togi, you can return to the game," Blue said. "I'm okay."

"I will score the winning tri for you," Togi stated with a grin.

"I hope not since we're on opposite teams."

Togi dashed out of the fale, and Blue could hear the teams welcoming him back to the match.

"You can return too, if you want," Blue said to Aumua.

"No. I want to be with you."

"Where'd you learn to hit like that?"

"I have big brothers."

Blue smiled.

"I'm sorry I missed your ceremony. I really wanted to see you dance."

Aumua grabbed his hand.

"I will dance many times for you."

Blue felt comforted holding on to Aumua's hand. The fire in his belly seemed to have subsided. He closed his eyes, hoping that Aumua would never leave. There was a pleasant calm that descended on the two. There were no aching stomachs, no weird dreams, no diarrhea, no rugby matches in the hot sun, and no cackling Lance and Maeva.

It was just peaceful... and Blue knew that it would remain this way until Taaiti arrived with her herbal remedies.

2

It was about a week after the rugby match, and Blue was feeling much better. He spent most of the past few days in his *fale* listening to music, and whenever he felt motivated, he would work on his novel. Aumua had gone with Maeva to Apia to visit relatives and shop for things she couldn't get in the village. Maeva would attend school until Friday and then journey back to Vaimasina with Aumua sometime after her classes had finished.

Since Blue and Aumua had started a relationship, he had never spent this many days away from his girlfriend, and he never realized how much he missed her companionship. Aumua was the type that rarely sat still. She was always doing something, whether it was practicing her dancing, singing, or making something useful out of pandanus leaves. Even when she went to take care of her father or was attending the cocoa plantation, Blue knew she was close by and could still feel her reassuring and devoted heart beating. But Apia felt like it was on the other side of the world.

With nothing to do and nowhere to go, Blue suffered a little depression and loneliness. Togi would often come by with Kobe and tried to persuade the volunteer to go fishing, but Blue always refused. There would be no way that anyone would ever get him to return to the water where man-eating sharks roamed. Togi tried to convince Blue that the shark that attacked them was an anomaly and probably wouldn't happen again in a hundred years. Blue didn't believe him.

He typed half-heartedly away on his computer. He paused long enough to think about St. Cecilia and how much he missed going there. Although he failed in his volunteer job, there never seemed to be a dull day at the school, and he always got involved with the shenanigans that occurred every day. Plus, he never took better naps than in his little classroom.

Blue contemplated if it was really time to return home, get a job, and try to save enough money to get his own place. He didn't know what he would do. The thought of playing piano for money did not even cross his mind. It all seemed daunting. He thought for a fleeting second that maybe his aunt could set him up with a journalist job with the Associated Press, just like her. Blue sighed. He knew that his aunt would dissuade him from working with the AP and encourage him to go out and make his own path to a career. Wasn't coming to Samoa supposed to be part of that journey?

It didn't take long for him to pause again from typing when he heard the scratching sound coming from the rafters of his *fale*. He had heard the noise a few times in the past several months, but every time he thought he found the source, there was nothing there. Most of the time he thought it was only rats visiting his *fale*, but they usually come at night. Blue listened very carefully. The noise sounded like long fingernails scratching against a hard surface.

The tin roof!

Blue ran out of his *fale*. He squinted from the glare of the afternoon sun. Once he got used to the brightness, he took a couple of steps to get a look at the roof of his fale. His heart dropped to his stomach when he saw a group of *Teine Sa* standing on the roof. Scarlett scurried around on her hands and feet like a spider, her nails clicking and clacking with every movement. Blue couldn't believe his eyes. He hadn't seen the *Teine Sa* for several months. This time, however, felt more ominous than previous engagements.

Blue rushed back into his *fale* and looked around for a weapon. The only thing he could find was a village-made broom, which he grabbed, then hurried back to the opening. Before he could make it back outside, Scarlett leaned her head upside down from the roof into the top of the opening and hissed at him. Her algae-corroded face forced Blue to fall on his backside. Scarlett began to climb inside the *fale*. Blue watched the hideous creature in a white dress crawl in the rafters of the *fale*. He understood now that the scratching sound that he had been hearing in the ceiling was ghosts.

Blue thought that it would be safer outside the *fale* and made a quick decision to shoot through the opening. He cursed himself for being lazy and not taking the time to open the other blinds earlier in the day. If they had been open, an escape route would have been easier. Nevertheless, he didn't want to wait and see what Scarlett would do, or if the other *Teine Sa* would come for him as well. So he grabbed his broom, closed his eyes, and rushed the opening while swinging away. As he exited his *fale*, the wild swinging of the broom made him stumble to the ground and fall right at Fiame's feet.

"Mr. Ronin, are you okay?"

"Yeah," Blue mumbled. He looked back at his *fale* and saw that there was nobody on the roof.

"What were you trying to hit?"

"Uh... mosquitoes."

"You need a broom to hit mosquitoes?"

"They were, uh, huge."

Fiame helped Blue to his feet. She then picked up the broom and handed it to the volunteer.

"You should go ask Savea if he has any insect repellent. That might work better."

"Yeah, I might need something stronger—like a flamethrower."

"I doubt he has one of those."

"Is there something I can help you with, Fiame?"

"I have to admit I went looking for you in your classroom, and then... I remembered," Fiame said, ending the sentence a bit somberly. "I was hoping you would be available to join Joseph and me when we meet with a member from a cocoa company at our plantation."

Blue judged the use of the word, "our," as inappropriate. The plantation belonged to the Tuputala *aiga*.

"Let me check my schedule for tomorrow," Blue said

half-jokingly, knowing that he had nothing going on these days. Fiame didn't laugh, and Blue believed that she probably thought he was being sincere.

"We could use your insight on the matter."

Blue wanted to ask, *what insight?* But he then remembered that months earlier, he promised Fiame that he would attend the meeting and decided that he would remain helpful as much as he could.

"What time?"

"Half past one."

Blue tried to calculate the time in Samoan time.

"I might have to move a few things around, but I will be there."

Fiame still didn't get the joke, but she was pleased with his answer.

"And you will help me persuade Joseph?"

"If it's warranted, I will do my best."

"*Faafetai lava,*" Fiame said and smiled gratefully.

Walking away, Fiame remembered something else and turned to Blue.

"Oh. Can you talk with Mr. Saitele?"

"He's still here?"

"Apparently, he continues to work on the piano and eat all my food," Fiame said with a sigh. "Normally, I don't mind feeding guests, but... but your dogs have more manners than him."

"I'll talk to him."

"I can't believe how much that man eats."

"Where has he been staying?"

"I think he sleeps at the church."

Blue felt it was his responsibility to deal with this. After all, he was the one that hired the man. Blue didn't like the thought of the piano tuner taking advantage of the village and the hospitality of the villagers. Nobody in the village would ever dare tell Saitele that he had overextended his stay, especially if he was a high-ranking chief or member of another village. However, Fiame knew that if a *palagi* were to say something to Saitele about his prolonged stay, the piano tuner would most likely listen.

Blue cautiously entered his *fale*, his broom held up, guarding his upper body. He jumped inside, swinging away like a desperate tennis player, but at what, he didn't even know. He stopped and looked around and saw nobody. He then looked up to each corner of the rafters and saw nothing. His dogs came galloping inside and crashed in the shade of the *fale*. Blue thought it would be best if he left for a while. He grabbed some money and headed for the opening.

"You guys keep the ghosts outta here," Blue commanded his dogs. They didn't even lift their heads.

When Blue got to the top step of the balcony of the church, he could feel the change in the heat. He didn't envy the piano tuner's job working in a cramped space with no ventilation. Nevertheless, Blue believed that it shouldn't have taken more than a day to complete the job. If he hadn't become sick and been fired from the Helping Hands organization, he could've monitored Saitele more closely.

Saitele looked like he was taking a break when Blue arrived. The piano tuner was sitting in a chair, legs stretched out and lying upon the ornately carved wood railing, eating an ice-cream cone.

"You must be finished with your work," Blue commented.

"*Leai*, the work is very delicate," Saitele said coldly. He was not a man of many words.

"You've been here over a week. Where'd you get the ice cream?"

"At the trading store."

Every so often, Savea would receive a few tubs of ice cream for sale. Naturally, the villagers loved it and would line up to get some. By the time Blue hears about it, though, it was sold out.

"Man, that looks good."

"If you hurry, you might be able to get some."

Blue knew that it would be a futile trek over to the store.

"So, how much more do you have to do with the piano?"

"A few more days. Maybe."

"Really?" Blue asked incredulously. Saitele took offense at Blue's tone.

"*Ioe*. I do impeccable work."

"This isn't a grand piano."

"It's old," Saitele said smugly. He finished his ice-cream cone, then licked each of his fingers. "And it needs some tender care."

Blue stared at Saitele. He would love to throw the piano tuner over the balcony.

"Can I play it?"

"Can you play it?"

Blue stared at him again. It was a good question, and Blue wondered what his skill level would currently be. He imagined it would be like a person being able to ride a bike even after years of not riding one. He had been playing at an advanced level for many years, thus he felt confident in his ability to regain that intensity. However, he promised himself he wouldn't play again. Plus, he also didn't want to indulge the piano tuner.

"You're right. I'll have to find the person who can play it," Blue said.

"I can play it."

"Right."

"It should be playable in three, four days."

"Well, I brought your pay—three hundred forty-five *tala*," Blue said and laid the money on the piano keys. "And you received your meal... several times."

"*Faafetai*. The next time I come I give discount."

Blue smirked and questioned himself what the discount would be.

What? You only want two meals a day?

"By the way, the Lafau family will not be preparing dinners after *Sa* for the next several days," Blue lied.

This piqued Saitele's interest. "Huh?"

"Yeah, I guess several family members went to visit relatives in Apia, being that it's the Lentenal season and all."

Blue wasn't sure if he was using the word "Lentenal" correctly, but it sounded good, and Saitele understood what the volunteer was saying.

"That's unfortunate," the piano tuner replied, bowing his head with dejection. "I mean, they have had such wonderful suppers."

"Yeah, well, you can always dine with Father Krimple. He would love the company. But keep in mind he has been fasting a lot lately—you know, because it's the Lentenal season."

The news was a crushing blow, and Saitele looked as if a sledgehammer had just hit him.

"Of... of course."

Blue left the piano tuner to ponder having a day—or two or three, without a feast.

It was an uncomfortable evening for Blue as he sat in his *fale*. The day's heat and humidity were burdensome and seemed to weigh upon him as if he was lying under a stack of wet towels. He thought about opening the blinds to let a breeze brush through, but he still liked his privacy, and it helped minimize the number of bugs that entered his place. Additionally, he didn't want his *fale* to look inviting to the *Teine Sa*.

Blue tried to work on his novel, and the music from the computer was turned up louder than usual. He truly didn't want to hear the scratching sound, mainly because he now knew what was creating it. From time to time, he would glance at the rafters, hoping to see that there was nothing on the beams. He would never forget the sight of Scarlett crawling around up there. He thought it was so unlike her. He could never have imagined that just a few years ago, while playing music with her, she would end up becoming an undignified, diaphanous demon. It was harsh. It was sad. It was unfair.

It had been well over a year now when Blue first saw her with the other *Teine Sa* in the jungle, and he questioned why she would want to torment him. He was always good to her. In fact, as far as he knew, he was her only friend. Sometimes he wondered, too, if she were his only friend. He never forgot that after his mother died, he went to Sabatini's Beach to contemplate and reminisce about her. It was Scarlett who came and sat with him. The two hardly said a word to each other that day. They simply watched the waves roll on the beach, gently lapping their feet.

Nevertheless, Blue believed that God would surely have a better use for Scarlett. She could be playing cello for the angels. Blue thought that, when she was alive, she sure as hell played the cello as if possessed by an angel. Instead, she was forced to roam around an island village in the middle of nowhere looking like a decaying sea creature in white. It was harsh. It was sad. It was unfair.

Blue was in a pensive mood for the rest of the evening. He didn't feel like writing or sleeping. He lay down on his cushy mat underneath his mosquito net and stared above him. He was alone, and he felt alone. Not even his dogs came home. But being alone and feeling alone were two different things, and the latter just made Blue overthink and question everything. The *Teine Sa*, for example, couldn't be real, could they? Loneliness always tried to overcompensate irrational thoughts and behavior. But it wasn't just a one-time encounter with the wispy women in white. Blue wanted to blame the heat, or himself getting sick, or Togi's weed for seeing them. And Scarlett?

What the hell? Why am I seeing her?

He thought again how it was harsh. It was sad. It was unfair.

He believed that maybe she had been nestled in his subconscious. It was only natural. Her death still lay heavily upon his mind. Maybe she had been trying to tell him something, like to go home or play piano again.

Couldn't she just tell me in a polite way instead of creeping about and scaring the shit out of me?

Blue then contemplated that, perhaps, that it was his

mother acting through Scarlett. No! He didn't want to go there. It was another untimely death of a wonderful, gifted woman who he missed too much. It was harsh. It was sad. It was unfair.

Loneliness jams jumbled thoughts, and Blue had to decipher which reasoning was rational. It wasn't easy; so much ran through his mind. He could feel each thought getting louder and trying to out speak and outplay other thoughts. It got so bad that he leaned up and blurted out:

"I have to return home! I have to return home."

As soon as he stated it, the loneliness went away. His mind became clear. He became at ease. No more heat, no more *Teine Sa*, no more illness, and no more Togi's weed.

Leaving the village would be hard, and leaving Aumua would be harder. He loved her. He would have to convince her to go with him. How? He could show her how they were meant to be together, and that she had to go with him and share her customs, her traditions, with the Western world. He could promise a prosperous life with periodic returns to Vaimasina.

Blue lay backed down on his mat and considered what he would tell Aumua when he saw her next. It would have to be right away. He couldn't wait. He smiled at the thought of life with Aumua at home. It would be easy. It would be happy. It would be fair.

Shortly after his epiphany of returning home, he fell asleep.

It was the sound of barking dogs late in the morning that awoke Blue. He waited a minute or two in hopes that they would stop so that he could fall asleep again. But they didn't, and he was forced to lie there and stare at the rafters.

A short moment later, the dogs suddenly ceased barking. Blue, then he heard a portion of the blinds separate behind him, which made him lean up. Thinking that Scarlett had returned, he quickly reached for his broom and held it up for protection. Fortunately, it wasn't Scarlett, or a ghost, that intruded his *fale*. It was Aumua who rashly pulled back the mosquito net, jumped on the volunteer, and kissed him.

"Aumua!"

"What's with the broom?" Aumua asked in Samoan. She typically spoke Samoan to Blue these days, and he did his best to keep up with her.

"Oh—uh, nothing."

"Did you miss me?"

"Like the stars miss the moon," Blue answered. He wasn't sure if he captured what he meant to say in Samoan. Nevertheless, Blue wasn't lying. The last few days without her had been lonely, even though he usually doesn't see her for most of the day. "How was Apia?"

"It was good. The university wants me to help teach dancing."

"Really?"

"Maeva introduced me to some members of the dancing faculty. They also want me to enroll."

The news didn't discourage him and his plan. There would also be many opportunities to teach dancing in the States, probably even more with better pay.

"That's awesome. Did you leave Maeva there?"

"*Ioe*," Aumua said with suspicion. "She has class."

"That's even better news."

"And I have more to tell you."

Blue couldn't wait to tell her that he had decided to

return home and that he wanted her to come with him. He thought about announcing his plan to her right then and there, but he wanted to be more awake and a little more dressed.

"I need to talk to you, too," Blue said with enthusiasm.

"How about we go to the pool?"

"Sounds refreshing. I could use a splash."

"Wonderful. I'll run over to my house and make something to eat."

Aumua kissed him on his forehead and rushed out of the *fale*.

As Blue got dressed and ready for the day, he practiced what he was going to say to Aumua. He was proud of himself for sounding quite convincing.

If I were a girl from a South Seas village, I would run away with my lover to another country.

It was about an hour later when Aumua arrived with a basket made of coconut palm leaves.

"I have *talo*, banana, rice, and I found some leftover *oka 'ia*."

Blue's eyes lit up. He loved eating the raw fish marinated in lemon juice and coconut milk, although, and he would admit it, that sometimes, it didn't love him back and would make him sick.

"I'm starving. Let's eat now."

"No. At the pool. Let's go."

As the two made their way along the village towards the forest, they playfully kicked, shoved, and hugged each other.

Blue's hounds came trotting around them and got caught up in the couple's friskiness with the hope that, perhaps, a dog pile may soon ensue.

When the couple neared the church, the distinctive purple-and-black Vaimasina bus was about to pull out and make its way to Apia. Blue noticed that Saitele was sitting at the window and looking hungry. Blue was so pleased to see the piano tuner on the bus that he reached into Aumua's basket and pulled out some taro.

"Saitele!" Blue called. The piano tuner turned to him when he heard his name. "*Faafetai.*"

Blue threw Saitele the taro, which he caught. The piano tuner smiled as if it was the best gift he had ever received.

By the time the bus drove away to the sound of Madonna's odd island version of "Like a Prayer," Saitele had already eaten half of the taro.

"Who was that?" Aumua asked with a confused expression on her face.

"Just a man who tried to eat the village."

"What?"

Blue put his arm around Aumua and led her across the grassy field to the bush.

At the edge of the forest, Aumua yelled at the dogs to go away, and they happily complied. The hounds rarely went into the bush, preferring to frolic and loiter around the village.

Sitting in the shade of a frangipani tree that was also engulfed by a large African Tulip tree, the two finished eating the contents of the basket. Neither said much while they ate, as they were both starving. Blue then lay flat on his back, replete with his lunch. When the wind and birds fell silent for a few seconds, he could hear the waterfall of the pool gurgling just a few feet away.

Aumua let her hair down and lay next to Blue, placing

her head on his chest. She closed her eyes as Blue stroked her thick hair. Blue then kissed and smelled the top of her head. He always liked how her hair smelled of coconut and gardenia flowers. It reminded him, despite her tomboyish figure, how feminine she truly was.

The wind picked up and jostled the leaves of the trees, allowing streams of sunlight to surge downward and briefly scorch the two lovers on the ground.

"I like the sound of your heartbeat," Aumua said. "It puts me to sleep every night."

"It's like a metronome."

"What's that?"

"Something that keeps beat and rhythm."

Aumua rolled over and was now face-to-face with Blue.

"I could not sleep without your heart while I was in Apia."

"Next time, I'll cut it out and send it along with you."

Aumua laughed and bopped Blue on the nose with her hand. They then passionately kissed.

"I wish we could just stay here in the shade and hold each other. Then, at night, we'd let the moonbeams dance around us," Blue said wistfully.

"We do not dare stay here after dark," Aumua reminded him. She remained pragmatic even during the romantic outing. "*Aitus.*"

"True. And if the ghosts don't eat you, the mosquitoes will."

Blue teasingly bit Aumua on the neck. Aumua laughed and kissed him so he would stop biting her. She then looked lovingly into his eyes.

"I can see in your eyes how much you missed me," Aumua stated.

"The soul only talks through one's eyes," Blue responded and wondered if what he had just said was a worthy quote for the ages. He didn't have time to ponder the thought, as Aumua leaned in to kiss him again. She only understood the words "soul" and "eyes," and cherished the moment when their souls and eyes came together.

It was Aumua who initiated their lovemaking. Blue readily exhibited how much he missed her, and Aumua was pleased to feel the sense of him longing for her. The couple knew that they had to be quick. Many villagers, particularly children, use the pool, and, naturally, they didn't want to get caught in a compromising position. Aumua grabbed hold of a couple of branches of the frangipani tree to help steady herself and to help speed up her climax. Blue felt like one of his dogs fornicating in the bush, but he enjoyed the impetuousness and the risky excitement of the moment. Their sweaty bodies only heightened the experience and made their thumping and determined drive flourish more easily. As the couple hit their carnal peak together, the tree shook intensely, and flower petals rained upon them.

In the aftermath of their lovemaking, Blue sunk in a supine position upon the ground. Aumua immediately put her clothes back on and lay next to him. She put one of the felled flowers behind her ear.

"Wow. I can't see straight after that," Blue commented.

"That's because you're in love."

"True. But it's also because of the sweat stinging my eyes."

Aumua smacked him.

"Hey, I thought you had something important to tell me," Blue said, leaning on his elbows.

"Yes, but you have to catch me first."

Aumua quickly stood and ran for the pool, where she jumped in with her clothes on.

Blue slowly stood and walked nonchalantly to the pool. He was completely naked. When the cool water hit his burning, sweaty body, it stung for a second before the chill felt nice.

Aumua swam all around Blue. She then surfaced behind him and spat water on his back. Blue quickly turned around and splashed water in her face. She laughed, dipped herself under the water, and then flung herself into his arms.

"I caught a siren," Blue announced, and Aumua spat water in his face.

"Siren?" Aumua asked with disgust. "They're scaly and fishy smelling."

By her tone, Blue wondered if Aumua believed that sirens actually existed. In a society full of superstitions, he wouldn't be surprised if she did. After all, there was a legend that her father made love to a siren and lived to tell about it. Obviously, he had a million questions to ask Aumua about sirens, but he decided to table it for the moment and ask the more important question.

"So, what news do you have for me? And when you're done telling me, I have something to run by you."

Aumua giggled and blushed.

"Well, I did not go to Apia just for a job," She started. "I wanted to check my body."

"Your body? Why? Is everything okay?"

"*Ioe*. I am with child," Aumua said softly.

Blue pretended not to hear her and continued to speak.

"I mean, a few minutes ago your body was terrific... what?"

"I have a child in me," Aumua said loudly and proudly.

Was she kidding?

"Your child," she added.

Damn me.

Blue was dumbstruck and speechless, but not really surprised. They had been living together for several months and having sex without protection. It was just a matter of time, he figured. A million voices ran through his mind telling him what to do or say, or what not to do or say. So many, in fact, that everything became jumbled and confusing. What would his mother have said, or his aunt? He stopped there. One thing became clear to him—the thought of asking her to move to the States with him was now completely pointless.

Aumua swallowed some water and then squirted it in Blue's face. She giggled gleefully and was obviously delighted.

Blue felt embarrassed about the situation. He never imagined that he would come to Samoa as a volunteer and then impregnate a girl. It was a stupid thing to do, and he became angry with himself. He just wanted to travel, volunteer, and write.

"How long have you been pregnant?" Blue asked.

"Just over three months."

"Three months!" Blue exclaimed with alarm. He wondered how on earth he didn't recognize any signs. She never displayed morning sickness, irritable behavior, or even craved weird food. "Wait—you played rugby last week."

"I didn't know I was with child last week," she said, and then added with a smile, "Well, I knew. But it didn't bother me."

Oh my God.

Children's amusement could be heard from the area of the bush near the frangipani tree where they had their lunch. At first, Blue thought it was the Samoan gods laughing at him, which would be nothing more than he deserved.

"Mister *Lanu Moana!*" called a voice. The words were repeated several times by different children.

"Mister *Lanu Moana!*"

Not wanting anyone to see his naked body, Blue sank under the water up to his eyes and ears like a hippopotamus. All of a sudden, the water started to feel very cold to him, and he didn't feel like swimming any longer. He wanted to go back to the comfort of his *fale* and think about how to proceed with the news.

"Thanks for the clothes, Mister *Lanu Moana!*"

Blue shook his head in disbelief. "Did they just take my clothes?"

Aumua shrugged her shoulders and then jumped on his back. She kissed him on his cheek.

"I think they just took my clothes."

"Tell me, please, your news," Aumua insisted.

Blue knew that it would be futile to ask her to come home with him. She would never leave her family and village now that she knew that she was pregnant, and so he had to make up something else to tell her. The only thing that came to mind was being invited to meet with the cocoa plantation buyer, which made him stiffen with shock in the water.

"Oh shit!" Blue exclaimed. "I'm supposed to be with your father and Fiame to meet a guy who wants to run the plantation."

"What time?"

"Half past one."

"I think it is past that."

"Shit!"

Aumua didn't like her man swearing.

"Calm your voice down," Aumua said, reprimanding Blue with a slap on his head. "We can go over there right now."

Blue began leaving the pool, but then realized he was naked.

"Can you check and see if my clothes are there?"

Aumua left the pool and walked over to the frangipani tree to look for the clothes. Not seeing anything, she turned to Blue and shrugged her shoulders.

"Only your sandals."

"Shit!

"Calm your voice down," Aumua said, scolding him again. "I will help you."

"How?"

"Come out of the water."

"What? Is anyone around?"

"No. Come out."

Blue hesitantly came out of the water. After not seeing anyone for himself, he quickly jumped behind an immature traveler's palm. The leaf line of the palm typically fanned in an east–west line and could provide a crude compass for travelers. But as he quickly learned, the tree also provided a good screen to hide behind.

He watched Aumua grab a knife from the basket that carried their food. She then looked around at the nearby trees, analyzing each one until she found the one that she was looking for, which happened to be a coconut tree. Without a second thought, she went to the tree and climbed it in just a matter of seconds, as it was only about ten feet tall. She began cutting a palm frond with her knife.

Blue was shocked, and yet oddly impressed, that she would do this in her condition.

"Should you be doing that?" Blue asked with a wry smirk on his face.

The palm frond fell to the ground, and Aumua shuffled back down the trunk of the tree.

"Doing what?"

It only took Aumua approximately ten minutes to make a simple but effective skirt by braiding leaves of the fronds together. She reinforced the skirt by entwining portions of the basket that was made from pandanus leaves with the coconut leaves, particularly around the waist.

Aumua brought the skirt to Blue and handed it to him behind the palm tree. He felt more comfortable remaining behind the tree, then put on the skirt there, even though he knew that his island girl had seen him many times in the buff.

"Well?" Aumua asked.

Blue stepped out from behind the tree wearing the natural makeshift skirt.

"It feels, uh, a little airy."

"Turn around."

Blue turned around to show his backside. His ass showed through the leaves. Aumua noticed that his ass showed a little. She acknowledged to herself that she probably could have used a few more leaves to cover it. Nevertheless, she covered her mouth and tried to keep from laughing.

"Can you see my butt cheeks?" Blue asked in a concerned tone.

"*Leai.*"

Blue tried to turn his head and look at his ass, as if he was looking for a "Kick Me" sticker on his back. Aumua turned away and laughed in her hands.

"You're laughing. Are you laughing?"

"*Leai.*"

"This is unbelievable."

"Here—your sandals. We should go."

They started making their way to the plantation. After every five yards or so, Blue felt the needed to adjust his skirt by pulling leaves out of the crack of his butt.

"I feel like I should be dancing," Blue said sarcastically. "Hey! Hawaii just called, and they want their hula girl back."

Aumua laughed, but not at the joke, which she thought wasn't very funny. Instead, she was laughing at her makeshift, handy-dandy work and the strange predicament Blue was in.

They reached the top of the hill that looked down upon the plantation within fifteen minutes, thanks in part to Aumua's shortcut through the forest. From there, they were glad to see that Joseph and Fiame were seated at the wooden tables of the open-wall hut with an unfamiliar Caucasian man.

As Blue and Aumua approached the table, it was the stranger who noticed them first. He stood very abruptly straight and introduced himself.

"Hiya. I'm Ringo, like the Beatles," Ringo said loudly in an Australian accent.

Ringo was a tall, burly man in his late thirties. He explained that he played professional rugby in his younger days for a team in Sydney but had to retire early due to persistent knee injuries. His clear commitment to keeping fit was evident, as he looked like he could still hold his own in a rugby match. His jovial attitude and booming voice, however, made it easy for him to transition into a second career as a salesman, which he had been doing for the past fifteen years or so. He had worked for many companies, but he seemed to have found stability with his latest job as a regional production manager for the Crighton Cocoa Company. His full name was John Ringo Atherton, and since he was a kid, he wanted everyone to simply call him Ringo. He believed that nobody would ever forget a name like that. The name Ringo was, in fact, what appeared on the back of all his rugby jerseys.

The company man was dressed in black slacks with a long-sleeved, yellow collared shirt. A matching leather black belt and shoes made him look sharp. Blue, however, couldn't help but notice how Ringo's ensemble made the salesman sweat profusely—beads of sweat left trails like a snail down his bald head.

"*Talofa*," Aumua said, shaking Ringo's hand.

Ringo offered his hand to Blue, who didn't take it.

Instead, he simply nodded his head. This didn't persuade Ringo from writing notes on his clipboard.

"Where are your clothes?" Fiame asked Blue in Samoan. She was slightly embarrassed in front of the important businessman that Blue would appear wearing a crude skirt.

"They were stolen," Blue answered in Samoan.

"Off your back?" Fiame pressed.

"Uh, no ... not exactly," Blue said, stumbling for a way to tell the truth.

Joseph chortled and raised his eyebrows. He had accepted the relationship between his daughter and Blue despite the two deriving from disparate cultures. He made sure to stand out of their energetic, yet exhaustive attraction for one another. In fact, Joseph believed that love was simply like a fleeting flap of wings that eventually flew away. He, however, hoped that the two would enjoy each other for as long as they could. After all, the chief had three wives and several lovers throughout his lifetime and could vividly remember the exciting and reckless moments with each of them. Although they had all flown away a long time ago, he was vicariously reminded of them through observing Blue and Aumua's affectionate connection.

"We had a couple of mishaps on our way here, and I had to make him the skirt so that he wouldn't miss this meeting," Aumua confidently said in Blue's defense. But she knew that fewer details would be best for everyone.

"I apologize for his appearance," Fiame said to Ringo. "It seems they ran into some trouble in the forest on their way here."

"Quite all right. Quite all right," Ringo replied with a wink of the eye. "I lost my shirt a few times in the bush, eh?"

"Mr. Ronin Blue is here for consultation. We trust and value his opinion. Aumua is the daughter of Joseph," Fiame explained. "She has been managing the trees for a couple of years. But with the plantation's operations becoming more demanding, we think my son, Lance, would be the ideal candidate to help Aumua and oversee the cocoa production."

Aumua and Blue looked at Fiame with a quizzical expression on their faces. Blue had no idea what went into the care of a plantation, but he knew Aumua was way more capable and experienced than Lance to handle the workload.

Joseph stared at the ground and said nothing.

"Right. And it's my job to bring out the plantation's fullest potential. Look—you already have quite a load to harvest. We want to get to them before the rats do. Once they break the pod wall, the beans will be compromised."

"We were planning on harvesting them in the next few days," Blue said, trying to sound as if the village was on top of things. He was also thinking about "Samoa Time" and wondered how many days it would take for a group to come and harvest the pods.

Aumua looked proudly at Blue. She liked it when he acted as if he was part of the village.

"Good on ya, mate. It warms my heart to see a village be proactive about their plantation. I can't tell you the number of cocoa owners that I've met who neglect their trees," Ringo said. "But I think here we'll have a beautiful and profitable relationship, eh?"

"Will you be supervising the work?" Blue asked.

"Me? Nah, mate. We'll bring in a team that will manage

the trees. We have an office in Apia. And, as I was telling Fiame and Joseph, we'll build a new facility that will replace your outdated hut for drying and fermenting. We'll bring in new tools for harvesting and reaching those pods that grow high in the trees. We'll introduce sustainable horticultural practices to prevent the risk of deforestation. How does that sound, Ronin, eh?"

Ringo's error of saying "Fiame" before "Joseph" completely threw Blue off. Being a visiting *palagi,* nobody would dare correct him, but Blue knew that everyone made a mental note of it.

Joseph stared at the ground and said nothing.

"It sounds, um... daunting."

Ringo laughed. "You mean, daring, eh? We dare to create meaningful bonds with the village, which will help improve quality and sustainability."

"And money."

"Yeah, mate. We will improve all the yields as well. I see the village being quite prosperous."

"Will you be able to put an air-con unit in every house?" Blue asked with a somewhat cynical attitude.

"Ha! Maybe two," Ringo jibed and wrote another note on his clipboard. "But this is what concerns me, Ronin. I can see that you have an aging tree population, which will eventually produce a very low pod count. I propose that we remove the older trees and replace them with new and different hybrid varieties. This will improve the overall cocoa cultivation."

"How long will it take the new trees to produce pods?"

"Good question, Ronin. I like doing business with a man in a grass skirt who asks good questions."

"And how long?" Blue asked unamused.

"Three to five years. And you have room to add even more trees. The potential of this plantation is mammoth and mind-blowing. Just mind-blowin', eh?"

"Well, why don't you come back to the village and let Aumua make you some *Koko Samoa*. Our cocoa is quite renowned throughout Samoa," Fiame said, trying to impress the businessman. But he didn't need to be impressed.

"Oh, crikey! I hear it's the best!"

"This is promising. Don't you think, Joseph?" Fiame queried in Samoan. "Mr. Ringo seems to really know his stuff about the plantation."

Joseph stared at the ground and said nothing.

Fiame became uncomfortable with the chief's silence. She knew that ultimately it would be Joseph's final decision on the matter. However, when the time was right in the next couple of days, she will try to persuade him to agree with the venture. She nervously shuffled herself. "Well, let's allow the chief to think about your proposition. You brought up many good ideas for him, Mr. Ringo."

"Right. I like that he's a man of few words," Ringo said.

Soon he will be a man of one word for you, Mr. Ringo," Aumua added.

"Huh?" Ringo didn't quite understand, but then it hit him. Eventually, it will come down for Joseph to say either yes or no. "Right. I hear you. I hear you."

"Shall we go have some of our delicious *Koko Samoa*?" Fiame enticed.

As Fiame, Aumua, and Ringo began to walk away, Ringo turned to the two men.

"I'll write a proposal and contract outlining what we

discussed. Together, we'll make every Samoan village jealous of Vaimasina, eh?"

Blue looked away, not enthralled by Ringo's comment.

Joseph stared at the ground and said nothing.

Blue watched as the three moved slowly but steadily along the well-worn path up the hill like a line of mules until they disappeared on the other side.

Blue sat next to the chief and periodically scratched his bum.

"These leaves really tickle my butt," Blue complained. "Feels like bugs are crawling all around down there..."

Blue had to stand up to thoroughly scratch himself.

Joseph finally broke his silence and said, "The trees are ageless, Mr. Ronin. They have been part of this land before us and will continue to be part of the land after us."

Blue looked at the matai, who was no longer looking at the ground. Instead, he was gazing at the plantation. Blue wondered if every tree had a story like every other living thing on the island. "Ringo might make every Samoan village jealous of Vaimasina, but he'll suck the soul right out of the village."

"Hmm."

"I don't trust him or his company's ambitions."

"He made some good points about optimizing the plantation better," Joseph admitted.

"Yeah, but we can do that as a village. We don't need them to come in with their people and their machines and their rules."

The old chief smiled. He liked enticing and exciting Blue's passion. Over the decades, Joseph had witnessed other volunteers who came to the village wilt and wither in the heat and the mundane, simple village life. It was easy to become complacent and lethargic, especially after a year or two. But he noticed that Blue kept his wits, enthusiasm, and desire to learn more of the cultural aspects of *Fa'a Samoa*. Or, perhaps, it was simply because Blue was in love with his daughter that kept him involved with village life. Be that as it may, Joseph looked at the volunteer who was now bending over and vigorously scratching his buttocks. He considered that any white man who agreed to wear palm leaves that tickled his fanny whenever a breeze blew was categorically devoted to the relationship with his daughter and to the village, and this was worthy of his respect. "Then we are in agreement."

"Hell yeah," Blue enthusiastically said as he straightened himself... "Uh, about what?"

"To keep the soul within the trees," the chief stated.

"Oh, Yeah ... Fiame won't be pleased."

"Hmm."

"But we can achieve the revenue that she's looking for. We just have to convince her of that."

Blue sat back down next to Joseph and took a deep breath.

"I wish I had underwear on," Blue lamented. "Damn kids."

"Don't we all," the *matai* added.

Blue cracked a laugh and looked at the chief. He didn't want to know what was going on underneath Joseph's *lavalava*.

"How long do you plan to stay after your sacking?" the *matai* asked.

"You heard about that?" Blue said naively. Of course, the

entire village had heard about him being let go by now. "I guess I checked too many boxes."

"Checked or unchecked boxes near the name rarely tells the truth about a man."

Blue wondered if Joseph was being poetic, philosophical, or if he just muddled his translation from Samoan to English. Regardless, Blue liked the *matai's* sentiment and wished he could write the words down because he'd never remember them.

"I'd like finish my second year," Blue said. "Doing what, I'm not sure. But I might, uh, have to stay even longer."

"Hmm."

"It would be the right thing to do."

"Responsibilities."

It was then that Blue realized that the chief knew about Aumua's pregnancy. There would be no sense in hiding the fact from the sagacious old man.

The two remained silent for a moment. Blue felt a little uncomfortable. After all, it was the chief's daughter he knocked up. He questioned himself what he would be doing now if had never come to Samoa. All kinds of images popped in his head from sitting at Sabatini's Beach to eating an In-N-Out burger. He pictured himself writing his novel in his room on top of his keyboard. It wouldn't have been the most rewarding year and a half, but he wouldn't be a stunned father-to-be.

He then selfishly couldn't help but wonder if he would ever finish his novel now that he had a child on the way.

Blue thought again how good that In-N-Out burger would taste.

Damn me.

A warm wind whipped through the valley, and Blue felt it part his palm leaf skirt and whirl around his genitals. He felt weird and exposed. He made a sworn promise to himself that he would never take his clothes off again.

"When I returned to Vaimasina from New Guinea in '44, I had nothing to live for," the chief said, breaking the uneasy silence. "I had lost my brother, who was cursed in the head before he was shot through the heart, and my best friend was laid up in an Apia hospital from bayonet wounds that punctured a lung. He would die a month later."

Joseph paused for a moment. He hadn't thought about his World War II companions for a long time. A lifetime had now passed, and when they were alive, it was simply a different era with a distinct collection of people and events.

Blue looked at the chief and hoped that the old veteran would continue talking about his time during the war, although he wondered why Joseph brought it up. Blue imagined an adventurous account full of battles against the Japanese and the intense environment of the Solomon Islands. He leaned closer to the chief like a five-year-old eagerly waiting for a bedtime story. But the *matai* didn't want to talk about the war. Not now. It wasn't the right time. He wanted to share another narrative that was more relevant, and perhaps, more didactic.

"In those days, my father was *matai* of Vaimasina, and he wanted desperately to groom me for position. But I was hellbent on being a hellion. I spent my days looking for challenges that were as dangerous as fighting Japanese. I fought a lot in those days. I fought Japanese, fought other villagers, and fought myself."

Blue chuckled to himself. It was hard to believe that this old man, who was now known for being a "sitting chief" and who typically didn't say much during village council meetings until it was time to make a final or important decision, was once a troublemaker.

"I spent a night in an Apia jail for getting into a fight."

The chief paused again. He picked up a fan constructed of pandanus leaves and bird feathers that Aumua most likely made for him and started fanning himself. The leaves of Blue's skirt were tickling the backside of his thighs, and he couldn't help but scratch himself.

"I had a jail-mate—the one I fought with—who told me about a peculiar young woman named Lanu'ese'ese from Amaile village. He said she was most beautiful woman he had ever seen. Nobody knew where she came from. She just showed up in the village one day. Rumors spread around that she was a daughter of the supreme deity, *Tangaloa*, which peeved the clergymen of the village greatly."

Joseph smiled. He enjoyed the stories that annoyed priests and missionaries.

Lanu'ese'ese loved the sea and was a great swimmer. She spent most of the day in the sea and sometimes wouldn't come back to the village at night. Villagers thought she was dead, and when they went to the beach to look for her, she would come out of the owater. Some people said she was part mermaid, which also peeved the clergymen of the village."

"Ha! Most religions eventually depend more on superstitions to keep hold of their flock," Blue added.

"Hmm."

"Sorry, I didn't mean to interrupt."

Blue stood up to scratch his butt. Some of the leaves began to fall from the ties.

"When young men throughout Samoa heard about Lanu'ese'ese, they headed to Amaile village to try to woo her and make love to her," Joseph continued.

Blue sat back down. The words "make love" piqued his interest.

"She would tell these hapless lovers that if they could catch her in the sea, they could have her. But nobody ever caught her. She outswam every suitor, and the ones who didn't gave in or were never seen or heard from again. It was believed that these men drowned, which peeved the clergymen of the village."

The chief put the fan down, and Blue picked it up to scratch an itch that started on his lower back and went down to the crack of his butt.

"It was a couple of weeks later when I thought I would try and woo the girl," Joseph said with a shrug. "I wasn't supposed to live through New Guinea anyway, so I had nothing to lose. Drowning seemed a lot better than taking a bullet."

"But you did live through New Guinea, and you came home. Didn't you take it as a sign that, I don't know, that you were meant for better things in life?"

"Not at that time."

"Okay, so you met your goddess in Amaile village, and then what?"

"I met her on the beach, and she was as beautiful as my jail-mate said she was. She looked at me and asked if I wanted her, and I said yes. She stripped off her clothes and slipped into the water like a slippery seal, and I followed her. I didn't hesitate. She was a good swimmer, but I was a good swimmer too. We swam a long distance, but I never caught up to her. I was so far out in the sea that if I swam any farther, I would grow too tired and drown, but it was also too far to swim back. It was then that I gave up and sunk further under the water. As luck or providence had it, a dolphin came by. I grabbed the back of its dorsal fin and rode it. Rode it a long way. Rode it fast until I caught the girl."

Damn me. He's like Aquaman!

"She was surprised, almost terrified, when I grabbed her around her waist. Turning in my arms to face me, her eyes slit like a serpent with disgust and disbelief. She hissed at me and showed her fangs, the smell of fish upon her breath. But she clamped onto me and kissed me. At first, I was revolted. Then she nibbled my neck and sung a sweet melody in my ear. A current carried us to a shoal. This was where I saw bones not consumed by the sea—human bones scattered across the shoal. I knew then that the men who were thought drowned met a different fate."

Joseph stopped talking and stared forward. The chief wasn't in a rush and held his pause until Blue couldn't stand it any longer and desperately asked, "So did you make love to her?"

Joseph smiled. "Yes. It was either make love to her or let her devour me."

"Holy shit."

"I still have the scratch marks on my back from her claws."

"Holy shit."

"The next morning, she was gone, and I never saw Lanu'ese'ese again."

"How'd you get back to the shore?" Blue

"Swam, I believe. But I do not remember. Some people said that a dolphin returned me to the village."

"Holy shit. You'd think the least Lanu'ese'ese could do for a good time was give you a ride back."

"I returned to Vaimasina, and months later I heard that Lanu'ese'ese bore a child—a boy. She left the child with the nuns and disappeared forever, which peeved the clergymen of the village."

"It was your child."

"Hmm."

"Holy shit."

"I had to return to Amaile village to claim the boy. At the time, hearing about the boy's existence invigorated me. He provided a meaning to my life that I had never known—that I had produced something incredible from an unlikely source and place. I knew the nuns would eventually send the boy to an orphanage in Apia. They had no choice. It would have been one less mouth to feed. Although it was difficult to prove the boy was mine, nobody was going to argue with the son of a *matai*, and they were happy to be rid of the child. But I looked in the boy's eyes to make sure and I saw myself. There was no mistake. For an instant, I lived my life over through his eyes. I took the boy back to Vaimasina and raised him. That's when I understood that living through the war and through all my foolhardy risks and undertakings was important. I was important- it took a child eyes to see my life full."

The chief paused. Telling the story seemed to tire him.

Blue had a million questions to ask. The obvious questions came to him first, such as if the boy had gills or webbed feet. But he refrained from asking such inane questions. Instead, he sat and pondered the story, wondering what was fact and what was fiction. It then occurred to him that it didn't matter. The only thing that was important was that the story was now lore embedded in the minds of the villagers across many villages in the region and passed down to the next generation. Joseph Tuputala had lived a long time, and had witnessed many generations who listened and learned about his legends.

"Now I must rest before I go to village. You may leave," the chief said straightforwardly. "Put on some real clothes before you chafe your ass."

"Oh, yeah," Blue responded. He knew when he was being dismissed.

When Blue returned to the grassy field at the village, he heard someone playing the piano in the church and accompanying a choir. He stopped to listen for a few seconds and was impressed with how well Saitele tuned the old piano. Blue didn't think that it could sound any better for its age. He was pleased with Saitele's job, and he felt that it was worth the money and all the food the piano tuner consumed in the village.

Blue's satisfied moment was quickly dashed when he became surrounded by laughing children who danced around him as if he were a pole on May Day. They called him, "Mister *Lanu Moana*" and tugged at the palm leaves of his skirt, which was now practically falling apart. He picked up his pace to avoid becoming a peepshow, only to be hindered by his hounds, which were excited to sniff at his skirt.

As Blue hurriedly made his way through the village towards his *fale*, he tried to be as inconspicuous as possible. But to his chagrin, it seemed that everyone was out and about on this day, and the commotion that the children and the dogs were making around him only enhanced his return to the village. As he passed people, they couldn't help but stare. Some, like Maeva and Lance, shook their heads with repugnance. Most people, however, simply raised an eyebrow, questioning what the volunteer was up to.

Blue practically leapt into his *fale* and quickly closed the blinds on the children and the dogs. He then squirmed out of the skirt. When he heard the children giggling as they watched him from a broken blind, he flung the skirt at the blind and yelled at them to go away. They did so laughing and calling him, "Mister *Lanu Moana*." He wrapped a *lavalava* around his waist and crashed on his mat.

Blue closed his eyes. He endured so much enlightenment throughout the day that the quiet nothingness of the dark, late afternoon in his *fale* felt rather peaceful to him. Exhausted, he closed his eyes and took a deep breath. All he had wanted to do today—the only thing he had planned— was to tell Aumua that he was returning home. He fancied a sweet homecoming with his girl, where the two would start a new life together. Now, home seemed as if it was a million miles away on another unreachable, uncharted island. And he had no dolphin to carry him there.

3

It was a few months later, after the "pool incident" and the meeting with Ringo, that the main harvest season of the cocoa pods had commenced, and Blue found himself engrossed with helping Aumua on the plantation. It wasn't exactly backbreaking work, but he was sweaty, tired, and hungry by the end of the day. He was also concerned with Aumua working so hard while she was pregnant. She was never bothered by the tedious chores it took to run a plantation, and she never wavered or complained about the work. Whenever Blue tried to get her to slow down and take a rest, she would laugh and continue with her task. Blue, who easily wilted in the heat and had to take breaks in the shade of the mango tree, always felt ashamed watching Aumua steadily work.

Fortunately, the couple was able to recruit several villagers who were dedicated to helping them throughout the entire day. They also had a few part-time workers such as Maeva, who would come and help when she wasn't in class, and Togi, who seemed to show up at different times every day, work for an hour or so, then leave. He certainly didn't have the stamina working with cocoa pods as he did working a fishing pole. Nevertheless, Blue was content with the group of workers, and the help reminded him of the old adage, "Many hands make light work."

Harvesting the cocoa pods took about two to three weeks. The pods typically grew directly from the trunk of the trees and were ready for picking when they changed colors. Blue learned how to use a machete to separate the pod from the base of the tree, and then toss it into a basket made of pandanus leaves. Sometimes, he couldn't help but pretend that he was playing basketball and was making the winning shot for the championship. Although he usually missed, the children that attended the harvesting were always ready to chase the wobbly pod and place it properly in the basket.

During a weekend, villagers that included Togi, Lemanu, and Savea helped Blue repair the roof of the open-wall hut next to the cocoa plantation by replacing the old coconut palm leaves with new ones. They had also built another open hut to help with the fermentation process. Blue mostly followed Lemanu's instruction on the repair and construction of the huts. The project went slowly at first. Togi typically spent the time strumming a ukulele, while Savea, who brought the supplies they needed, would have to leave when his wife, Vaveao, came calling for him to mind his stores. She was very irritated at having to walk a long distance from the village to retrieve her husband. The two invariably argued before Savea gave in and left. Nevertheless, Lemanu grew tired of the time wasting and would eventually bring his family members to quickly finish the job.

The extra hut added much-needed space to for those who harvested the pods. They would remove the beans from the pods, pack them in heaps, then cover them with banana leaves. This process, which took from three to seven days, would force the layer of pulp that surrounds the beans to heat up and ferment them. Aumua believed that this way of fermenting the beans enhanced the Vaimasina cocoa flavor. She handled the discarded husks and distributed them throughout the fields to return nutrients to the soil. Nothing was wasted. The beans were then left to dry in the sun for several days.

Blue often believed that Aumua had a sixth sense for knowing when the beans were ready to be packed in sacks and sold or used. If the beans dried too quickly, some of the chemical reactions that started in the fermentation process would not be allowed to complete their work. If this happened, the beans would become acidic and have a bitter flavor to them. On the other hand, if the beans dried too slowly, molds and an unpleasant flavor easily develop. However, Aumua knew exactly when to stop the drying process, and she would prove her intuition to Blue every time she made him *Koko Samoa*.

From time to time, Blue noticed Ringo appearing on the hill overlooking the plantation, scrutinizing the labor, and jotting notes on the paper of his clipboard. Blue thought that the Aussie's body language looked like that of a petulant troll. Blue wondered about Ringo's jolly and gregarious personality when the salesman wasn't trying to sell a new contract and concluded that the Aussie acted the same no matter where he was or whom he was with. In fact, Blue believed that the salesman was probably even more outgoing with a few beers in front of him.

After examining the plantation, Ringo would seek out Fiame and continue to persuade her to sign a contract before he headed back to the office in Apia. Even when she was at St. Cecilia, he would not hesitate to find her and interrupt her day. Despite his abrupt, yet enthusiastic, manner, she would graciously stop what she was doing and listen to him, nodding in accordance with his recommendations. However, the principal knew that the final say in the matter would ultimately fall upon Joseph and the Tuputala family.

It was at the end of the harvest when Joseph made the final decision not to partner with Crighton Cocoa Company, and he wanted Blue to tell Ringo that the salesman's services would no longer be required, so he could stop coming to Vaimasina.

It didn't take much for Blue to find Ringo, who happened to be at St. Cecilia talking with Fiame one late afternoon. The salesman was dressed more sportily in slacks and a polo shirt. The Western clothes still made Ringo look hot and uncomfortable to Blue. Nevertheless, Blue thought it was best to get the bad news over with as quickly as possible and send the Aussie on his way in his air-conditioned car.

Approaching the two, Blue got a little nervous. Ringo was a massive man, and despite the jolly nature that the Aussie typically displayed, Blue didn't trust his reactions after hearing the bad news. Blue questioned himself whether or not if he should've brought Togi along for extra muscle.

"*Talofa*," Blue said, announcing himself.

"We were just talkin' about you, mate," Ringo said with a wink of an eye.

"The Crighton Company needs an answer about partnering," Fiame added rather impatiently.

"You probably saw me standing on the hill and beaming like a Samoan god, eh?" the salesman said with a laugh. Blue and Fiame didn't laugh. "After watchin' you the past month, I wholeheartedly believe that we can increase your productivity."

Blue thought there was no doubt that they could increase productivity, but he questioned if it would be more economic than doing things the traditional way. Besides, the integrity and the flavor of the cocoa was going to be the same no matter how they harvested the beans and processed them.

"That's why I came to you. We decided not to take your offer," Blue boldly blurted out.

It wasn't the smile on the Aussie's face that dropped as quickly as a manic clown that bothered Blue. It was the dejected exhale that emanated from Fiame's disposition. He knew how badly she wanted this deal to happen.

"That's disappointing, mate," the salesman stated. "I feel sorry for this village. We could've doubled your productivity."

"Perhaps. But I think we do pretty well."

"Yeah, but we could've done it faster."

"It's not a race."

"Add more trees and more workers. The money would be flowing in, eh?"

"Well, we made our decision."

"Right. And who are you?" Ringo asked with a bit of a bite in his tone. "You're just some wily, yella Yank. What are you even doin' here, mate? You look like a ghost in a black sheet factory."

Blue winced at the metaphor, which he felt was as bad as the ones he usually thought of, but without the accent. He was also miffed by Ringo's sudden transformation in attitude. The insult stung him. He had always believed that he had assimilated well into the village way of life. It wasn't easy at first, but currently, he felt like he had some kind of purpose and routine. In fact, Blue would bet the house (or *fale*) that he understood the *Fa'a Samoa* much more than the ex-rugby player.

"I like to think that I'm a member of this community. Today, I'm just a messenger."

"I've seen your kind before. You beachcombers. Livin' off the village and pretendin' to act like you care about the place."

"Dude, I'm just relaying what I was asked to tell you."

"From what some people have been tellin' me around here, you're a bit of a softy. I heard you got the stuffin' knocked out of you durin' a rugby match by a girl, eh?"

"Who told you that?" Blue inquired.

"Some big bloke with tats."

Damn it, Togi.

"Your accusations and insults are totally unfounded and highly uncalled for, Mr. Ringo," Fiame said in Blue's defense.

"Mr. Ronin has been a valuable asset to the village for over a year now."

Blue was a little flattered that Fiame would vouch for his integrity despite believing that the decision that the Tuputalas had made regarding the plantation was a wrong one.

"I hate to see a *palagi* have such influence on a village. I see it all the time I'm in Samoa."

"It's not me who made the decision," Blue added.

"Ah, the hell with you. I'll come back next year, and you'll be begging to sign a contract."

Ringo walked away in a huff but stopped and turned back to Blue.

"I think I liked you better when you wore a grass skirt."

Blue and Fiame remained silent as they watched the Aussie go to his car, which he rudely had parked in the middle of where children usually play. Not that the children minded, as they climbed all over the car and used it as if it was part of the playground. Some of the children even climbed through the window and sat at the wheel, pretending that they were driving the vehicle.

Ringo shooed the children off his car and was helped by Lance Lafau. They opened the driver's door, and an endless pile of kids filed out one by one as if it was a clown car at the circus. The children scrambled away, excited about their next adventure, while the two men conversed. Ringo obviously gave Lance the update and pointed accusingly back at Blue. Staring intensely at Lance, Blue wondered if he was hasty in blaming Togi for telling Ringo about his embarrassing moment during the village rugby match. But after a second thought and despite wanting to find Lance at fault, he still blamed Togi.

Blue wanted to flip off Lance with his middle finger, but he knew better than to provoke him, especially with Lance's mother standing right next to him. The thought that Lance wanted to do the same to him naturally crossed Blue's mind.

Ringo then shook Lance's hand. He got into the car and peeled out of the village, while *veavao* birds scattered for their lives, and the Aussie narrowly missed hitting a pig and a couple of chickens.

Lance gave Blue another one of his classic, scathing stares before heading towards the church.

"I did rock the grass skirt, didn't I?" Blue asked Fiame, who only grunted watching the missed opportunity drive away. "Even though it tickled the hell out of my fanny."

There was a slight pause before Fiame let out a laugh. The laugh was short, but audible. In fact, it was the first time that Blue had ever seen her laugh, and he wasn't exactly positive if she was laughing at his little quip. Blue thought that the principal had been consistently stoic, calculating, and methodical—always planning ahead while never seeming interested in a joke or having fun. Blue was somewhat relieved with the way Fiame laughed.

It was a laugh that put closure to a long and drawn-out idea that she firmly believed in but sadly had no control over.

It was a laugh that meant she had come to terms with another disillusionment.

It was a laugh that stated that she would remain a champion on concerns and issues that would benefit the survival of the village.

Blue watched the principal return to her office and shut the door. It was at that moment that he believed that Fiame was, indeed, the heartbeat of the village, and it could not exist without her.

Piano music began to play from inside the church, and Blue smiled at how well the instrument sounded. He also remembered that Aumua had mentioned to him that the choir was going to rehearse for the upcoming Teuila Festival, as the choir was, once again, asked to perform on the opening night of the festival. Although he was itching to do some writing, he decided to take a few minutes of his time and walked to the church to listen to the choir.

It had been several months since Blue had stepped inside the church. His eyes took a moment to adjust from the brightness of the day. Even the stained glass windows at that moment seemed dimmed, disinterested, and devoid of being able to tell the story of St. Cecilia. It was as if the show had closed for the evening.

Once Blue's eyes adjusted to the light of the church, he sat in a chair near the altar that faced toward the back of the church and its entry door. The choir members were leisurely arriving, and after a chat with other members and non-members, they made their way up the stairs. Blue thought about moving the piano to the community room, where it would be cooler for the choir to practice. But then he thought that would be a bad idea as the piano would have to be returned to the church for Sunday Mass, and he would probably be one of the men to move it.

Children, still in their school uniforms, played in every corner of the church. They were typically not allowed in the church unless it was for some kind of Mass. But they took full advantage of being there, especially since they were mostly unsupervised. They scampered up and down the center aisle, climbed over and under the pews, and splashed holy water at each other from the several stoups that were placed at the doors. Blue even saw some children sitting on top of the balcony wall, dangling their bare feet, and yelling at their friends below. God's house was a playground, and Blue believed that it wouldn't be long before Father Krimple would put a stop to this behavior and have them kneeling in the pews to pray.

Thinking of Father Krimple made Blue wonder where the priest was now. He scanned the entire interior of the church before finding the clergyman sitting in a pew near the confessional box. The priest was engrossed in an intense, but somewhat private conversation with Maria, who was then very pregnant (her due date was just a few weeks behind Aumua). From time to time, little Isaac would run up to them and try to climb between them, only to be brushed away and told to go play with his friends. Blue smiled at the trio and thought that they made a handsome family before remembering that Maria was married to Lemanu and Father Krimple was a priest.

After his consultation with Maria, Father Krimple made his way towards the altar. He saw Blue sitting in a chair and placed another chair next to the volunteer. As he sat down, he nodded to Blue and took a deep breath. He didn't say anything for a moment and stared towards the main door of the church underneath the balcony.

Aumua entered the church showing her many months of pregnancy. She paused and said hello to others who asked her how she felt. She most likely had to remind them of her approximate due date. Maria then greeted Aumua, no doubt sharing a few pregnancy stories before the two expectant mothers ascended the stairs together.

Blue squirmed in his seat. Ever since Aumua started showing that she was pregnant, he had purposely avoided Father Krimple. Blue was embarrassed to be near the priest, knowing that having a child out of wedlock was frowned upon. Blue hated to disappoint Father Krimple, especially because he believed that the priest was a good friend to him. The villagers on the other hand, didn't really seem to care and were quite accepting of the situation, which made Blue feel much more relaxed. Even the very devout and pious ones showed a tolerance towards the fact. Everyone believed that any child born in the village was a blessing and would potentially make the village stronger.

"Maria told me that Lemanu hasn't been home the past week," the priest said in English. In fact, it seemed that the only time the two spoke English was when they were together.

"Doesn't he work in Apia?"

"Yes."

"Maybe he has been tied up with work."

"He beats her, Ronin. He has for a while."

Blue often knew something wasn't right with Lemanu and Maria. She rarely smiled, and often didn't show for choir practice and other group gatherings, opting to stay home with her children.

"Shit."

"And I'm such a coward that I haven't tried to stop it."

"Lemanu would break every bone in your body if you confronted him."

"Probably. I tried a different approach by talking about the wrongs of domestic violence during Mass. It's a big issue throughout Samoa."

"Did Lemanu respond to your talks?"

"I think for a while, but he would often return from Apia drunk, and the trouble would start over. I just feel bad for the children."

"I gotta ask, Father K. Do all their children belong to Lemanu?" It was a bold question. However, Blue believed that their friendship had grown enough that he could ask it.

"Go on. Of course, they're his."

"All?"

"What—what kind of question is that?"

It was at that moment that little Isaac climbed the pulpit and began to recite the Lord's Prayer in broken English, which he butchered. His friends, however, found it to be hilarious.

"Isaac! Get down from there!" Father Krimple shouted in Samoan.

Isaac hopped off the pulpit and ran to his friends, who goaded him to do it again.

Father Krimple took another heavy breath.

"I guess you should know," the priest said.

"Wait. You really don't have to tell me anything."

"No. I want to. I mean, you're part of the village and you should be in the know like everyone else."

Blue was flattered at the comment that he was part of the village. It was the second positive confirmation of his acceptance that had received today. However, he really didn't want to hear about a torrid affair between a priest, a Caucasian priest nonetheless, and a village woman.

"I think I already know."

"Maria and I had an affair shortly after she married Lemanu."

Damn me.

"Lemanu was working overseas in New Zealand, and she attended my Bible study class. She was a very smart, intuitive young woman. She questioned every phrase, psalm, and passage. I was so intrigued with her. I mean, for one thing, she's beautiful. But, after a few months, I just fell for her. I fell deeply for her. I know. I know. I know. What a weak priest. I understand if you think I'm a scumbag."

"I... I don't know. You're a human being first, a man second, and a priest third. And a human can't help but... love."

"Lust?"

"Perhaps that's a bit of a strong word for your circumstance. A human loves in many different ways and for many different reasons."

Blue thought his response sounded cliché. Although the conversation had made him feel a little uncomfortable, he would bet that the gossip during the affair spread quickly through the village.

"I couldn't wait to be with her. Our meetings would continue after everyone else left. We would proceed with our chat long into the night in the community room. Eventually, we would move into my office where our talks became much more, as you can imagine."

"Well, air-conditioning has a way of heightening one's libido."

The priest let out a quick chortle.

"Go on. That's what I like about you, Ronin. You know

how to make the best of a bad situation. You're unassuming and nonjudgmental. I see why the village really likes you. I'm glad you came to Vaimasina and that we've become good such friends."

"And Lemanu knows that Isaac is your son?"

"Yes, he knows. Lemanu has been a good sport. I mean, he could've easily ripped me to shreds. But during confession one day, he confided that he was having an affair with a woman in Apia, and he felt that Isaac was a way that God punished him for his adultery."

"Whoa. Even little island villages aren't immune to sordid intrigue."

"That's why we always need God."

"I suppose. Well, it's, uh, not easy for a Westerner as yourself to live in the Pacific for as long as you have. Maugham, or mom, I could never pronounce his name—but he once wrote, 'The Pacific is inconstant and uncertain like the soul of man.'"

"Did he mean the ocean, the island, or both?"

"Oh, uh, I don't know..."

There was an awkward pause as Blue thought about the priest's question. Although Blue addled his brain, he couldn't remember where he read the quote, and so he left it at that.

Vaveao Suisala, who conducted the group, decided it was time to get started and signaled to her husband, Savea, to begin playing the piano. The choir began to rehearse their first hymn of the night and chose the song, "Be Not Afraid," by the Jesuit priest, Bob Dufford. Everyone immediately stopped talking, paused for the piano intro, and then began singing. The sentimental song sounded superb within the stone and sand of the church. The harmonies between the men and women were exquisite and transformed the old place of worship into an ethereal realm that possessed no boundaries, only a vacuumed space of pleasant serenity and quietness.

Blue had never heard anything like it.

Blue and Father Krimple sat staring at the ground and were lost in thought. Blue enjoyed the sound of the piano since it had been tuned despite Savea's slipups of the notes. Father Krimple on the other hand, tried to recognize Maria's voice and remembered a time when the young lady sung to him. The choir, however, had one voice, and it was next to impossible for him to single out the sound of his former lover.

"Sometimes I think that I should quit all this and be with Maria," the priest said rather wistfully. "After all, I'm not even a Catholic."

Blue shook his head in disbelief.

"Whoa. What?"

"It's true," the priest sighed. "When I left Canada, I was about your age and made my way to the Pacific. I was a practicing Episcopalian at the time, but not a priest. I bounced around from Fiji to Tonga to the Cooks before settling in Samoa. When I finally came to Vaimasina village, I knew that I would never want to leave. I immediately fell in love with the people, the parish, the village, their... *Koko Samoa.* I've been here for sixteen years."

"How'd you become Father Krimple then?"

"The priest at the time was a salty, crusty ole man from Ireland named Father O'Malley. Believe it or not, he had a mouth like a sailor and was the most disagreeable human being I had ever met. He was pushing ninety and complained about this and that, and was always displeased with the villagers. Nothing was done right in his mind. He berated and belittled them. He never even learned how to speak Samoan after spending fifty years on the island. I always thought that the villagers deserved better, and I couldn't wait for the ole curmudgeon to die. Do you think that was unchristian of me?"

"Oh, uh... I don't think I'm in any position to determine... I mean, I wasn't there."

"When he passed away, we buried him in the small church graveyard that's now overrun with bush. I don't think the man had any family. The diocese didn't seem to know, or care, that he passed away. I guess I took advantage of the villagers, being a white man and all, and said that I would volunteer to run St. Cecilia. I learned how to be a Catholic priest."

"And the diocese still doesn't know?"

"If they do, they haven't taken any action over it. Vaimasina is not exactly on the tip of anyone's tongue. I think they're just happy someone is out here doing the Lord's work. I wouldn't trade it for the world."

"Who are you, Father K? Do you fight crime at night too?"

Father Krimple laughed.

"No. I only fight angry wives and superstitions."

"And do the villagers know you're not Catholic?"

"I think so."

"Shit. They know everything."

"They do. But they liked me, and I loved them. We've had a wonderful relationship over the years."

Blue couldn't believe the disclosures that he was hearing this evening. Blue had a hunch about Isaac being Father Krimple's son, but he had no idea that the priest wasn't Catholic. He wondered how the villagers protected Father Krimple when someone from the diocese came to visit the village, and he thought how this would make a lively and zany television show.

"Is it a sin to act under the pretense of a Catholic priest?" Blue asked.

"Go on. That's a question I struggle with every day, my friend. But everything I've done and will do is through the love of the people of Vaimasina. The villagers know that it will be I, and I alone, who will have to face God's judgment someday. I try to anticipate that God will be just and understanding."

Blue shrugged his shoulders. He never believed in a just God and thought that religion in general was just one big, tangled yarn of hypocrisy. Nevertheless, Blue thought that if there should be any man getting through the gates of heaven, it should be Father Krimple. Blue had never seen anyone who was entirely devoted to serving God and man to the point that he had to invent a profession as a priest to do it.

"My only regret right now is falling in love with Maria," the priest lamented, staring at the choir. "I envy you, Ronin. Soon you'll be able to go home to your family."

Blue looked at the priest and wanted to tell him that the word, "regret," seemed a bit harsh.

One should never regret falling in love.

However, the volunteer understood what Father Krimple meant. The priest would never give up his calling to be with the Maria. There were just too many consequences that would fall upon him for such a rash act. Blue felt sorry for him. He knew that Father Krimple had been living in a quandary—damned if he did and damned if he didn't. Nevertheless, if Blue was in the priest's sandals, he would be damned with the church and the village and be with the woman he loved. Blue then asked himself, *was this what he had done with Aumua?* Did he be damned everything to be with her? Regardless, now Blue appreciated his relationship with Aumua. He could love her without any costs.

Blue gazed towards the balcony and immediately locked eyes with her. She paused her singing long enough to smile at him. Blue returned the smile, and he swooned, lost in her gaze as if the two were the only ones in the place. Staring at Aumua, Blue could feel the jealousy of the priest and he was proud of that. Blue had heard the adage that a pregnant woman always glowed, but Aumua simply sparkled. Perhaps it was the light in the church as the day began to surrender itself to the night that made Aumua look effervescent and glittery. Whatever it was, Blue felt a loving calm that overtook him, and he was comforted that everything would be all right. All doubt was conquered. He wasn't apprehensive about bringing a life into this world because it would be a safe, supportive world, and Aumua was going to be a kind and loving mother. He began to anticipate the birth of his child.

Although it wasn't technically nightfall, Blue would remember this moment as a night of revelations for the rest of his life. It was a night of honesty, self-awareness, and acceptance. The latter genuinely intrigued Blue. Despite the villagers' idiosyncrasies and staunch commitment to their traditions and religion, they were willing to bend the rules to ensure a happy and thriving community. Most importantly, it was the night that Blue, for the first time, recognized that he was truly and unequivocally in love. And it excited him.

It was a couple of months later, on Halloween night, when Aumua went into labor. Blue tried to convince her to go to the hospital in Apia to give birth, but she insisted on having the child in the village. In fact, she decided to give birth to the child in her and Blue's *fale*. She was in good hands, however. Taaiti and her two daughters acted as midwives, and Aumua's older half-sister, Lupesina, was there with her two daughters to help in the process. Other women, such as Maeva, Iris, and Vaveao, would come and go from the *fale*, bringing and taking away food and supplies. All the women agreed that it would be best for Blue to wait outside.

It was a still, quiescent night as Blue paced around the *fale*. The moon was in its new phase, which allowed the stars to dazzle and daze anyone who bothered to look upon them. It was as if the stars were desperate to have someone —anyone—watch them like an out-of-work actor. Blue, however, never bothered to look up, much to the disappointment of the stars. He was too worried about the event that was unfolding in his *fale*. Every time a woman exited the building, Blue would look at them in want of hopeful news. Unfortunately, they would shake their head and say, "Not yet," and Blue would resume his pacing.

His patrolling wore a new path in the grass around his

fale. Togi nonchalantly joined Blue, smoking marijuana. He stood still watching the volunteer pace around the *fale* a few times.

"Bro, you making me dizzy," Togi said and took a long puff of his joint.

Blue stopped and stood next to his friend. Togi passed the joint to Blue, who took a big hit and returned it.

"*Faafetai.*"

"You look as if you could use a puff or two."

"Yeah, at least two," Blue agreed and took the joint from Togi again.

"No moon tonight, bro. You shouldn't be out here by yourself, or ghosts will get you."

Blue wasn't sure if Togi was kidding with him or not. But he did find it somewhat amusing if Togi was sincere, which meant that this giant of a man was scared of the dark.

"It's Halloween night," Blue stated and took another drag of the joint. "Let the ghosts sing."

Halloween wasn't really celebrated in a homogeneous village like Vaimasina, as every night seemed to be taken with caution. In the larger town of Apia, however, All Hallows' Eve had become a little more widespread with its diverse population of many expats who enjoyed seeing the holiday's popularity grow each year.

"No moon is good sign you have a boy," Togi said proudly.

"As long as it's healthy."

"You teach him to fish."

"Dude, I hate the water."

"I teach him to fish."

"If it's a boy, you can teach him to fish."

Togi smiled. He was delighted about the possibility of teaching the ways of fishing to another young member of the village.

"He will be a good fisherman like my boys," Togi added.

When Iris emerged from the *fale*, Togi quickly smothered his joint and tossed it on the ground. She quickly sighed when she saw Blue standing with her man. If Togi wasn't fishing, he was more than likely hanging out with the volunteer. She increasingly became frustrated and jealous that her man spent more time with the American than her.

"What are you doing out here in the dark?" Iris asked irritably.

"I was told to wait..." Blue started to say before being cut off.

"I know why you're here," she said curtly before turning her attention to her husband. "Are you smoking again?"

"No," Togi said.

"I can smell you from here."

"You smell like a bloodhound."

Blue grinned and tried to keep from laughing.

"Mr. Ronin, was he smoking his marijuana?"

Blue shrugged his shoulders. "What's marijuana?" Togi couldn't help but laugh.

"Oh, you two," she said with disgust.

Aumua moaned in the *fale*, and Blue remembered the bigger picture.

"It'll happen any moment," Iris said to Blue. "We have a crib you can use."

Blue translated what she said from Samoan to English and felt a bit comforted that everything seemed to be going without any complications.

"*Faafetai.*"

Iris beckoned Togi to return with her to their home, and the fisherman responded.

"Bro, maybe my sister will give you two boys."

"Then there will be a lot of fishing going on."

"Yeah," Togi said with a smile. "I'll build them a canoe."

"*Sau loa!*" Iris urged, and the big Samoan hurried to catch up to his wife.

Blue was alerted by Aumua's moan and went to the *fale* to make sure she was all right. He stopped just outside and heard the women encouraging Aumua to push and telling her how beautiful it was that she was bringing life into the world. Blue eased his anxiety and backed away from the *fale*.

As if tired of being ignored, a star fell from the cluster and fizzled out over the ocean. Blue didn't see it, and thus, another star gave its life in hopes of attracting attention to the rest of the sky.

A breeze swished through the village and stirred the stagnant air. Blue closed his eyes to let the wind cool his clammy face. He heard familiar music, which was carried by the gust. But he couldn't quite place the tune, not that he cared at that soothing moment.

When the breeze died away, the music continued. Blue opened his eyes. He recognized the tune, which was the "Danse Macabre" by Camille Saint-Saëns, an appropriate piece for a Halloween night. It was an odd version that was played with a cello, and Blue knew instantly that his old friend-turned-demon was producing the music. He turned and looked across the grassy field and could barely see a diaphanous Scarlett playing the piece at the edge of the jungle.

Blue wondered if Scarlett was mocking him, or if she was simply providing background music for the night of the dead. Blue watched and listened to her as her playing somewhat intoxicated him.

Damn me—she's good... even in death.

Blue reminisced the Halloween night during his senior year in high school when he was at Scarlett's house rehearsing for her college entrance audition. He was dressed as The Terminator. He wore an eighteenth-century-looking costume but with a leather jacket and sunglasses. A violin represented a weapon.

"What are you wearing?" Scarlett asked. She was annoyed at the distraction enough to stop playing.

"It's Halloween. I'm the Bachinator."

"The what?'

"I'll be *baach*," Blue quoted from the movie, *The Terminator*, and laughed. "Get it?"

"No."

"I'm the Terminator and Johann Sebastian Bach. Get it?"

Blue instantly thought that saying it out loud sounded lame, but he cut himself some slack since it was Halloween.

"What's the Terminator?"

"You've never seen the movie?"

"No."

"Then my costume is wasted on you."

"I think it would be wasted on a lot of people."

"You think?"

"Yes."

"Shit," Blue said with a bit of concern. He scrutinized his costume. "And I'm going to a party tonight."

"I thought we were practicing tonight?"

"We are. But it's Halloween. I'm gonna head out early."

"Hands on the piano!" A voice came from outside the room. Scarlett's grandmother was never caught off guard.

Blue sarcastically placed his hands behind himself on the piano.

"Speaking of ole ghouls..." Blue added with insolence.

"Leave her alone."

"Why don't you come to the party with me?"

"Where is it?"

"It's at the resort where I work. Just throw on a costume."

"I don't know what I'd be."

"Anything. Just go as Yo-Yo Ma."

Scarlett giggled. Blue liked to hear her giggle. It made her seem human.

"We can play Halloween music at the party," Blue said, excited by the idea.

"What's Halloween music?"

"I don't know... like the Dance Macabre or something."

"I can't go. My parents aren't home."

"That's the best time to go."

Scarlett giggled again.

"My grandmother would catch me. I'm never out of her sight."

Blue sighed. He knew it was true. He believed that if Scarlett left, the old woman would use a witch's spell to bring her back.

Blue looked at his music companion and felt sorry for her. She had never been allowed to live a normal life. He knew he would feel bad if he left her earlier than he was supposed to, and he came to the realization that he was going to miss the party.

"Maybe we can tell each other ghost stories later," Blue sighed, wondering if she knew any.

Scarlett's smile was quick and satisfied. She began to playfully perform the "Danse Macabre" on her cello, and it sounded even more haunting on the instrument.

It was another groan from Aumua that broke Blue's transfixed attention on the spectral Scarlett. As Blue turned towards his *fale*, Father Krimple was standing right behind him and practically scared the volunteer to death.

"Damn, Father K!"

"Happy Halloween!" the priest exclaimed.

Blue looked back across the grassy field to see that Scarlett had vanished.

"You're a little jumpy tonight," Father Krimple said. "But go on. You should be. Your child is gracing the world for the first time."

Blue liked the phrase that the priest had used, "gracing the world for the first time."

"It should be any minute now," Blue said.

"Quite. Over the years, I've had a habit of showing up at the moment of delivery. I guess God gave me a birthing intuition."

Blue shot him a curious look.

What does that mean?

"Er... for paperwork," the priest continued. "I record the date and time of the birth."

"Oh."

"You'll need to notify the registrar of birth to the Samoa Bureau of Statistics within three months. It usually costs about fifteen *talas* for the certificate. If you don't have the money, I will pay it for you."

"I have the money."

"I trust you'll baptized the child soon?" the priest asked in a tone where only an affirmative answer would suffice.

Blue, of course, knew Father Krimple was egging him on, but he also knew that it would be a moot point to answer negatively. Aumua was going to baptize the child with or without Blue's consent.

"I will do whatever Aumua wants."

"Go on. Aumua is so splendidly devoted to the Lord, don't you think? I have no doubts that she'll want her family serving God and worshipping together every Sunday, right? Are you willing to share that same spiritual piety with your new family, Ronin? Will you let the Lord into your life?"

The many questions made Blue feel uncomfortable. He nervously twitched and looked around for a distraction that would allow him to not have to answer any of the priest's hard inquiries.

Hey! The Spanish Inquisition just called, and they want to hire you.

Fortunately for Blue, a commotion could be heard coming from the *fale*. Aumua made a painful and prolonged shriek that signified the final push of the birth. Blue left the priest and hurried to the *fale* but stopped when all went eerily silent. He wondered if something had gone wrong. He waited for sound, any sound, but nothing came. He asked himself if God had taken away his Aumua, or child, or both.

A couple of important people had already unjustly been stolen from him, and he quickly speculated if he was cursed or not. Blue, accusingly looked back at the priest, ready to put the blame on him and his Almighty Father.

A joyous cry then came from Aumua and the ladies attending her that seeped through the surrounding slats of the blinds and drowned the silence. Relieved, Blue dashed into the *fale* to see his woman holding a baby girl.

Blue knelt down next to Aumua and the baby. Aumua managed a smile for Blue through her sweaty, exhausted disposition, and Blue had never seen anything more beautiful. He brushed the hair away from her face with his hand and then touched his nose to hers. The two remained nose-to-nose until the baby squealed.

Aumua then handed the child to Blue. He had never held anything that small that had a heartbeat. She was born with tan skin, black hair, and black eyes, and looked more like her mother, which Blue thanked the heavens for. Maeva jibed Blue and asked if he was the actual father. Everyone in the *fale* laughed until Father Krimple entered and crossed himself. Perhaps he didn't care for the joke. Nevertheless, he looked at the child and proudly blessed her. Blue tried to position his arms delicately so that he wouldn't drop the child. Maeva, naturally, couldn't help but remind the volunteer how to hold a baby properly by supporting the head. Others soon gathered around Blue to take a look and hopefully get a chance to hold the baby.

However, Blue pushed his way through the crowd and made his way out of the *fale*. He left the group like a boy who didn't want to share his new toy with his siblings. Then Togi and Lily returned with a small crib, and Togi asked if it was a boy. Blue shook his head negatively, which made his friend frown with disappointment. Lily, on the other hand, told Blue that the baby was exquisite, and the volunteer smiled because he was thinking the same thing.

Blue carried his daughter out to the middle of the grassy field. A breeze circled around the two, and the baby opened her eyes and started to cry. Blue looked at his child and was simply awestruck. He had never heard anything so lovely. The crying was music to him. It was a stunning, lively orchestral piece. The moment reminded him of the Hans Christian Andersen quote: "Where words fail, music speaks." He thought his daughter was composed of beautiful yet unheard of and unwritten notes—rare notes that could only be captured and used once.

At that moment, Blue thought of only one name for her: Mele, which he pronounced as "May-lay." He liked its poetic, melodic cadence and believed that it could be the name of a star. Later that night, he would share the name with Aumua and the village, and they would cherish her as if she was a brilliant heavenly body from the cosmos.

Scarlett appeared at the edge of the forest and began to perform the "Danse Macabre" again. Blue didn't care. He was solely transfixed on his daughter.

Blue's hounds came lumbering out of the darkness. They were instantly attracted to the small, smelly thing that Blue was holding. They sniffed, asking if the child was a toy, food, or both. Blue raised the baby higher and used his legs to push the dogs aside. He then told the dogs to go away. He was helped with an incensed wail from Mele that spooked the dogs. The hounds paused their enthusiastic investigation of the child. Blue yelled at them to go away again, and they bounded towards the village, hurdling one another until the darkness swallowed them.

Blue finally looked skyward, and the stars awoke, pleased that someone had actually paid attention to them. They shoved themselves to get into position to perform like a traveling troupe of actors. Realizing that they had a momentous occasion beneath them, the stars shined and twinkled, and every twenty seconds, one would gloriously fall to earth. Blue pretended to catch them all, so that one day he could give them to Mele.

4

―――――――

Almost a year had passed since the night of Mele's birth, and the months simply seemed to roll into each other. In fact, there were times throughout the year that Blue had no idea what month, or even what day, it was. Not that he minded. Blue liked the pace of the tropical village. On those unbearably hot days, he would visit Father Krimple and hope that the priest was in his air-conditioned office. Blue would try to talk to the clergyman for as long as he could until the priest kicked him out and scolded the volunteer for keeping him from his duties or an important meeting. Blue didn't mind the reprimand. He enjoyed his chats with the priest.

Blue spent his working days helping Aumua with the cocoa plantation. He continued to be impressed with her work ethics. She had no trouble harvesting more cocoa pods and carrying more baskets while holding Mele than Blue could do in a day. Regardless of being outshined by his woman, the plantation gave Blue the opportunity to provide assistance to the village and a sense of belonging, which made him feel as if he was part of the community. And since there was only one main harvest and a few smaller ones throughout the year, he could devote many hours to working on his novel. This, however, was probably more of a pipedream than reality. He could never resist saying no to Togi and other villagers who interrupted him and needed his help for one matter or another.

Perhaps what Blue loved the most about the past year was living with his family in his *fale*. He relished the evenings when Aumua tried to teach Mele the traditional ways of the village. She even began to teach their daughter how to dance, even though the child hadn't begun to walk. While Aumua and other villagers fussed over Mele, Blue would write until Mele would crawl to him and tried to engage her father into doing something more fun, which the volunteer readily obliged. Whenever the excitement level rose, Blue's hounds would leap into the *fale* to participate in the playtime. Blue believed that the dogs' participation was just a front to steal dirty and soiled nappies for a quick and easy snack.

The one thing that Blue noticed and was very relieved about was that Scarlett and the rest of the *Teine Sa* were not seen or heard since Mele was born. Blue wondered if it was the happiness of his life and home that kept the ghoulish, white-dressed women confined to some kind of a worldly dungeon of the forest. But Blue never forgot about the scary specters, and it wasn't like the adage, "out of sight, out of mind," that he took relief from. Indeed, Blue thought about Scarlett often and always checked his surroundings each time he went to the pool, the plantation, the forest, the church, and his *fale*. He had no doubts that the *Teine Sa* would someday return to him. The bigger question, however, that still prowled his mind was: Why?

It was about half past three in the morning in the middle of October when Blue groggily awoke to the sound of someone scratching on the blinds of his *fale*. At first, he was terrified that the *Teine Sa* had returned just as he predicted and rose from his mat, but then he became more at ease when he heard the voice of Togi.

"Bro. *To ka palolo.*"

Blue groaned and fell back on his mat. He knew it was once again *palolo* season.

For a couple of early mornings during the month of October, particularly after the full moon, the village comes alive with the hunting of worms in the shallow coral reef of the lagoon. It was practically a festival for them. Samoans considered the often vibrant, blue palolo a delicacy. Most of the villagers of Vaimasina got involved with the hunt. Not only do they eat the worms on the spot, but they would also catch enough to take home and fry them with butter and onions. They would then place the blend on a savory base like taro. In the years when the abundance of captured *palolo* was great, the villagers would take the tasty worms to the market in Apia to sell for good money because of its high demand and value.

Blue was able to avoid the *palolo* hunt for the past three years with assorted reasons, but he knew Aumua wasn't going to let him skip the annual experience this year. It was a village event, and Aumua always participated because they required everyone's efforts for a successful outcome.

She felt it was her way of giving back to those who helped her with the cocoa plantation.

Aumua kicked Blue to get up and get ready, then dressed Mele. Blue slowly rolled over. Aumua kicked him again.

"Get up," Aumua ordered.

After she finished dressing Mele, the baby crawled to Blue and pounced on top of him.

"Okay. Okay. I'm up," Blue moaned. He then took hold of his daughter and raised her above him. "You ready to catch some *palolo*?" When Blue placed her back on the ground, she demanded that he raise her again, which he did. After several times of this, Blue's arms got tired, and he finally gently placed her on the ground and quickly stood up to end the game.

Togi, Keanu, and Kobe entered the *fale* with specially made funnel-shaped baskets with handles for *palolo* catching. They also carried several leis made of *moso'oi*, which was a special flower that was supposed to attract the worms to the surface. They were eager to get to the reef. The two squirmed impatiently and acted as if they were late. They believed that if they didn't leave immediately, all the worms in the sea would be caught.

Blue put on shorts and a T-shirt. He was grateful that it wasn't a cold morning. In fact, it was one of those rare moments when he didn't mind the balmy temperature of the dark morning.

Aumua picked up Mele and rushed out of the *fale*. Togi, Keanu, and Kobe wanted to follow them, but they waited for Blue.

"Where's your net?" Togi asked Blue impatiently.

"I don't have one."

"Then you will be the bait."

The thought of returning to the water after his shark showdown a couple of years ago still haunted him, so Blue didn't like the word "bait."

"Wait? What kinda bait?"

Togi placed several leis around Blue's neck and even tied ones around the top of the volunteer's thighs.

"Worm bait," Kobe said and laughed.

By the time they got to the lagoon, most of the villagers were already in the reef catching *palolo* using flashlights and nets. A few villagers were using canoes and went a little farther in the hopes of finding a lucrative worm spot.

Blue was hesitant to go into the water, but he was practically dragged in by Togi and his sons. As they passed Aumua, Blue saw the abundance of worms that she had already caught. In a bucket, they looked like an undulating brain as they slithered and slimed on top of each other. Every so often, Aumua would pause and take a few to eat. She would also hand Mele a worm for her to slurp, which disgusted Blue.

"Uh, hello. A zombie just called and he's jealous of the brain you're eating."

Nobody paid attention to the volunteer.

Blue then looked at Togi and Kobe, who both had a handful of worms writhing from their mouths.

"Good Lord."

"Bro, over here," Togi called.

Blue didn't want to go any further than necessary in the reef. He was already in knee-high water, and each step made him more nervous.

Children swam and waded by and laughed at the volunteer for wearing an overabundance of leis.

"Stand next to me, bro, and get your flowers closer to the water," Togi ordered.

"How long does this take?"

"You're like a mistress, bro, smelling all pretty," Togi said. "The worms love it."

"Come on, this doesn't work."

"Just stand still."

Kobe called for his father a little distance away. He had found a spot with a flashlight where the *palolo* was in abundance. Togi and Keanu hurried over to him, but Blue remained where he was.

"Jackpot, bro!" Togi yelled. "Come over here!"

"Hurry!" Keanu added in Samoan. "*Vave!*"

Blue sighed and started to move towards them.

After a few steps, Blue felt a sting on the bottom of his foot. At first, he thought that he had just stepped on a piece of coral, but it wasn't long before he realized that it was something much worse.

"Mr. *Lanu Moana*, over here!" Kobe beckoned.

Blue tried to move on, but had to stop, as the pain became much worse. He grabbed his foot and lifted it out of the water to look at it. The pain was excruciating. It was like he stepped on a plate of upright nails. His foot had already started to swell, and the discomfort began to shoot up his leg.

"Togi!" Blue called. "I think I stepped on something. I can't walk."

Togi looked over at his friend and saw that he was struggling to stand on one foot. He tugged Kobe's arm, and the two headed back to Blue. The two were a little annoyed that they had to leave a good spot.

"I stepped on a rock or something, and now my foot hurts."

Togi gave Blue a concerned look. He told Keanu and Kobe to swim away from the area, which they did immediately.

"I think you stepped on a stonefish."

"I don't feel so good."

"They're poisonous, bro."

Damn me.

"We better get you ashore for help," Togi said with apprehension.

"I can't walk, dude."

Togi looked around to see what villager was close and saw Savea. He called for the store owner to come over and help.

"What's wrong?" Savea asked.

"He stepped on a stonefish."

A sense of terror came over the store owner.

"In these waters?"

The question was a valid one. Stonefish were rarely found in the reef near Vaimasina and, indeed, in the waters around Upolu Island.

"Help him up." Togi directed.

The two men picked up the volunteer and began to carry him back to shore.

When Aumua saw that Blue was being carried, she hurriedly rushed to them to see what was wrong.

"He stepped on a stonefish," Togi said excitedly.

"Here?" Aumua responded a bit confused, as nobody

from the village had ever encountered a stonefish. "Oh my God."

The men placed Blue on the beach. A fever overtook the volunteer, and he felt a little nauseous. It wasn't uncommon for victims of a stonefish sting to feel some numbness and tingling near the entry point of the poison, and Blue complained that he couldn't feel his foot anymore. Although he had never heard of a stonefish before, he detected everyone's concern and became scared. He started to have tremors—perhaps from an allergic reaction to the venom.

Villager after villager came out of nowhere and gathered around Blue. They seemed to quickly multiply like crabs from an upturned rock in the sand. They asked questions as to what happened and gasped when they heard what caused the volunteer's dilemma.

"Let's get him to our *fale*," Aumua ordered. "I'll get Taaiti."

This was the first time that the sound of the vane traditional healer's name provided a brief sense of relief for Blue.

Togi and Savea carried Blue to the volunteer's *fale*. Other villagers tried to aid the men by stepping in to grab Blue's leg, arm, or a foot, but they were more of a nuisance than support. Togi was constantly telling people to back away. But whenever someone dropped away, another person stepped in. Despite being in severe pain, Blue couldn't help but to feel a little touched at the enthusiastic, yet clumsy interest of every villager wanting to help him.

As the villagers laid Blue on the mat of his *fale*, he fell flat on his back. He stared at the rafters and wondered if this was the end for him. It was very likely that he was having an allergic reaction to the venom. He started to have aches and chills, and his eyes began to burn. He rolled over to his side and saw that everyone was staring at him.

"I guess this is one way of getting out of *palolo* fishing," Blue jibed.

Nobody laughed, and Blue thought it was a tough crowd as he usually did whenever he told a joke.

"No worries, bro. *Palolo* will be back tomorrow," Togi reassured his friend, not that Blue cared.

A bleary-eyed Blue looked at Taaiti entering the *fale* with a bag made out of pandanus leaves wrapped around her shoulder. The old lady was wearing a traditional grass skirt, and he thought that she had entered his home naked from the waist upwards. She had an assortment of necklaces made of shells and flowers draped around her neck. This, naturally, prompted Blue to jest to himself:

Hey! The 1972 National Geographic magazine just called, and they want their villager back in their photo.

It wasn't funny, but Blue, nevertheless, laughed hysterically, which caused some concern to those who were around him.

Behind Taaiti followed one of her daughters and Aumua, who was carrying Mele.

Taaiti's daughter was holding a tray of assorted herbs that she would need to help the volunteer.

The traditional healer and her daughter knelt next to Blue, and the old lady started chanting in Samoan. Blue wasn't sure if it was the poison that was distorting his comprehension of what Taaiti was saying, but he certainly had a hard time understanding her.

Taaiti lifted Blue's poisoned foot, grabbed a small bottle

of hot water off the tray that her daughter was holding, and poured it on the wound. She also forced the volunteer to consume leaves from the *matalafi* plant, which was known to be used for treating aches, pains, swelling, fevers, and more.

Taaiti then took an 'ava coconut shell full of liquid off the tray and poured its content on the area where the poisonous spine punctured his skin.

It hurt.

"What was that?" Blue asked, lifting his head and expecting to hear that it was some kind of traditional medicine.

"Vinegar," Taaiti answered.

Blue rested his head back down on the mat, a bit disappointed. But it didn't matter. The word, vinegar, would be the last word the volunteer heard before he fell unconscious.

When Blue awoke twenty-four hours later, he was in an Apia hospital. Aumua, Mele, and Maeva were sitting by his side. Blue blinked his eyes, trying to get his bearings. He didn't recognize the ceiling, as it quickly dawned on him that wherever he was, it wasn't his *fale* in Vaimasina. Perhaps the biggest giveaway that he was in a strange place was the fact that he was lying in an actual bed. It had been years since he felt the padding of a Western-style mattress. Even the pillow was softly cushioned and cradled his head like an egg in a nest.

Aumua was glad and relieved to see Blue awake. She kissed him on the cheek and rubbed her nose against his nose. She then picked up Mele and held her close to Blue to do the same.

"Where am I?" Blue asked groggily. He could still feel a tingling from his hip down to the bottom of the foot where the venom entered his body.

"You're in hospital, dummy," Maeva answered in an unsympathetic tone. "You were dying, so we got Savea to drive you and us here."

Blue was surprised to hear that the villagers would allow him to be brought all the way to Apia. Typically, they would let Taaiti perform her magic and make everything better. The stonefish poisoning, however, was something unusual and even caused a little uncertainty on the part of the traditional healer.

Blue leaned forward in his bed.

"I was dying?"

"Your legs were twitching like an upright cockroach," Maeva facetiously added.

"No. Stop teasing him, Maeva," Aumua said with a hint of reproach. She then turned her attention back to Blue. "Taaiti stopped the poison, and it was Father who told us to bring you here."

Blue was intrigued and somewhat flattered about hearing that it was Joseph who told them to take him to the hospital. An order from the *matai*, the big man, who usually wasn't involved with trivial events such as this, made Blue feel more like an essential part of the village and that the chief truly cared for his well-being.

"Your father told you to bring me here?"

"It's the only place that has the antivenom," Aumua said.

"You stepped on four spines," Maeva revealed. "You'll be pissing poison out for days."

Blue looked at the affected, bandaged foot. He lay back down. His head was spinning, and his entire body felt achy, stiff, and just weird.

"I have to go to class," Maeva said. She then patted the toes of the bandaged foot. "Try not to step on anything with spines on the way home, or you'll really look like a dying cockroach."

Maeva raised her arms in the air and wriggled them as if she was in the last throws of death. She then giggled and exited the room.

"Don't pay attention to her, Ronin," Aumua said calmly.

"I never do."

Aumua placed Mele on Blue's chest and then lay down next to him. As long as no one touched his sore foot, he didn't mind the crowdedness. He was used to it in his *fale*. Mele was fascinated with Blue's shell and coconut necklace and started to play with it.

"I was very worried about you," Aumua confided. "People have died from stonefish stings, especially those who were allergic to the venom. Thank God they had an antivenom."

"That'll be the last time I wear a bunch of leis in the water. I couldn't see where I was walking."

Aumua snickered and then said, "Strange how we are always looking for an antidote in life."

Whoa. That was profound.

Blue wanted to make sure that he understood her Samoan.

"What do you mean?"

"I mean, when we are sad, we look for what makes us happy. When we hurt, we want something to take the pain away. Those who are poor search for ways to get rich. Life constantly asks for an antivenom... a remedy."

Blue had to admit that his woman was being quite thought-provoking. He always thought of Aumua as being one with the earth, as well as being rooted with traditional customs and values. Acting as a poet, however, was new to him, and he was delighted to see this side of her. Since he first met her, she had become much more complex and insightful. He had also noticed how sagacious, like her father, she had become over the past couple of years.

"Well, you certainly cured my loneliness."

Aumua slapped Blue on the chest. "How can you be lonely with all the villagers around you?"

"True. They are nosy."

Aumua slapped him again.

"Father Krimple thinks you and I are truly blessed, and I do too. I think it is your mother, Ronin. She faithfully watches over you. Sometimes, when you fall asleep in the shade of a banyan tree on our plantation, I see her sitting next to you. She cradles your head. It comforts me to see how she protects you. I feel she protects me and Mele as well."

Blue tucked Aumua's head under his chin and kissed the top of her head. He closed his eyes and tried to visualize Aumua's imagery of his mother being near him as he slept under a banyan tree. The protection from the ancestors was a big part of the *Fa'a Samoa*, and even in death, they were alive all around them. He understood how Aumua would be so proud to see his mother watching over him—that's what the ancestors were supposed to do. Blue believed that if his mother could also still safeguard him from another realm, she would do it. She was simply that type of person... and she would probably whistle a Broadway tune as well.

Blue smirked, as he believed he heard a humming of the melody of the song, "Someone Like You," from the Broadway Musical *Jekyll and Hyde*, which his mother loved to sing.

The thought of his mother being in the hospital room and lovingly cradling his family made him forget his pain. It was the perfect antidote now, until he fell asleep.

A couple of days later, Blue was released from the hospital. He didn't return right away to Vaimasina. Instead, he and his family spent a few days at Aumua's aunt's house in Apia. Hearing that Aumua's child was at the house, relatives from around Apia came to meet the youngest member of the *aiga*. Naturally, the relative's visit was accompanied by a bountiful of food, and Blue ate until his strength recovered. Although the relatives were mainly interested in getting to know Mele, a few of the male relatives were intrigued with Blue's struggle with the stonefish and asked the volunteer all kinds of questions. They then argued like a group of opposing politicians for the reason why such a creature which hadn't been seen in ten, twenty, fifty years, would suddenly be found in their lagoon. Eventually, they came to an agreement that put the blame on global warming, rising sea levels, and Blue's *Teine Sa*.

5

Blue certainly had his share of getting himself in unusual predicaments the past few years while living in Samoa. Although he tried his best to anticipate and mitigate these pesky occurrences, an awkward quandary unfolded out of the most innocuous day that Blue was completely unprepared for, and it would leave lasting repercussions.

The day was bright, blistering, and without any breeze. In fact, it was one of those days where most of the villagers only wanted to take a nap in hopes that nighttime would bring some relief from the uncomfortable heat. Blue was working in the cocoa plantation, collecting a modest harvest of cocoa pods. He was still having issues with his foot and leg, and at times, there was a numbness that hindered him from doing any activities that required the use of his leg. Thus, the volunteer decided to head back to the village and join the rest of his fellow villagers to rest in a shady place. Even

Aumua had already left the plantation to seek refuge from the heat of the day.

Upon arriving in the village, Blue decided to first go to the Internet Café to check his emails, which he hadn't done for a few weeks. Blue noticed Chief Joseph sitting in his *fale* while Lupesina brought him his lunch that consisted of fish, taro, rice, papaya, pineapple, and bananas. It looked tasty, and it made Blue hungry. Lupesina would also occasionally pick up a handmade fan and used it to cool herself. Juggling food, fans, and coconuts, she looked like a street performer that needed an extra pair of hands. Although Joseph graciously accepted everything that Lupesina did for him, he rarely moved a muscle to make his daughter's job easier.

It's good to be the king.

Blue was going to stop and say hello, but he knew that if did, he would probably end up staying there for the rest of the day. So he kept going. He just wanted to check his emails, then find a cool napping place.

When Savea saw Blue outside the trading store, he quickly grabbed a box and hurried to the volunteer.

"Mr. Ronin, Mr. Ronin!" Savea shouted. "I have something for you."

"What is it?"

"It came by post."

Blue hadn't received any mail since he arrived in Samoa. Sometimes he wondered if the few people he knew back home even remembered who or where he was.

Blue saw his Aunt Ophelia's return address on the package. Savea eagerly waited for the volunteer to open it.

Togi then approached the two to see what they were discussing.

"He got a package," the trader said.

"What's in it?" Togi asked.

Blue realized that not many villagers received mail packages over the course of the year. And when one does come in, everyone wants to know the contents.

"He got a package," Togi stated to Fiame and Vaveao, who happened to be walking by the group. The two were taking a break from school and were heading to the store to get a beverage.

"Oh, I love packages," Vaveao exclaimed and rushed over to the group. "What is it?"

"Open it, Mr. Ronin," Savea demanded.

"Mail is usually private," Blue responded.

They didn't understand and continued to look at him full of excited curiosity.

"All right," Blue uttered in a defeated tone.

He had trouble opening the package because it was well-taped. He tugged and fumbled the box until Togi stepped in and took it from him. After a brief struggle using a machete, he was able to open the box and then handed it back to his friend.

Blue pulled out the protective packaging, as everyone leaned in to get a better look.

"Oh my God," Blue said a bit overdramatically. "This is gonna change my life."

Blue pulled out a small box of flea ointment to control fleas and flea eggs for his dogs. He must've complained about the fleas on his hounds to his aunt in an email, and she thought that she would help him out.

"What is it?" Fiame asked.

"It's to help kill fleas on my dogs," Blue said with excitement. "This will be a game changer."

The group was disappointed with the contents of the box. They were truly hoping that it would be something much more interesting.

Nevertheless, the thought of his aunt responding to one of his emails helped Blue remember the reason why he came to this part of the village. He left the box and its contents with the group, who scrutinized the flea box. Blue quickly went into the Internet Café.

Because the internet was slow, it took a few minutes for the computer to log online. As he waited, Blue looked back outside and saw Savea applying the flea ointment on his legs. Naturally, this made Blue go to the doorway.

"Hey! That's for dogs!" Blue shouted.

The group laughed, and Savea placed the little plastic bottle back in the box.

Blue returned to the computer, which was now ready for the internet. He logged into his email. It was slow, but it opened. He didn't have too many unread messages. There were a few from his aunt, some spam, and three messages from his girlfriend, or fiancé, Harper. He was glad to see that there were only three, which meant that she hadn't been sending him letters as often as she did the first year and a half while he was in Samoa. Blue thought that maybe she'd got the hint that he didn't have any plans to return home and that she should stop trying to contact him. He then felt like a coward for not contacting her to give her an update of his life in Samoa.

Is she still waiting for me?

It was an odd question that Blue asked himself, but he

knew the answer. Harper was not the type of girl to wait for anyone. She had her own agenda and aspirations, and people simply joined her journey. They wanted to be with Harper even if it meant that they had to wait for her acceptance.

Blue browsed Harper's subject lines. The first one said, "Coming home?" He ignored it and felt timorous again. He should answer her. It would be the right thing to do.

Isn't it obvious?

Blue scanned the next subject line and read, "Save the date." He didn't open it, thinking that it was probably one of the gorgons getting married, or it was some kind of party invitation, or something.

The third subject line made Blue pause for a second. "See you soon."

Blue was about to delete the message, but it gave him a peculiar feeling like sensing an unseen presence in the same room. He opened the email. Horrified, he quickly stood.

"Shit."

He read the message again.

"Shit. She's coming to Samoa. Shit."

He read it again and repeated the date that she was planning on arriving.

"That's today! Oh shit."

Blue rushed outside. The group was still talking about the flea ointment.

"Togi, did the bus return yet?"

"Yeah, about twenty minutes ago, bro."

"The bus is here?!"

"Yeah. That reminds me. There was a pretty, white girl asking for you." Togi remembered.

"*Ioe*, I saw her," Vaveao agreed.

Damn it, Togi.

"What did you tell her?" Blue asked.

"I didn't see a white girl," Savea answered.

"Not you. Togi, what did you say to her?"

"I told her I didn't know where you were. But if she wanted to find you, she should ask my sister at the community room."

"What?! Oh shit."

"We just saw her heading towards your *fale*," Fiame added.

"Is she your sister?" Vaveao asked.

"No... Oh God."

"If she's a friend of yours, we'll give her a welcome ceremony," Fiame added.

"Oh my God," Blue uttered.

"We always welcome our guests, Mr. Ronin. It's a Vaimasina tradition. You know this."

"Oh shit..."

Blue started to head to his *fale* but stopped and went back to the group. He grabbed his box out of Savea's hand and continued. The group curiously watched Blue run away in somewhat of a panic. He tried to move as fast as he could, but the numbness in his leg considerably slowed him down.

En route to his home, a million thoughts ran through Blue's mind. He was genuinely worried that his two worlds would collide, and he knew that something would have to give—perhaps, even the loss of Aumua. He was apprehensive about Harper meeting Aumua and Mele, and he wasn't in the mood to spend the rest of the day explaining his actions and life choices.

There goes my nap.

Blue started to profusely sweat as he approached his *fale*. He paused before entering and hoped that Harper wouldn't be inside.

Maybe he misread the email, and Harper wasn't coming.

Maybe she stayed in Apia and will send for him.

Maybe she decided to postpone her trip and hadn't told him yet.

Maybe there's nothing to worry about.

Blue entered his *fale* and sighed.

Damn me.

Sunlight poured in through the open blinds like a spotlight to reveal Harper's silhouette. One would think that she would be interested in exploring the village, but instead, she gave all her attention to a cell phone that she was holding. Occasionally, she would type on the phone with her thumbs. She didn't know that Blue was standing at the other end of the house. This gave the volunteer a moment to examine his girlfriend or fiancé, who looked the same as the last time he saw her in the restaurant.

Harper was wearing jean shorts and a pink, cropped crewneck shirt. She had sandals, which she slipped her feet out of to scratch the flea or mosquito bites on her ankles with her toes. She slowly and sensually moved her foot up and down her ankle. To Blue, she was still sexy even when she wasn't trying to be. Although it was probably the lighting, her hair looked darker, but it was put up in a bun on top of her head, no doubt to keep her neck cool. A large Louis Vuitton luggage bag was leaning against one of the poles of the *fale*. She looked as out of place as a polar bear in the desert. Nevertheless, he heard the melody of the song, "Surfer Girl," by the Beach Boys.

It was Blue who initiated the greetings.

"Harper?"

Harper turned around and smiled.

"Charlie Brown!" Harper declared and quickly rushed to Blue. She hugged him first, then kissed him on the lips.

The kiss made Blue think of Aumua. He then looked around the *fale* and noticed that Aumua and Mele's clothes and personal belongings were gone. Aumua must've heard that a friend of Blue's was here, and she retrieved her and Mele's stuff before the visitor arrived. Blue thought he was living in some kind of bizarre world, and it kind of freaked him out.

"Oh my Lord. Look how skinny you are! You feel like a bag of bones."

"You look, uh, the same—great!" Blue said with a worried tone.

"What's with the scruff?" Harper asked, feeling his unshaven face. "I like a clean-cut Charlie Brown."

Blue mumbled to defend his appearance, but the words didn't come out.

"And you're so dark like the natives here."

Blue didn't like the use of the word native. "Uh, villagers."

"Yeah, like the villagers."

"It's hard to escape the sun," Blue said.

"You're so weird. I'm *jelly* of your tan, dude. I should come here more often to work on my tan. It beats the tanning salon."

Blue always thought how lame it was for her to use a

tanning salon, especially since she lived in a city that had more sunny days than cloudy ones. In fact, he particularly hated it when she would fry herself to the point that left lightened goggle stains around her eyes that made her look like a scorched raccoon.

"And what are you wearing?" Harper asked and took a couple of steps back. "A skirt? I gotta get a photo of this. They won't believe this back home."

Harper snapped a couple of photos from her phone.

"It's a *lavalava*. It's cooler than pants."

"I think pants are way cooler."

"No, I mean lit- "

"A *wavawava*," Harper laughed. When she tried to be funny, she had a way of actually being more obnoxious. "You look cute in your *wavawava*."

Blue rubbed his eyes.

Somebody kill me.

"So this is where you live? It took me a while to find it. Some girl told me you lived at the other end of the village. Some witch lady then pointed over in this direction."

Blue thought that Aumua was a crafty one. She had sent Harper out of the way so that she could clean out the *fale*.

"Yeah, uh, this is where I live."

"But there's no bed."

"I sleep on the mat."

Harper started taking pictures of the place.

"This place is so foreign, but it's cool."

"What kind of phone is that?"

"This is the new iPhone. It's so cool. You can use it for pictures, and it has all kinds of apps. I totally spend, like, twenty hours a day on it. We all do. When you come home, we'll get you one, and we'll text each other. It's awesome because we can secretly talk to each other anywhere at any time."

Smartphones hadn't reached Samoa just yet. For the first couple of years in Samoa, Blue noticed that there were a few villagers that possessed cell phones, but these were mostly people who worked government jobs in Apia. However, during his recent trip to Apia, he had noticed that more and more young people were transfixed to cellular devices, and he wondered how long it would be before the phones hit Vaimasina.

"Let's go to the beach!" Harper said enthusiastically.

Before Blue could say anything, Harper was outside the *fale*. She had seen enough of Blue's place and wanted to see a tropical, South Seas lagoon.

At the beach, Harper had stripped to a bikini that she wore under her clothes. Blue wondered if the girl wore the bathing suit on her journey across the Pacific. He looked nervously around like a meerkat on guard, hoping that nobody would see the scantily clad surfer girl. Aside from some fishermen out near the reef, there was nobody else around.

"Wow. This is so dope. Look at the water. I've never seen so many shades of blue before."

Harper took a few more pictures. She then raced to the water, dove in, and began to swim. After wading for several yards, she looked back at Blue.

"Hey! Do you surf those waves out there?"

"Not unless you want to get crushed by coral."

"Oh, this is, like, so awesome. It's like bath water! Are you coming in, Charlie Brown?"

Blue was a little annoyed. He thought that since she hadn't seen him in three years and flew about 4800 miles, the least she could do was to hang out with him. But Harper did what Harper wanted to do. And at this moment, she didn't want to hang out—she wanted to swim. Watching her swim in the lagoon, Blue wondered how long she was staying.

Harper splashed and screamed while gamboling in the water. She couldn't believe all the fish she was seeing. Now and then, she would implore the volunteer to join her, but her pleas went unanswered.

Then, out of the tree line, Togi appeared with his family that included Iris, Keanu, and Kobe. Togi, Keanu, and Kobe were carrying traditional fishing poles. Iris was several months pregnant with their third child (no doubt it will be another boy). At times, the boys would scamper in and out of the water, and Iris would tell them to be careful.

Togi saw Blue staring at Harper in the water and quickened his pace to greet his friend.

"Bro, everyone's talking about the girl," Togi said in Samoan. Although Togi liked speaking English with Blue, he played it safe in front of the stranger, even though she wouldn't be able to hear him from where she was in the water.

"An acquaintance from home," Blue responded in Samoan. He felt bad that he labeled Harper as an "acquaintance."

"I can't believe you're not coming in," Harper said, returning to Blue. "If I lived here, I'd be in this water every day."

Blue cringed as Togi's family approached him at the

same time Harper got out of the water. Harper's bathing suit seemed to have shrunk after getting wet. She tossed her wet hair like a model on a beach shoot.

"Is that a mermaid?" Kobe asked in Samoan.

Iris placed her hand over Kobe's eyes.

"Bro, she looks like a girl Keanu Reeves would marry," Togi stated, his eyes bulging lustily.

Harper noticed the family was standing with Blue and turned her attention to them.

"Oh, hello. I'm Harper. Ronin's girlfriend."

Blue took some consolation from Harper's greeting. At least she didn't say that she was his fiancé. Nevertheless, Blue wondered how much meaning of the word "girlfriend" they were processing.

"Is she swimming in her underwear?" Keanu asked.

"People do that where she's from," Blue answered, defending Harper's appearance.

"Aww, you speak their language. That's so dope," Harper said, "How do you say 'cute ' in Samoan?"

"*Aulelei*," Blue answered.

"You have a real *aulelei* language," Harper declared to Togi's family. The boys laughed. Iris slapped them on their backs for being rude.

Blue handed Harper her clothes with the hope of her putting them on. When she did, the group was able to relax.

"The welcome party is after *Sa* tonight in the *fale tele*," Togi said to Blue. He continued to speak in Samoan.

"Really?"

"We'll give her a proper Samoan welcome," Iris added.

"I know you will."

Blue knew that if there were a party, the entire village

would come. The last thing he wanted was for Harper and Aumua to be in the same place.

"We always show how grateful we are when a visitor comes here," Iris followed up.

Damn me.

Blue's stomach began to twang and twitch, and he coughed up a ball of nerves.

"What are you guys talking about?" Harper asked.

"The village is giving you a party this evening. But, if you're too tired, we can tell them to have it another time."

"I'm not tired. I slept the entire way here."

"We catch fish for party," Togi said nervously in somewhat broken English. Blue looked at him queerly, knowing full well that Togi can speak English much better.

"That's so cool! Can you catch a tuna? That's my favorite."

"He's just fishing in the lagoon..."

"Togi catch tuna!" Togi exclaimed. He grabbed his boys and swept them away as if he was embracing a challenge.

"*Feiloai mulimuli ane,*" Iris said, and headed in the same direction as her boys.

"What did that mean?"

"See you later."

"I can't believe you know their language. Didn't you take Italian or Latin or something in college?"

"Yeah, something."

"You almost failed the class."

Blue grinned. He knew she was correct, but did she really have to remind him of it? Besides, he reminded himself that it's not like she knows how to speak another language.

"My Charlie Brown is no linguist," Harper said in a taunting and teasing tone.

"You know the real Charlie Brown grew up to be a professor of comparative literature. He spoke Greek and Latin."

"You're kidding."

Blue shrugged his shoulders.

"Oh my God! I gotta figure out what to wear tonight," Harper exclaimed. She had already forgotten about linguists, Charlie Brown, and comparative literature professors. "Help me pick an outfit."

She started making her way back to Blue's *fale*.

Blue paused before following her. He felt like vomiting. He wanted to slap himself to ensure that he wasn't dreaming. He looked back at the lagoon and could see Togi with his family in *Calypso*, fishing poles trailing in the water. Narrow puffs of gray clouds jutted skyward on the late afternoon horizon. Blue wanted to be anywhere else than where he was. He wished he could walk across the water, climb a cloud as if it were a beanstalk, and hide on another plain. Blue even took a few steps into the water but stopped when he heard Harper ask a question from beyond the coconut trees.

"Dude, which hut is yours?"

Blue dropped his head and sighed like, well, like Charlie Brown.

When Blue and Harper arrived at the *fale tele*, half of the village was already there. Children were running and playing in and out of the place, adults, particularly the *matais,* were seated and conversing with one another, and some of the women were practicing dance moves with their daughters and nieces. Harper felt bad for arriving late, but Blue assured her not to worry and that everyone was on Samoan time. He told her that the rest of the village still hadn't shown, most likely because they were still cooking.

"I can't believe this is all for me."

"It's amazing, and you'll never forget it," Blue commented. He was a bit gratified that the village would go through this much trouble for his friend. "My welcome party was... uh, unforgettable." He thought about how much he vomited and had to be carried to his *fale*. He didn't worry that something like that would happen to Harper. Things like that don't happen to people like her.

Harper wasn't a shy person and was quickly mingling with people in the *fale tele*. Blue cringed when he saw the look on some of the villagers' faces after Harper introduced herself as his girlfriend from California. Nevertheless, Blue was pleased that she was wearing an outfit that was more acceptable than her beachwear earlier in the day. Harper was wearing a floral pink and green, one-piece tank-top jumper that seemed comfortable and cool, especially for the humid and stuffy evening. In fact, Blue was impressed with her outfit, as it looked like she went shopping for it before her departure from San Diego.

Chief Joseph finally decided that it was time to begin the formalities. Everyone took a seat except for those who stood near the openings of the *fale* in hopes of capturing a cool breeze. For the next thirty minutes, welcome speeches in English and Samoan were given by the *matais*. Blue translated the Samoan phrases to Harper. When there was a pause in the speeches, Harper leaned to Blue and asked how he learned the language so easily. Naturally, he thought of

Aumua and him on their long strolls in the forest. Although it had only been a day, he started to miss Aumua and Mele. He wished that they would come home tonight, but he knew that they would stay clear until Harper returned to California.

Just as with Blue's welcome ceremony, the next step was participating in the traditional *'ava* drink. When the coconut shell of the muddy water came to Harper, she inquisitively looked at it like a child looks at vegetables and hesitated before bringing the shell to her lips.

"I'm supposed to drink this?" Harper asked Blue. Those who understood her laughed at her remark.

"Yeah. It's an honor."

"It looks like poo water."

Everyone laughed again, and Blue was a little embarrassed by her remark.

"Just down it in one gulp."

It took Harper several sips to drink the contents of the shell. Everyone applauded.

"My lips are numb."

"That's normal," Blue said, thinking about the very few times he got to make out with her.

After the *'ava* ceremony, dancers entered the *fale tele* and performed a *siva*. Aumua was one of the dancers and performed her role without looking at Blue. This upset him. Whenever Aumua performed, she always found Blue in the crowd and smiled at him. The moment was uncomfortable, and Blue wished he were anywhere else in the world. When the dance finished, they invited Harper to accompany them to another dance. Harper craved being the center of attention and had no trouble accepting their offer. She jumped right in front of the group, and Aumua quickly taught her a few moves. The villagers cheered the visitor's valid attempt to dance along with the group. Watching Aumua and Harper dance side by side made Blue queasy.

As Harper took her seat after dancing, a group of children that included Mele gave Harper gifts of traditionally made leis and a headdress. Blue was thrilled to see that Mele was walking, although she easily plopped on the floor every now and then. Eventually, Mele crawled into her father's lap.

"She's so damn cute," Harper said.

"Her name's Mele, which means music."

"What a pretty name."

Aumua briskly approached the group and picked up Mele, and told her daughter not to bother the guest in Samoan.

"Are you her mother?" Harper asked.

Aumua smiled. She hadn't spoken English for a while since Blue had learned to speak Samoan. She stumbled over her words in her head as she tried to translate them from Samoan to English. This created an awkward pause.

"Yes, she's the mother," Blue interjected nervously.

"I'm Charlie Brown's fiancé," Harper said with a laugh.

Blue cocked his head. It was the first time that he had heard her call him his fiancé. He wondered if she was joking. There had been many times when he couldn't tell if Harper was kidding around. Aumua, on the other hand, squinted her eyes, trying to understand what Charlie Brown's fiancé meant.

"I am Aumua."

"Aumua's such a pretty foreign name. Isn't it pretty, Ronin?"

"Yeah, uh, very."

"You are Harper," Aumua stated.

"Yes. How'd you know?"

"She heard the speakers say your name," Blue replied.

"But she came in with the dancers after the speeches."

Blue got a little flustered.

"Well, uh, I told people your name."

Harper quickly lost interest and turned her attention back to Aumua.

"Your daughter is so cute."

"Thank you."

"But you look too young to be a mother," Harper added.

"Samoans have a very youthful appearance," Blue interposed.

"That's awesome."

Blue looked tensely at Aumua.

"And is Mele's father here?" Harper asked, mispronouncing, "Mele."

"He's, uh, not here at the moment," Blue answered impatiently. "He's miles away... in the deep blue sea."

"That's too bad. I bet they look awesome together. Everyone always told me how beautiful my family is. We were very photogenic. People couldn't wait to get our Christmas card every year 'cause it was a photo of my family." Harper leaned into Blue. "He's not a deadbeat father, is he?" Harper asked and then snorted.

Aumua gave Blue the side-eye, as she most likely never heard of the word "deadbeat." Despite thinking that

Harper's snorts were still sexy, Blue couldn't think of a more nightmarish situation than that moment.

"I go now. I help with food," Aumua said.

As Aumua smiled and walked away carrying her daughter, Mele pulled a flower off her mother's headdress and placed it into her mouth.

"That was so friggin' adorable."

"Yeah."

Blue took a deep breath. He thought about the adage that he "dodged a bullet." He felt, however, cowardly for not telling Harper that this was his family and how much he adored them. If there was a time to disclose his relationship, this was it. But he squandered the opportunity, and now he felt as if he had alienated his woman and daughter.

It wasn't long before a group of villagers led by Iris, Vavaeo, Maria, Lupesina, and Aumua brought in trays and plates of food. It was an endless train of food that kept coming through the opening of the *fale*. They brought out all the main dishes fit for a special occasion: *palusami*, *fa'apapa*, and *sapasui*. Another popular dish was *oka i'a*, which many villagers ensured that the guest of honor should try. Iris had passed on to the others that it was Harper's favorite- tuna marinated in lemon juice and coconut milk and served with onions. The village staples of taro, sweet potatoes, and an assortment of fruit accompanied all the dishes. It was a bounty of food, and Harper wondered how all of it would ever be consumed. But Blue assured her that there would be nothing left except the bones of the chicken and fish.

Bringing up the rear of carrying dishes like a caboose was Togi. He was holding a plate with something wrapped in a banana leaf and was eager to find Blue.

"Bro! Bro!" Togi shouted. "We caught it!"

Togi raced over to Blue and held out the plate.

"Caught what?"

"Open it, bro."

Blue peeled back the banana leaf and flinched at a mangled but cooked fish.

"What is it?" Blue asked.

"It's the stonefish. We caught it. It's the one that poisoned you," Togi proudly stated.

"How do you know it's the one that stung me?"

"'Cause, bro, it was missing four stingers."

Blue didn't want to argue with that logic. Besides, Togi seemed intent on believing that it was the fish that poisoned his friend and was very pleased with himself that he was able to catch and cook it.

"Is it still poisonous?" Blue asked.

"Nah. Togi took stingers out," Togi answered in the first person. "Try it."

"It looks disgusting," Harper said.

Togi's smile turned to a frown. Blue knew that his feelings were hurt. He grabbed a hunk of the fish with two of his fingers and put it in his mouth.

"Hey, that's not bad."

Togi smiled.

"I bet Kobe and Keanu helped you catch it," Blue said in a placatory tone.

"Yeah, bro. They're good fisherman. I teach them."

Togi walked away, eating the stonefish and licking his fingers after each bite.

"You eat with your hands?"

"Yeah, it's a little hard to get used to at first. But

eventually, when you're starving, you don't care," Blue said. "They'll probably give you a fork."

Indeed, a few minutes later, Vaveao brought the couple plates piled high with food and a fork for Harper. Blue pointed out to Harper the *oka i'a* and reminded her that Togi caught the tuna that was in the dish. As a vegan, Harper seemed to enjoy the cuisine.

"So... uh, I forget. How long are you staying?" Blue asked innocently.

"Till I talk you into coming home."

Blue wanted to tell her that he was at home.

"But I have to head back in a couple of days. I'm a lawyer now, Charlie Brown."

"Really?"

"Took me a couple of times to pass the state bar exam."

"What kind of lawyer?"

"An environmental attorney. You know I love taking on green initiatives, animal protection, and preserving wetlands. Right now, we're working on saving the Corazon Lagoon from contractors who want to build more houses."

Blue was a little jealous of Harper starting a career. She always did outshine him in studies, personality, and accomplishments, despite acting like a dumb blonde. Blue had no doubt, however, that Harper would follow in her father's footsteps and become a lawyer herself. Her father incessantly doted on her and had spoiled her since she was born. Blue wondered how much influence her father had on her getting her first job with a law firm.

"I work downtown in a high-rise building. My office looks towards Coronado Island. It's so cool."

"I'm getting closer to finishing my novel," Blue stated as if trying to compete with Harper's success.

"Oh, yeah, your Titanic thing."

"Not Titanic. It's an adven ..."

"What is that guy holding up?! Oh my God, is that a sea turtle? That's so dope!"

Blue looked over to a crowd that had gathered around Lance Lafau. He had lifted a sea turtle out of a large bucket. Although the turtle was a juvenile, it still weighed about thirty-five pounds.

"I love sea turtles!"

And before Blue knew it, Harper had walked away, attracted by the dangling turtle in Lance's hands. Blue didn't think it was rude of her to leave in the middle of a conversation because Harper always walked away when something or someone else caught her attention.

Blue saw Chief Joseph sitting by himself, watching the villagers eat and frolic like a king watching over his court. It wasn't long until Lupesina delivered him a second helping of food, which he methodically devoured, picking his favorite fares first. Blue went and sat next to the *matai*, but he knew better than to start a conversation until Joseph was ready to converse. In fact, the chief didn't say anything at first and, instead, concentrated on consuming his meal. After licking his fingers, Joseph acknowledged the volunteer.

"Two women," Joseph said.

"Not intentional, I assure you."

"Mmm."

"Harper just showed up unexpectedly. But she's just a friend now."

"She spews white and gold."

This sounded odd to Blue when he translated it to English in his head.

"Yeah, like a Christmas ornament."

"Mmm."

"I promise you that I'm devoted to Aumua and Mele."

"She's not here to just visit you?"

"I don't think so. I haven't seen her in three years."

"Absence invigorates nostalgia and longing."

"I think she's disappointed in my appearance and what I've become."

"Appearances can be altered. In time, she'll remember your veritable nature. If not, she will leave."

"She plans to leave soon," Blue assured the *matai*. "She has a profession, and that usually trumps everything else. Besides, this place is too rugged and short of Target stores for her."

"Hmm."

The two heard Harper cry out in excitement as she held the sea turtle and declared how slimy it felt.

"She looks like she wants to take it home as a pet," the chief stated.

"Should I tell her that the turtle will be dinner someday?" Blue sarcastically asked.

The two smirked at each other, and Blue wondered what the next few days would reveal.

A couple of hours later, Blue and Harper made their way back to Blue's *fale*. Harper became a little frisky, tugging on Blue's beard and long hair.

"That was dope. Your villagers really know how to throw a party."

"They're natural party throwers."

"We should have a party on the beach."

"If you ask, they'll do it."

"I don't know what I was eating, but I can see why you're so skinny."

"I weigh about the same as I did when you saw me last."

"You're so full of it," Harper said, then jumped on his back. Blue struggled to carry her. She kissed the top of his head. "Eww, you need a shower. You smell like I do after surfing for hours—a mixture of seaweed and sand."

"That's just my South Seas musk."

"Eww."

Blue's hounds came bouncing to the couple out of the darkness. They liked that Blue was giving his girlfriend, or fiancé, a piggyback ride and started jumping at Blue's waist, nipping at his hands and arms.

"*Alu ese!*" Blue yelled.

"Oh my God! Whose dogs are these?"

"They're kinda mine. But they mainly belong to the village."

"Do they bite?"

"Nah. They're just very exuberant. They probably came from eating out of Father K's garbage pile. They're not beneath living off the land."

"That's so gross."

Blue carried Harper into his *fale* and plopped her down on the mattress. The dogs followed them inside and found a place to roll up to go to sleep.

As Blue rolled over to face her, she looked earnestly into his eyes. She began to rub his beard again.

"Somewhere in there is the college boy I knew."

This sounded strange to Blue. He knew that Harper was

not a sentimental person and never once spoke intimately to him. He thought how much the girl had, perhaps, matured since the last time he saw her, and he questioned if she truly missed their college days romance.

Nevertheless, she kissed him on the lips until Blue pulled away.

"Now I remember that wishy-washy Charlie Brown kiss."

Blue became annoyed at being called the Peanuts character. He believed that he had grown emotionally and physically the past two years. He didn't feel as if he was running from anything anymore. He tried to justify his current situation, believing that, although he hadn't started a profession and wasn't really making any money, he had become an asset to the village. Besides, he believed wholeheartedly that he could kiss a girl way better than Charlie Brown.

For crying out loud, Aumua never complained about his kissing.

Blue lost all sense of time while in the presence of the beautiful beach girl who was sitting seductively in the middle of his *fale*. After all, this was supposed to be his girlfriend, or fiancé, or whatever, and he told himself that he was expected to act accordingly. Blue whipped off his T-shirt and thought that maybe he could get to second base. Harper was always the quintessential tease. She always seemed to find a way to cool his pistons when they got hot and heavy.

Blue noticed the dabs of sweat that shimmered on her skin just above her cleavage, and he leaned in to lick the beads of perspiration. He couldn't remember if he had ever seen her topless before. He must've felt her breasts at least one time when they were dating, but he wasn't sure. Harper gasped at the congenial foreplay, and her hands lustfully ran through his thick and matted hair. She kissed the top of his head.

Blue thought he had heard her say his name in a passionate tone.

But it only lasted for a second or two, as Harper pulled Blue's head off her chest. "The walls seem thin. Do we need music?" Harper asked, looking around the *fale*.

At first, Blue thought that this was another ploy to stop the passion, but then realized that she was right. He knew that the village grew large ears in moments like this. As Blue lifted himself up, Harper fell on her back and exhaustively exhaled.

Blue went to his computer and fumbled to open it. He opened his iTunes and searched for the perfect music to set the mood and drown out the potential sounds of lovemaking. It took him a while to find the right music, and he got anxious that he was taking too long. He slightly chuckled when he came across the group, Guns N' Roses.

Welcome to the jungle, baby.

Shifting the computer quickly to the side, Blue knocked a toy of Mele's made of seashells onto the floor. It shattered into many pieces and was the one and only remnant that showed that someone else had been in the *fale*. As Blue picked up a few of the shells, it was like a spell had instantly burst, and the seductive moment had snapped. He recalled Aumua helping Mele pick the shells at the beach and then bringing them back home to make the toy.

Blue felt his bare chest and realized that he couldn't do

what Harper wanted him to do, if in fact, she really wanted to go third base—whatever that was. Besides, he was not that kind of guy, and he knew it wouldn't be fair to Aumua and Mele. They were his true love. He wanted to save his home run for Aumua.

Blue finally decided that he wasn't going to be a Charlie Brown anymore. He wanted to be strong-willed, telling Harper that their relationship wasn't right, and she should return home. It was time to tell her about his family and how much he loved them.

"Harper, I gotta tell you something..."

Blue determinedly marched over to the mattress only to see that Harper had curled up and fallen asleep. The long day of travel and village activities had caught up to her. Blue was peeved for either not being able to tell Harper the truth or for not being able to get to third base with her once again. He truly believed it was the former.

Blue covered her exposed back with her shirt and let down the mosquito net. He then grabbed a mat and laid it out near the dogs. As he lay his head down, he smiled, thinking that the only noise the villagers would hear coming from his *fale* this evening would be the sound of the dogs snoring above the Guns N' Roses song.

The next day, Mother Nature decided to break the stagnated air and doused the land with a cascade of water. The rain was hard and driving. When it clattered against the tin roof, it awoke Blue and Harper. Blue, of course, was used to it, but Harper had never heard anything so loud and ominous.

"Is it a hurricane?" Harper asked. She quickly donned her bra and T-shirt.

Blue opened some of the blinds and looked outside.

"No. But it's gonna pour all day."

Harper didn't believe him. She wasn't used to the kind of rain like a South Seas downpour. Blue, however, was correct. The day's shower was endless and inexorable.

A couple of hours later, Harper paced back and forth in the *fale* like a sentry guarding the castle wall. Blue sat on the floor typing occasionally on his computer. He was too distracted watching Harper to get any real work done on his novel.

"What do you do when it rains like this?" Harper peevishly asked.

"This."

"That's so boring."

"I like the rain."

"You're so weird. I don't know how you can just sit there and loaf the day away."

Blue understood Harper's statement. He knew that she had never sat still for a second, especially alone. She always had something to do with others, either planned or on a whim.

"Loafing is the most productive part of a writer's life," Blue quoted. "Uh, James Norman Hall."

"I've been worried about your loafing."

Blue scoffed.

You've never worried about anything in your life.

"It's been over three years. I thought your volunteer job ended after two."

"It was extended," Blue lied.

"And you never respond to my emails. I thought you

were dead. Myna and Cherry said that you been eaten by a shark or caught some gnarly tropical sickness."

Blue raised his eyebrows.

"I'm totally fine."

"Dude, you're not fine."

"I like the rain."

"When you first said hello to me yesterday, I didn't even recognize you."

"I could say the same thing about you. It's been three years."

"You're so weird. I haven't changed at all. These days, I surf in the morning before work. Then I meet with Myna and Cherry, and we go to dinner. Sometimes after dinner, we meet everyone else and have a bonfire on the beach. We all miss our Charlie Brown."

"All?"

Blue never really felt like he fit into Harper's wide circle of beach friends and found it hard to believe that any of them thought about him.

"Yeah, everyone asks why haven't you come home."

"I like the rain."

"I told them that I'd go and see what's going on with you. Everyone told me not to get brainwashed by villagers. They think you're part of some cult now."

"Do you think of me as your boyfriend still?" Blue bluntly asked.

"I have a few boyfriends, but you're my favorite Charlie Brown," Harper said with a laugh.

Blue wondered what she meant by the word "boyfriends." Were these guys lovers, or were they just friends? Was he just a friend all this time? Perhaps he filled some kind of void or a sidekick role for Harper. Why did she get partially naked in front of him last night? It wasn't like she got drunk off the *'ava*. He thought that maybe it was her way of teasing, "See what you're missing back home!"

There was an awkward pause as Harper stared spitefully at the rain falling steadily on the village.

Then, out of the rain, a tall, imposing figure wearing a dark purple cape with a hood, jeans, and shoes with four-inch heels appeared.

"Oh!" Harper cried out.

"Where is this beautiful star-girl I keep hearing about?" the figure ardently asked in English while entering the *fale*.

Blue instantly recognized Misi Sau's voice and quickly stood.

It had been almost six months since Blue had seen Misi, who had been traveling and performing in Singapore and Thailand, respectively.

Misi looked at Blue and then at Harper.

"Oh dear. I have been gone a long time."

"*Talofa*, Misi," Blue said.

"Oh! Darling, no, no, no, no. You have to lose the beard. You look like a castaway."

"That's what I told him," Harper added.

Misi examined Harper. "What are you up to, deary?" Misi asked Blue in Samoan.

"I know. I know. She showed up unexpectedly," Blue responded in Samoan. "Now, I wish she'd leave."

"Ah-ha. The air is rather stifling in here."

"I just can't stand it," Blue said in English and began fanning himself with a fan that Aumua made.

"That's what Charlie Brown would say," Harper stated with a mocking giggle.

"Oh, God. I wish lightning would strike me dead right now," Blue added in Samoan.

Misi scoffed and turned to Harper. "Oooh, I love your hair color. Don't you think I would make a sexy blonde, Mr. Ronin?"

"Sexy or naughty- that's what you do best."

"You flatter me," Misi said with a laugh. "And who might this blonde, baby doll be?"

"I'm Harper. Ronin's girlfriend."

"You don't say," Misi stated, a little confused. Misi then looked at Blue, who surreptitiously shrugged his shoulders and negatively shook his head back and forth.

"Oooh. What kind of a girlfriend, pray tell?" Misi asked.

"I'm not so sure anymore," Harper responded.

"Well, you know, he's quite the ladies' man here in Samoa."

"Him? I find that hard to believe. I mean, he's cute in a wishy-washy way. All my friends say so."

"But have you ever heard the dear boy sing?" Misi asked.

"Ronin sings?"

"Like a *mao* bird."

Blue snorted. Harper winced with surprise.

"I wanted to take the crooner on tour with me. But he sadly declined. Darling, I was heartbroken. We would've made an indomitable duo on stage. I just returned from Thailand, and they don't know what they missed."

"Ronin on stage? You're pulling my leg, right?"

Blue thought about the countless times he performed piano for an audience and various panels of judges.

"You really don't know your friend," Misi affirmed. "He's really full of magical moments."

Harper shook her head, dumbfounded. She never believed that Blue had an ounce of talent in anything. Blue, on the other hand, reveled in the compliment that Misi provided. He rarely received such respect.

Another awkward pause ensued that even made Misi felt a little uncomfortable.

"Well, the person that I'm looking for isn't here," Misi declared and then turned towards Blue to ask him in Samoan. "So where's your beautiful woman and daughter?"

"At her father's house, most likely," Blue answered in Samoan.

"This will pass," Misi added, still in Samoan. "Just don't do anything stupid. Right, darling?"

"Yeah."

"It usually is," Misi added. "Well, I'm not leaving until I see your star-child." The *fa'afafine* then spoke to Harper in English. "Harper, darling, don't ever cut your hair... and define your boyfriend meaning. Ciao."

Harper watched Misi exit as luridly as she entered.

"She was, like, so weird," Harper said.

"She's not a she."

"What?"

"Or a he pretending to be a she."

"What'd you mean?"

"Misi's a third gender- what they call a *fa'afafine* in Samoa."

"*Fafa*- no friggin' way..."

Blue could tell that Harper couldn't wait to tell her friends about meeting a *fa'afafine* as soon as she returned home. He could already hear the inappropriate and idiotic remarks her friends would make after Harper told them about Misi.

Harper returned her attention to the steady downpour as Blue fought the uncomfortable, muggy atmosphere to type a few words on his computer.

"God, I hate the rain," Harper stated with exasperation.

"I'm sorry."

"I bet you get bored here a lot."

"Rarely."

"Then you're brainwashed. Myna and Cherry said that you're probably part of some village cult."

"Well, am I?"

"From what I've seen? No. But it's still boring."

"If you get bored, you take a nap."

"So don't you want to go home at all? I mean, really? It's a pretty place and the people are nice, but there's not much going on. Do you just wanna stay here instead of hanging out with me?"

"I like the rain."

Harper stared at the volunteer with some concern and defeat. Blue wondered if she had instantly taken Misi's advice on defining what a boyfriend is.

When Blue awoke the next morning, Harper and her luggage were gone. A light rain was still falling, and he could hear the bus spurning its engine. He rose and opened the blinds just in time to see the bus spinning its wheels in the mud. After grinding, shifting, and gyrating, the bus finally freed itself and moved forward with a jolt. Although Blue couldn't see Harper, he knew she was on the bus and would abhor every minute it took to return to Apia.

Blue took a deep breath. For the first time in a few days, he felt relieved and relaxed. A welcome breeze whooshed through the *fale* and pushed the clammy, oppressive air to the sea. Blue was optimistic that the day would be the beginning of a time when he would finally be free from a girlfriend and especially a fiancé, that he never truly had. Most of all, he reveled in the thought that he would be relieved from receiving and reading fewer asinine emails.

Years later, Blue would learn that after Harper left Vaimasina, she stayed for a couple of days at a resort in Apia. When she returned to the States, she told everyone what a beautiful place Samoa was and how much fun she had swimming, snorkeling, windsurfing, and sunbathing with a couple of Australian men. She hardly mentioned Blue's name at all to her friends, with the exception that she told everyone that he wasn't interested in returning home anytime soon. Harper, however, did make a big deal about holding a real sea turtle—the same turtle that Blue would eventually partake in eating during a *toonai* many months later.

6

———————

A couple of months later, after Harper's visit, Blue was feeling distraught because Aumua had not returned to their *fale*. Every time he met with her, he would ask when she was coming home, but she would act demure and tell him that she was living at home. Despite his supplications, she would simply smile and gently let him know that she wasn't ready. Blue hated it when she was literal, and he despised it even more when he returned to an empty, quiet *fale*. Ironically, the tranquil environment was what he had originally craved to work on his novel. And although he grew accustomed to the idiosyncratic sounds that Aumua and Mele had made, he never thought that there would be a day without hearing their noises. Now, the silence was excruciating and louder and more annoying than when they were in the *fale*. In fact, he couldn't write at all. He would spend the nights listening to music, or if it were windy, he would walk to the beach to escape the mosquitoes and watch the stars dance.

Christmastime swept through Vaimasina like a fervent trade wind and blew rampant across the villagers. Like most villages in Samoa, the villagers celebrated a "13 Days to Christmas" that was filled with the church choir concerts of Christmas carols and social events. Blue spent most of the holiday season at the Tuputala homestead, where he would try to spend time with Aumua and play with Mele. In addition, he was able to dine at Fiame's house on several occasions after Sa. When Togi and his boys had a good fishing day, Blue was invited over to Togi's *fale,* where the "catch of the day" was shared with him. Keanu and Kobe would proudly point to which fish they caught. They then would enthusiastically engage in how they caught each fish, only to get into arguments when their stories inadvertently contradicted each other.

On Christmas morning, Blue awoke early from a streak of sunrays that burst through the broken slats of the blinds and melted upon his face. After being in Samoa for over three years, he never got used to the hot and humid Christmas weather. Not that living in San Diego County was full of cool, snowy, and sparkling holiday weather, but temperatures would at least drop by thirty degrees once the sun went down. Blue always equated Christmastime with a cozy fire that his mother and aunt would build in the fireplace with the sudden cold weather. In Vaimasina, however, if there was smoke, it meant that either food was being cooked or trash was being burned.

It wasn't long after Blue awoke that he could hear singing coming from the church. He heard beautiful variations of several non-secular Christmas carols rejoicing the birth of the baby Jesus. The singing was so loud and passionate that it persuaded the volunteer to rise, wash his face, dress in the finest *lavalava* he owned, and make his way to the church.

His hounds greeted him on his way and were excited to see him moving about at such an early hour. Perhaps they anticipated receiving a special holiday treat. Indeed, they were correct as Blue tossed them sticks of beef jerky that he recently bought at the trading store. The dogs merrily took their individual piece to a nice shady spot under a pandanus bush to blissfully gnaw on the stick as if it were a rawhide.

Blue furtively entered the church and sat in the back pew. It was the first time since arriving in the village that he attended a Mass. Nobody stared at him or gave him any kind of a disparaging side-eye. After all, he had heard that back home, many Catholics only attended Mass twice a year—at Christmas and Easter. Although he didn't pay much attention to the scripture readings or Father Krimple's sermon about keeping the Christmas charitable attitude throughout the entire year, he did get caught up in the pageantry of the spirit and traditions of this special, annual Mass. With each song that was sung, he tried to pick out Aumua's angelic voice in the choir. Before he knew it, the final song was performed as the priest and his entourage of altar boys and girls and scripture readers made their procession down the aisle and outside the church.

Blue hung around greeting people with a *"Manuia le Kerisimasi"* or "Merry Christmas" and liked that everyone was in a cheerful mood that was appropriate for the day. He could tell that some of the parishioners were happy that Mass was over and were excited about the Christmas feast that was nigh. As he watched the children play with some of the toys they received from Santa earlier in the morning, a tap on his shoulder forced him to turn around. It was Aumua holding Mele, who was dressed in a red dress.

"*Manuia le Kerisimasi*," Aumua said with a smile. She was excited to see that Blue had attended Mass.

"Merry Christmas," Blue answered in English. "And look at my little Christmas angel," Blue added in Samoan to his daughter. He then took Mele from Aumua and held her up high. "Did Santa bring you lots of presents?" Mele nodded her head, then gave Blue an ornament made from a coconut shell that resembled a star. "Wow! Did Santa bring this for you?" She shook her head.

"I made," Mele said. "For you."

"We made ornaments for people," Aumua added.

"Someday we'll get a proper Christmas tree to hang it on," Blue stated. "Would you like that? I'll hang it nicely in our house. You and Mama will have to come and see it, okay?"

"Yes, and you play music on your computer," Mele said with excitement.

"Of course, lots of music. Maybe you and Mama will come over today?"

Aumua's disposition changed, and she wasn't smiling anymore. "I don't think so," she said and quickly took Mele back from Blue.

"Aumua, when are you coming back home?"

"Not today. It's Christmas. You are welcome to come to our house to celebrate."

"It's been months. Your home is with me."

"My home is with my family."

"That's me."

"We are not married."

"That doesn't mean we're not a family."

"I'm not sure where your home is, Ronin. I feel sorry for you. But when your girlfriend came, I saw where you belonged. You look like you belong together. I saw that Mele and I are too different for you and that you should go home and be with people like you. You should be with your family."

"You are my family, Aumua!" Blue declared in an aggravated tone. "Don't you understand that I have nothing back home?"

"You have a girlfriend—Harper."

"She left me. I realized we were never meant to be together ... you and me and Mele should be together."

"I'm sorry, Ronin. Come to Christmas dinner later."

Before Blue could say anything else, Aumua was called away. Blue watched her walk away with Mele. The feeling of loss percolated in his stomach like boiling water in a teakettle. He didn't want to give up so easily. He felt that he should say more to her. He wanted to try to make her understand that he would never see Harper again, and that she and Mele were the only two important people in his life.

Determined to make things right again, he started for Aumua but stopped when Father Krimple grabbed his arm.

"*Manuia le Kerisimasi*, Ronin."

"Huh? Yeah. Same to you."

"This has to be the best Christmas Day of all because you came to Mass."

"Please don't say that it's a Christmas miracle," Blue said, a bit peeved. "I hate that phrase."

"But isn't it, though?"

"What?"

"A Christmas miracle."

"Come on, Father K. I only came to listen to the music."

"Go on. You could've easily listened to the music outside the church."

"And I also wanted Aumua to know that I was there," Blue added. "You see? I had ulterior motives than worship."

"At least you're honest."

"It's Aumua and Mele I want for Christmas—not to celebrate Jesus's birthday."

"Ah. God gave us a great gift today—the greatest gift of all. Accepting this gift will give you strength, wisdom, forgiveness, and love—all of which you'll need to secure your relationship with Aumua."

Although Blue didn't want to admit it, the priest made sense. However, Blue left Aumua alone the rest of the time at church. Hours later, he showed up at the steps of the Tuputala's *fale*. He could smell the food cooking from his home, which made his mouth water. He brought with him a wrapped Christmas gift for Aumua and Mele that he had bought while in Apia when he had his teeth examined and cleaned at a dentist's office. For Aumua, he had bought a new *lavalava* with a matching shawl, and a ukulele for Mele.

The volunteer didn't enter the *fale* or attend the Christmas party. He couldn't bear the thought that Aumua didn't want to live with him. He thought about what Father Krimple had said to him earlier in the day, and on this evening, he simply didn't possess any of the abilities that God might give to him to help him win back the mother of his child. It saddened him.

From afar, Blue watched the festivities in the *fale*.

Christmas music was blasting and competing with other music that came from other homes in the village. He saw children chasing each other with long strands of tinsel, and people wearing festive hats and eating and drinking a variety of cuisines and beverages, including alcohol. A group of villagers were decorating a small palm that acted as a Christmas tree. Nevertheless, what Blue noticed most of all was Aumua merrymaking and having a good time with her friends, particularly Maeva and Lance Lafau.

As Blue watched the party, he felt like he was standing there with the Ghost of Christmas Past, who took him to another Christmas that was long ago during his senior year in high school. He couldn't remember a lonelier Christmas than that year. His mother had already passed, and his aunt was on assignment abroad. Vivi, the neighbor who watched Blue, had already fallen asleep. Thus, Blue decided to go over to Scarlett's house. He never knew Scarlett and her parents to be an active family, and he thought that his appearance would be welcomed. He didn't even mind if Scarlett's parents asked him to practice with their daughter. Anything was better than sitting at home. Besides, live college auditions were coming fast, and it was the only thing on the family's mind. When he arrived at the house, a raging family gathering that included aunts, uncles, cousins, and friends was already in full swing.

Before he knocked, the door was swung open by Scarlett, who was glad to see him. Blue almost didn't recognize her at first. She wore makeup and let her hair down—a rarity ever since Blue had known her. She was wearing a red-and-green plaid skirt with a red sweater.

"You got my invitation!"

"Yeah, uh... what?" Blue didn't remember receiving any letters.

"You're a little late."

"Late for what?"

"But don't worry, Ronin, everyone's still waiting."

Blue was still confused. "Uh, waiting for what?"

"Our Christmas concert, dorkus. Come on."

Blue took off his shoes at the door, and Scarlett led him into the living room, where countless rehearsals had taken place. Everyone cheered in Chinese as the two entered the room. Blue realized quickly that he had walked into a family Christmas party. People were sitting in chairs, on the floor, and in makeshift seats of pillows and ottomans. The room was decorated in the colors of the season, and a ten-foot Christmas tree adorned with glass balls and shiny garland stood in the corner. Blue was just there a day or so ago and he couldn't remember the room having one decoration.

Blue sat at the piano and Scarlett placed the Christmas music in front of him, which was already in order to guarantee a smooth recital. Blue had played holiday music with Scarlett the past week or so, but he thought it was just for fun. Then it dawned on him that they had never played anything just for laughs. It was always for some personal gain, some competition, some goal, or some achievement.

Scarlett sat with her cello and gave the audience an introduction in Chinese. The only word Blue understood was his name. She then attacked the first song, *Sleigh Ride*, and Blue quickly had to keep pace.

Shit—thanks for the warm-up.

The songs weren't the simple versions for avid musicians. On the contrary, they were more advanced renditions, and Blue had to concentrate to stay in rhythm and tone. Nevertheless, the audience accompanied the musicians by singing in Chinese and English on the popular and upbeat songs. The more melodious, melancholy tunes, such as *Silent Night* and *Away in a Manger,* were listened to in silence and made half of the audience tear up.

Blue was heartened and impressed at how such a large family had come together to celebrate Christmas in Scarlett's home. He couldn't remember if this was an annual thing or if this was a once-in-a-lifetime event. But it didn't matter. The fact that they were celebrating together on this day and having a good time was what was important. Indeed, Blue was a little jealous of the whole event because he had hardly any family to celebrate Christmas with. When his mother was alive, Christmastime, especially Christmas Eve, was a lot of fun. Many of his mother's acting colleagues would come over, and the hot chocolate would be flowing. They would recite poems, act out skits, and sing carols.

After the concert, Scarlett became the center of attention among the guests. Blue could only understand the words Juilliard, Mannes, Eastman, and Boston, and assumed that they were talking about the conservatories that Scarlett was auditioning for. Blue noticed that Scarlett's grandmother, however, was staring discontentedly at him, and he was compelled to place his hands back on the piano keys. He tried not to look at her.

Blue felt awkward sitting at the piano with no one interested in talking with him. He thought about the couple of music schools that he applied to, and how he made it to the audition phase as well. He, however, had no intention of going through this stage of his applications. Blue was never really interested in pursuing music as a career, and he didn't have that desired drive to differentiate himself from the other applicants during the auditions. He hadn't had the heart to tell Scarlett, who, he believed, wanted him to attend the same conservatory as her and play piano for her forever.

Nobody seemed to notice when Blue silently slipped away from the shindig. In the front yard, he grabbed a solar-powered lantern with a Christmas tree pattern, put on his shoes, and walked away from the house and into the darkness. He didn't feel like going home to an empty house, and thus he decided to make his way to the trail that would wind down to Sabatini's Beach.

When he arrived at the beach, he sat down in the sand and stared at the black water. It was a crisp, cool Christmas night, still and silent, and Blue felt like he was part of a carol. Even the waves strolled placidly in rhythm within the cove so that he couldn't tell if the tide was coming in or out.

About fifteen minutes later, Scarlett approached him holding a flashlight.

"What are you doing here?" Scarlett asked.

"Staring."

"It's freezing."

"It's Christmas...and baby, it's cold outside."

"Ha. Everyone liked our concert."

"That's because we're awesome, Scar."

"My father wants us to perform our audition pieces."

"Now? It's Christmas."

"Yeah, he thinks it would be advantageous for us to play them in front of an audience."

"It's Christmas."

"Everyone wants to hear them."

Blue became peeved. The audition pieces were work, a lot of work, and he believed that he deserved a break, especially on Christmas. "Do you ever wonder what's on the other side of the ocean?" He asked, hoping to change the subject.

"China."

"It's not all China. There's a bunch of islands out there."

"We should get back."

"Don't you ever feel like blowing off everything and going and exploring those islands?"

Scarlett stood up, ignoring the question.

"Everyone's waiting."

"How 'bout we just blow off the music and go skinny-dipping? Swim to an island."

"Don't be a dork."

"We can't play music every second of our lives," Blue stated and stood up. "Let's do something fun. I mean, all we do is hang out in your living room."

"And freezing our tushes off is fun?"

"Yeah, it's Christmas. Christmas is fun, not full of chores."

"You think our music is a chore, Ronin?"

"Yeah," Blue said, feeling a bit ornery. He was also reacting to the differences between his and Scarlett's family dynamics. Although Scarlett's family was success-driven to the point of obsession, at least they were together tonight. "Don't you ever want to play what you want to play?"

"I play what is expected of me."

"Exactly. And nothing more."

"I got an audition for every school I applied to, and so did you."

"Yeah... you sure did."

"Come on. It's freezing out here."

"I'm sorry, I don't feel like it."

"Why?"

"It's Christmas."

"My father hasn't been happy with your commitment. He doesn't think that you're trying very hard, which is a shame because you're so talented. But he wants to replace you."

"What do you think?"

"I think my father's right. You haven't really been with it lately."

"Well, shit. Maybe you *should* find a replacement, because I'm sick of it."

"If that's how you feel, then maybe it's best," Scarlett said with some venom.

Perhaps it was the tension between the two teenagers, or it was that Blue felt sorry for the girl who didn't seem to have her own free will, but Blue was compelled to kiss Scarlett on the side of her cheek. Regardless of what it was, she responded by slapping him on the side of his cheek.

"What are you doing?"

"Sorry, I... uh..."

"I'm heading back home."

Scarlett grabbed the Christmas lantern and headed back to the trail that would lead to her house.

Blue sunk deeper into the sand.

"Don Juan just called, and he wants his lips back."

He stared out at the dark sea. A faint light from a distant boat bobbed on the horizon, as an onshore breeze chilled his bones. Blue wished he were out there, far away, on the other side of the ocean. Now, anywhere seemed better than where he was. He thought about how his mother would want him to go out and explore the dark sea and seek an adventure... with a song in his heart, of course. And this thought comforted him. All of a sudden, he didn't feel cold anymore. It was like he was being cuddled by a warm hug from his mother. This, he believed, was what was missing tonight. He could see and feel the warmth of an unseen person's exhaled breath in the cool air, but it didn't chill him. On the contrary, he smiled and embraced the heartfelt hug and reminded himself that this was what Christmas was all about.

Blue did not return to Scarlett's house that night. Whatever consequences may come from his absence, he felt he would deal with later. His mother had once told them that the ocean has a lot of wisdom that it wants to share, but you have to listen for it. Thus, Blue remained on Sabatini's Beach and spent the rest of Christmas night wrapped in the warmth of his mother's arms, listening to what the sea had to say.

———————

It wasn't long until the Ghost of Christmas Past released Blue from the sobering event that took place at Sabatini's Beach years ago. Blue brought his attention back to the party that was occurring in the Tuputala's *fale* and instantly became aware that only Joseph noticed that he was standing outside. The chief didn't point Blue out to the crowd or call the volunteer inside to join the fun. It was like he knew that Blue didn't feel comfortable joining the festivities. So, the *matai* gave Blue a quick nod of his head as if silently saying Merry Christmas. Blue nodded back and left the presents on the steps of the *fale* before rushing away towards the beach.

Like he did at Sabatini's Beach on Christmas night many years ago, Blue sunk in the sand. The environment was different, however, than the one at Sabatini's Beach. The warm water of the lagoon massaged his feet as it washed passed him and then retreated to where it came from. A half-moon orchestrated the sound of the surf slapping against the reef. The air seemed to languish, but every so often, a swirling gust that came from an unexpected direction created a misty and stimulating whirlwind. Blue breathed in the salty air and exhaled. He closed his eyes and hoped that his mother would soon embrace him. He needed to feel her touch even in Samoa.

As Blue patiently waited for his reassuring Christmas hug, he heard someone cough about twenty yards away. At first, he thought it was just the sound of the lagoon as the water rocked the canoes and boats. But he heard the cough again—a long, choking, disgusting sound. Blue looked to his right and saw Father Krimple sitting in the sand with several Vailima and Fosters beer cans strewn around him. The priest downed another can and half-heartedly tossed it in front of him.

"Father K?" Blue asked. The priest choked again. "Are you all right?"

"The jig is up. Isn't that what you Americans say?"

"Uh, I think you Canadians say that as well."

"The jig is up!"

Blue stood, moved towards Father Krimple, and plopped down in the sand next to his friend. The priest opened another can of beer and took a sip. "Want a drink?"

"No, thanks."

"You don't drink, do you, Ronin?"

"Nah. Alcohol's too expensive and it makes me barf."

"Go on... Well, I cleaned out Savea's stock."

Blue thought that Father Krimple's behavior was extremely odd, especially since he was beaming when he saw the volunteer had joined Christmas Mass earlier in the day.

"You don't, don't have any vices, do you?" Father Krimple added, "Oh, wait—besides knocking up a teenage village girl."

"Are you sauced, Father K?"

"...the least of my problems."

Blue stared out at the reef and waited for another breeze to help cool him down. He thought that maybe the less that was said, the better it was. But it was Father Krimple who spoke again.

"The Lord favors the villagers and frowns upon us white men on this holy night."

"Why do you say that?"

"Because, my friend, I am a fraud, and you are an anti, athe..." the priest couldn't find the word. "Anti—antichrist.

"Whoa. That's harsh."

"Atheist."

"A little better."

"The diocese has finally learned that I'm not Catholic. Yesterday, I received an email, which I didn't read until this afternoon, to cease my congregational tasks and step away from the church after the Christmas season has ended, on the Epiphany. For fifteen years I, I dedicated my church to this life..."

"You mean, life to this church," Blue corrected.

"Yes, that too."

"Who do you think spilled the beans on you?"

"I think the diocese always knew. They just couldn't find someone to come out here to take my place. But I don't know... don't know. I think Lance Lafau might've had something to do with it, too. He never trusted me, even as a child. It doesn't matter. It was just a matter of time before they took it all away from me."

Blue could see Lance waiting for the right time to tattle on Father Krimple to the diocese. He was that kind of person. Blue shook his head in disgust. "I'm sorry to hear this, man."

"All good things come to an end. That's what you Americans like to say, right?"

"I bet you Canadians say that too."

Father Krimple flung another empty can towards the water. Blue was dumbstruck by the priest's downheartedness, which was completely out of character. Father Krimple was the epitome of positive attitude and reinforcement.

"What are you gonna do?"

"I have to leave the village."

"Can you leave Maria and... uh, Isaac?"

Father Krimple bowed his head. An uncomfortable pause ensued. Blue couldn't tell if the priest was praying, or if he fell asleep. Perhaps, the thought of losing Maria and Isaac hadn't hit him.

"I pray that Lemanu will return to Maria and Isaac."

"It's been months since Lemanu has been here. I doubt he's coming back."

The buzz from the alcohol delayed Father Krimple's response. But Blue could tell that the priest thought long and hard about it before replying.

"Always faith the keep. The Lord will bring him back when the time's right," Father Krimple stated.

The priest then leaned back and lay flat on the beach as Blue stared towards the ocean. The Christmas music from several village homes seemed to get louder, drowning out the sound of the waves smashing against the reef.

Blue looked skyward. Passing clouds uncovered a very bright star, and Blue wondered if it was the star of Bethlehem. He was about to ask Father Krimple, but paused when he heard the clergyman begin to snore. Blue stayed by his friend, attempting to identify the Christmas carol drifting from the village.

Fifteen minutes later, Father Krimple awoke with a loud, abrupt snort. He shot upward as if awaking from a nightmare. Blue could see the priest slowly and painfully come to the eventual realization that his frightening dream was now the reality. A minute later, he noticed that Blue was still sitting next to him.

"Don't tell any of the villagers about my impending departure. I want to quietly exit like I came here."

Blue didn't answer. He knew that the villagers were going to find out sooner or later. In fact, they probably already knew.

"What are you doing here anyway?" the priest asked. "You should be with your family on this night of Jesus's birth?"

"Just waiting for an *aitu*- a special *aitu*."

Father Krimple sneered.

"Go on. Aren't we all?"

The two would remain on the beach until dawn the next morning. Father Krimple reminisced about his time in Vaimasina, as Blue confided in his friend about his mother, Aumua, Scarlett, and even Harper. And through all these stories, Father Krimple kept mentioning how blessed Blue was for having these women in his life.

The two didn't fall asleep until about four in the morning. Before Blue closed his eyes, he knew he would be saddened with the priest's leaving, but he also had a notion that Father Krimple would only be as far away as Apia, and this somewhat pleased him.

Father Krimple did not leave the village as quietly as he had hoped on January 7, the day after the Epiphany. Indeed, the villagers of Vaimasina found out about his departure and the reason for it. Nevertheless, they threw him a large going-away party in *fale tele*. There was music, dancing, games, and, of course, food—lots of food. There was no animosity shown towards the likeable, but phony priest, as everyone knew he lived a lie because he loved the village. The diocese, on the other hand, had a bit of a cleanup to proceed with, particularly with the very few baptisms (including Mele's) and marriages that Krimple performed during his tenure as a priest. This would take over a year to review, renew, and reconcile. Be that as it may, Krimple's revelation would produce more gossip among the villagers that would eventually spill over to other villages. As Krimple gave his last humble goodbye, everyone thanked him for his service and dedication to the village, but most of all, they thanked him for being a trustworthy friend.

7

The water of the Vaimasina pool was cool, refreshing, and proved to be an exceptional escape from the day's heat. For the past year or so, Blue enjoyed taking the time to swim there, as he had fond memories of frolicking in the pool with Aumua. Plus, he preferred cooling off in the pool rather than in the lagoon, where unfortunate events seem to happen to him. Aumua and Mele would join him on occasion, especially Mele, who loved to swim and play in the water. When Aumua was with Blue, the volunteer would try to persuade her to come back and live in his *fale*. Although there were times when it seemed that she would agree to return to his home, she ultimately rejected the offer. This didn't mean that Blue rarely got to see the mother of his child. Rather, Blue saw Aumua every day, and she would treat Blue as if they were in a long-distance relationship, even though they lived about sixty yards from each other.

Fortunately, Blue and Aumua's "distant" relationship

didn't have any adverse effects on Mele's development. She was growing into quite a pleasant, perceptive, and precocious young girl. Blue enjoyed being and playing with her, and she loved to tease and test her father because she thought he was so gullible, mostly because he acted that way. Nevertheless, Blue could see that his daughter, who was very much like her mother, had a natural affinity towards the cultural arts of crafts, music, and performance. In fact, on this day at the Vaimasina pool, Mele was sitting on a boulder strumming the ukulele that Blue had gifted her during what the villagers would come to call "the Christmas when Father Krimple left."

"Tell me again, Papa, about the time you fought the shark," Mele pleaded in Samoan.

"I've already told you a hundred times, Mele."

"I like to hear it again. Do you think the shark wanted to jump in the boat and fish for humans?" Mele giggled.

"It almost did."

Blue was floating on his back like a piece of driftwood. He squirted a mouthful of water in the air. As he looked skyward, he noticed a large flock of birds of various species flying overhead. He couldn't remember ever seeing birds migrating during this time in Samoa, but thought that this was perhaps something that happened every odd number of years. The noise that the birds produced even made Mele stop playing her ukulele and look to the sky.

"They sound like they're singing."

"Yeah... strange."

"I wish I could understand them. What do you think they're singing about?"

"They're probably reminding the bird in front of them not to stop."

Mele giggled and strummed the ukulele.

Blue watched the birds fly. There were hundreds of them. In fact, there were so many that at times they shaded him from the afternoon sun.

"I wish I could fly... and sing like them."

"Someday you will, Mele. Someday..."

Blue's concentration on the birds was broken when Fiame approached the pool with a group of about seven Australian and Japanese tourists. Blue spat water in the air in defiant abhorrence of their arrival.

This was a new program that was started about five months earlier and opened Vaimasina to tourists. Fiame created it to help increase revenue for the village. The program cost forty *talas* per person and would sometimes include a fishing trip with Togi, an *'ava* ceremony with Savea, and a dip in the pool or lagoon followed by an *umu* lunch. It took much persuasion for Joseph to agree, but she was dogged and was able to acquire the support from other *matais* and the Samoa Tourism Authority.

Blue, naturally, hated the idea of allowing tourists to gawk around the village. He found them to be incessantly in the way, and he thought it made the villagers look like cast members of a gaudy and over-exaggerated stage production. Blue had never witnessed such bad acting as when some of the villagers tried to go out of their way and over-impress the tourists for tips, which disgusted Blue. Although he expressed his frustrations about the tourists to Fiame, her only and repeated response was that everyone would soon get used to them.

Before Fiame noticed Blue in the water, she had told the group the history and folklore of the pool. She even managed to incorporate the famous legend of "Sina and the Eel," the widespread Polynesian story of how the coconut tree was formed. As the director of this venture, Fiame was in her element. In fact, she rarely had time to run the school anymore. There were rumors that she would step down as principal, and Vavaeo would take her place.

"I am the beautiful Sina!" Mele exclaimed in Samoan as she stood on the boulder. "I will dive in the water and meet the eel demon, *Tui Fiti*! I will cut off his head and plant it in the earth! From it, a coconut tree will grow and give me water!"

Mele dove into the pool. As the tourists applauded, Blue rolled his eyes. He was a bit embarrassed.

"You're not supposed to be in the pool between twelve and half past one today," Fiame said in Samoan to Blue.

"What? There's no sign-up sheet designating certain times to swim here," Blue responded in Samoan with some sass.

"There is. It's hanging in the community center."

Damn me.

"Well... I, uh, haven't been there in a while."

"Please vacate the pool, Mr. Ronin, so that our guests can have a swim."

"They don't want to share the pool?"

"No. They paid to have the pool to themselves."

Blue saw the determination in Fiame's eyes. He sighed and started to swim to the side.

"Mele, get your uke!" Blue yelled.

Mele swam to the boulder, hopped out of the water, and

grabbed her instrument. She had recently made a shoulder strap, or cordage called an *'afa*, out of sennit, which was dried coconut fiber. Mele wrapped the ukulele around her shoulder and then hop-scotched across the rocks to meet her father at the other end of the pool.

As Blue exited the water, Fiame stared at him. "You will get used to them," she said.

"When did our pool come to be used by only people with money?"

"It's just for a short time today."

As Blue waited for Mele to catch up to him, the tourists began to undress until they were wearing nothing but their bathing suits.

The capitalists just called, and they want their pool back.

"You know, I would like to have tours of the cocoa plantation. Are you willing to show our guests the site and tell them the history of it?" Fiame asked. "It would be a great way for you to get involved with our new endeavor."

"I, uh, I'd have to ask Aumua."

"I already did, and she thinks it's a wonderful idea."

"She did?"

"*Ioe.*"

"Well, I'll talk to her about it."

"*Faafetai.*"

Blue saw one of the Australian tourists trying to give Mele a five-*tala* tip for her outburst on the rock. Blue intervened and told Mele not to take it.

"Thanks, but that's okay," Blue said in English to the tourist. "She doesn't need that."

The tourist shrugged, put the money away, and then

wasted no time jumping in the water with the rest of the group.

Mele came to her father, and together the two started walking back to the village.

"Mr. Ronin, I strongly encourage you to put a shirt on Mele when out in public," Fiame demanded. "How old is she now? Six?"

"She's four."

"Right. Well, although we like to show our traditional ways, we also want to display that we are a modern, Christian village."

Blue looked at the female tourists who were wearing skimpy bikinis that barely covered their breasts and butts. He wondered if Fiame noticed it, or did she only see the money.

"Modern. I see."

"Thank you for understanding."

On the way back through the forest, Blue thought about how "modern" Vaimasina had become over the past year, as Mele fluttered in and out of the foliage like a butterfly. A cellular phone tower was erected about two years ago, and more villagers had their noses planted on their cell phones. Blue thought the cell phone usage was part of the globalization that was taking place throughout the Pacific Islands region. This kind of globalization, he believed, also contributed to the spread of Westernization with quick and irreversible vicissitudes in cultural, social, and education of individuals.

But he mostly feared that the Samoan village lifestyle that was based on traditional culture, or *Fa'a Samoa*, would fade away and be replaced by a Western lifestyle. This was a shared belief between Fiame and Blue, and they would spend hours talking about it late at night when Blue felt up to it. Both agreed the village (and Samoa) shouldn't develop dependency, thus undermining sustainable practices. Nevertheless, for the past couple of years, Blue could feel a change, or a merging of two cultures sweeping over the village, and it was still up in the air whether or not it was a good thing.

At the grassy field, Blue and Mele parted ways. Mele saw a group of children playing around the *fale tele*. She handed her father her ukulele and rushed over to join them, as Blue reminded her to be careful and to make sure to go home before *Sa*. He wasn't sure if she heard a single word he said.

Blue then noticed his hounds galloping towards the forest, followed by several other village dogs. Blue whistled for them to come to him. They stopped to scratch their necks and lick their nether regions. Once they satisfied their itches, they continued towards the forest and disappeared within the tree line. Blue thought they were acting odd since they rarely went into the jungle.

As Blue got closer to his *fale*, he noticed Lance Lafau and the Bandana Man moving boxes out of Savea's trading store. Blue had managed to mostly stay away from Lance the past couple of years, except when the troublemaker visited Aumua. Blue was pleased when Aumua turned down Lance's advancements towards her. But, of course, that didn't deter him from continuously trying, which greatly irritated Blue. During one of his trips to Apia, he, perhaps by accident, saw Lance canoodling and smooching with Maeva, and it only confirmed to the volunteer what a couple of scumbags they were. Blue wondered if the two were even still together, or if they had moved on to other lovers. Regardless, he didn't think Aumua knew anything about their affair, but he felt that he didn't have to say anything about it because Maeva wasn't going to put up with any of Lance's womanizing antics.

Blue had a hunch that Lance was up to something nefarious whenever the Bandana Man was in the village. Blue surmised that the two scalawags used Savea's store to hold the stuff that they swiped in Apia, and they used the place as a base to carry out their latest illegitimate venture of smuggling exotic animals, which was mostly birds and lizards. Blue only came to this conclusion because when he went into the store the past few weeks, he could hear birds squawking in the storeroom and saw lizards zipping along the counter.

Blue couldn't believe that Lance had the temerity to conduct his foul business in his own village under the noses of his family. He wondered how much anyone in the village knew about what Lance was up to, particularly when the Bandana Man came to visit.

"Savea, what's with all the creatures?" Blue asked, plopping a bundle of bottled water on the counter.

"It's Lance's new business deals."

"Aren't they supposed to be in a cage or something?"

"Yes, but not yet."

Blue practically ducked out of the way when an exotic-looking redheaded parrotfinch with blue feathers flew by his head and landed on a bag of chips on the counter.

"They're all over the place," Blue observed.

"There was one cage."

"Should you put them back in it?"

"Yes... no. It broke."

"The cage broke?"

"No."

"It didn't break."

"Yes. The cage has a hole in it."

Blue stared at the storekeeper, who smiled at him. A lizard ran up his arm.

"Well, okay. You, uh... you seem to have this under control."

"Yes, very much," Savea said with an unsure tone. "They make plenty of *talas* for Lance."

"I think what Lance is doing with them is illegal."

"They make plenty of *talas*."

"I have no doubt. But I don't want to see you get in trouble. Tell Lance to get his birds and lizards and keep them somewhere else."

"Yes, I will—when I put them in cages."

"But you don't have cages."

"Yes, it's broken."

Blue didn't want to get involved further. He grabbed his bundle of water bottles and exited the store just as another pretty lorikeet landed on the storekeeper's shoulder.

The next day, Blue wanted to check his emails at the Traitors Internet Café. As he approached the place, he witnessed Lance and the Bandana Man arriving. Blue could hear the two men yelling at Savea and calling him words such as "idiot," "stupid," and they even used English for "moron." He hated Lance for taking advantage of Savea's naivety.

Blue waited around to make sure that the two miscreants didn't harm Savea. Then, a few minutes later,

Lance and the Bandana Man exited the store carrying makeshift cages of teabag boxes, plastic containers, and coffee cans. As Lance and the Bandana Man placed the boxes and containers in the trunk of a car, Lance noticed Blue staring at them and immediately took offense. Blue quickly walked away.

"Hey- *palagi*!" Lance yelled.

Blue stopped walking and turned to the two thugs. They were already heading towards him and were both sucking on cigarettes like a couple of gangsters. Blue noticed that the Bandana Man had picked up a crowbar from the trunk of his car and was carrying it in an intimidating way.

"What are you staring at, *palagi*?" Lance asked in English. He always spoke in English to Blue. "You need to mind your own business."

"I'm just heading home," Blue said in Samoan.

"Speak in English, please. Your accent is sickening."

"You shouldn't use Savea's store to hold your contraband," Blue said accusingly in English. "You're just gonna get him in trouble."

As Lance confronted the volunteer, the Bandana Man circled them like a prowling jungle cat waiting for the most opportune moment for a mauling. Blue didn't believe that they would hurt him in the middle of the village.

"Why are you still living in this village?" Lance asked and rubbed his bald head. "Everyone is tired of you."

Blue fantasized putting Lance in a headlock to rub the shine off his bald head.

"Dude, I just want to go back to my *fale*."

"Answer me why everyone wants you out of this village?"

Blue contemplated the question for a few seconds: Was Lance telling the truth, or was he just being a prick?

"Tell me, bro," Lance goaded.

"I ain't your bro."

The Bandana Man then came up from behind and placed the crowbar over Blue's head and against his neck as if trying to hold the volunteer back from attacking.

"This isn't necessary. I'm just going home," Blue said in a muffled voice. He looked around the village to see if anyone was witnessing this random act of violence, but he didn't see anyone.

There's never a villager around when you need one.

"Tell me! Tell me why you're still here!"

"I don't know... I, I stay maybe... because I have a daughter here, dimwit!"

Announcing that he had a daughter reminded Lance that Aumua was the mother, and this really irked him. Angrily, Lance put his cigarette out on Blue's chin, which forced the volunteer to yelp.

The Bandana Man tightened the crowbar around the volunteer's neck.

"We'll get rid of you soon, just like we did with that fuckin' phony priest."

"It was you who *narked* on him?" Blue asked.

"Everyone knew about him. He wasn't fit to be pastor of our parish. I just did something about it. We don't need you *palagi* anymore sucking up our resources."

Blue vehemently lunged at Lance, but was held back by the Bandana Man.

"Asshole!" Blue shouted.

The Bandana Man took his cigarette and burned Blue's neck and forced him to hold back.

"Damn it!" Blue uttered.

At that moment, a small tremor rolled through the village. Although the men didn't feel anything unusual, the trees in the area reacted, dropping loose leaves and branches. The coconut trees, in fact, near the Bandana Man's car, lost several coconuts that fell upon the hood and trunk. The ones that smacked the trunk hit and created holes in the boxes, allowing its content of birds and lizards to escape.

The Bandana Man let go of Blue and rushed towards the car. Lance looked to see what the fuss was and saw a couple of birds flying away from the trunk.

"Oh, shit!" Lance added and followed the Bandana Man to the car.

Blue enjoyed watching the two men scramble around the car trying to recapture their cargo. They even had to get on their knees to grab a lizard and cussed when they got bitten. The event amused Blue, but he knew better than to stick around too long. Lance typically possessed more bravado when the Bandana Man was with him, and Blue didn't want to add more fuel to Lance's hatred towards him. Blue decided that the emails would wait, and he would head back home. He couldn't help, however, looking back at the two men who were now trying to catch birds with a net. They stumbled on top of the car and practically knocked heads as they fell to the ground. Blue scoffed at their misfortune.

Ringling Brothers just called, and they want their clowns back.

Blue shook his head, thinking how bad that joke was.

Blue then saw that the new priest, Father Edgar, stepped in and tried to help the two reprobates and thought how ironic the scene was from his point of view—a man with one foot through heaven's gates unknowingly helping two men who already sit at Satan's brimstone table.

Blue had indifferent feelings for the new priest, who was very young (he still looked like a teenager) and was, in fact, recently ordained before he took over from Father Krimple. Blue felt that Father Edgar, who was Samoan and the only one who accepted the challenge to come to Vaimasina, was devoid of creativeness and had a direct approach to running the church. This pleased many of the villagers who desired a more structured and disciplined faith formation. He spent most of his day trying to sort through Krimple's files, notes, and plans, which made him grumpy. Father Edgar didn't have much of a sense of humor, and he certainly didn't have the charisma and impetuous conduct that Krimple possessed. It didn't help that the new priest was naïve, and Blue knew that villagers would take advantage of this.

Blue watched the three men for a moment before becoming bored with their ineptness and headed for home.

In his *fale,* Blue looked at his cigarette burn marks in a mirror that hung on a post. He winced when he touched them. He wished that Lance would go back to Apia and spend most of his days there. He didn't like it that the bald bully was spending much more time in the village for the past couple of years. And now that the Bandana Man was coming around, it felt more dangerous for him to walk around the village.

After examining his wounds, Blue lay on his mat with

his computer and tried to get some writing done. Despite being entertained by the bumbling idiots, he was in a bad mood and had trouble getting back into his novel. He swore under his breath and promised himself that he wouldn't go over to Fiame's house for *Sa* and dinner. Besides, he didn't exactly like the way Fiame treated him at the pool as if he was just some slacker who was in the way. He began to question his role in the village once again. Did he belong there anymore? Did he ever fit in? Is this the reason why Aumua won't move back to his home? Maybe Lance was right when he said that the village wanted him to go home. The thought of the village turning on him and wanting him out truly bothered him.

He slammed his computer shut. He rolled over on his mat and stared into the rafters of the *fale*. He didn't even feel like going to the Tuputala's house for dinner. It was just going to be a night by himself.

He stared at the rafters, seething and feeling sorry for himself, until he fell asleep.

He dreamt hard that night in a fitful sleep. They were mostly little vignettes that made him awake and shift his body, only to quickly fall asleep again. However, it would be the last nightmare before he awoke that he would remember for a long time.

He was underwater in the Vaimasina pool. Mele was sitting on the pool's floor, strumming her ukulele. Several fishing hooks then dropped in the water, and Blue dodged a few of them. He then swam to the surface and lifted himself into a boat where a bunch of Japanese tourists were getting ready to swim, and Fiame was telling them to watch out for eels. Blue saw Aumua sitting next to Lance and laughing.

Blue wanted to impress Aumua by catching a colorful bird for her. As he looked around for a bird, Aumua asked him where Mele was. Blue suddenly remembered that she was still underwater and that he better bring her up or Aumua would hate him forever. He was reticent to jump back in the water for fear of eels. Blue continued to procrastinate when he saw Father Krimple floating by on his back. Before he jumped into the water, a fishhook was pulled out of the water, and on the end of it was an eel wrapped around a ukulele. Tourists screamed. Lance laughed. Aumua stood and called out Mele's name.

Blue awoke.

Blue stared at the rafter of his *fale*. It was later in the morning, around 8 a.m., than when he usually awoke. He thought about his dream for a moment and shook his head.

Damn me.

He started a joke... *Freud just called...* but he never finished it.

Blue rolled off his mat and noticed that he was still in his bathing suit. He stood and stretched his back. He grabbed a bottle of water and guzzled down the rest of its contents. As he went to his washbowl, he grabbed a T-shirt and put it on before he washed his face.

Staring at the bowl of water, Blue noticed the water was vibrating. Something felt off, like he was the only person left in the world. He went to the edge of the *fale* to see if anyone else was moving throughout the village. It was a bright, sunny morning, but still-oddly still. He didn't hear or see any other villager.

Then the furniture in his *fale* began to shake. As he turned to see what was causing his furniture to rattle, an earthquake rocked underneath as if the entire village was built on rolling pins. Such a violent quake caused Blue to desperately cling to a *fale* post for survival. He had never experienced anything like it. Even living through several quakes in San Diego County, he had never felt anything this strong. Blue sunk down the pole holding on with all his strength. He thought about diving under a desk or a table as he was taught to do in school back home, but his *fale* had no such items, or at least not big enough to protect his entire body.

The quake felt like it lasted an eternity. He saw a house in the village flattened like a house of cards, and he hoped that nobody was inside. Being that it was early in the morning, the chances of someone being inside the squashed house was quite good. He saw another house roll to one side and crash to the ground. Coconut trees tossed coconuts like hand grenades into houses, *fales,* and parked cars. A few coconuts landed by Blue. The destruction really scared him. He saw several villagers running towards the grassy field, and he wondered if he should do the same thing.

He decided to make a run for it. It was difficult to let go of the steady pole, but he managed to pry himself free and stumbled outside the *fale*. He fell to the ground. A *fetau* tree uplifted and almost crashed upon him. Blue used the tree to hoist himself to his feet and quickly staggered towards the grassy field. It felt as if he was running against gravity as the rocking earth forced him to move in all kinds of directions rather than a straight line. But after a struggle, he made it to the field and fell flat on the ground. Unless the sky fell on him, he felt safe.

After a minute and twelve seconds, the shaking didn't

come to an abrupt stop as much as Blue and everyone else in the village hoped it would. Instead, it lingered with several rolling sensations of aftershocks for about ten more minutes until it seemed to tire out from exhaustion, then finally ceased.

Blue looked at the other villagers on the grassy field. They appeared to be thunderstruck and stunned, but relieved to escape the village. Blue assumed that they were in no hurry to go anywhere now. He noticed one child pointing at the village and said something about a house on fire. Blue looked to where the child was pointing and saw that it might be the Tuputala's house. His heart sunk to his stomach, and he wasted no time hurrying to the house.

On his way back to the village, Blue stumbled over the uneven grassy field. He then had to dodge the oncoming hordes of villagers who were making their way to the grassy field. He didn't see Aumua and Mele among them. Another minor aftershock struck forcing villagers to collapse on the ground and cover their heads. It slowed Blue down, but he was determined to get to the mother of his child and his daughter. *Veavao* birds scrambled along the ground, but Blue didn't think that was too odd because those birds always dashed in various directions throughout the day. He pushed onward, only having to jump from side to side from the numerous chickens and pigs that had enough sense to follow the villagers to safety.

Arriving at the Tuputala complex, Blue was pleased to see that the *fale* was still intact. The house, however, was indeed on fire. Before he barged inside, Lupesina came rushing out with her teenage son and two younger daughters. They practically ran into Blue's arms. She was coughing and had a large, bleeding gash on her head.

"Mr. Ronin!"

"Lupesina, your head—are you all right?"

"It hurts a little, but I'm fine."

"Are Aumua and Mele in there?"

"No."

"Where are they?"

"I don't know. They left the house early this morning."

"They didn't say where they were going?"

"No... they're probably at the beach."

Blue looked towards the beach. They often went to the beach in the morning to practice dance before the heat of the day slowed everything and everyone down.

"People are gathering at the *fale tele*," Blue said.

"What about the house?" Lupesina asked.

"I'm sorry. It's a goner. But go! There might be more aftershocks. Go!"

Lupesina didn't argue. She grabbed her three children, and together they made their way to the grassy field.

Blue ran down to the beach and stopped in his tracks when he saw the lagoon. He was horrified to see that the lagoon was draining away towards the reef and the open ocean. The receding water exposed the lagoon's floor where a myriad of fish that didn't withdraw with the water helplessly flopped and floundered. Coral and sea rock was exposed, and the sea floor looked like brown slush that baked under the intense sun. It quickly reeked of death and decay. Several villagers couldn't help but be attracted to the bare lagoon as if they hit the jackpot and took advantage of catching a bonanza of fish. Some were also easily pulling out octopus and crab and praising each other for their good fortune.

Blue understood the signs that something ominous was about to happen. He had seen enough documentaries on cable television to know that the receding water was a natural warning that a tsunami was about to hit the shoreline. He could barely hear the rumbling sound of the oncoming giant wave out at sea, but he couldn't quite see it. His feet felt as if they were cemented in the sand, not wanting to move until he got a glimpse of the wall of water. Then he saw it: large, fat, and frightening. Although it was probably traveling around thirty miles per hour, it looked like it was coming in slow motion. Blue knew that nothing in this world would be able to stop it. He was mesmerized to see something so awesome coming right for him.

It was the voice of Togi that broke Blue's hypnotic trance and he saw that his friend and his sons, Keanu and Kobe, were in the lagoon spearfishing three to four fish at a time.

"Togi! Get out of there! Run to high ground!" Blue screamed, pointing to the ocean.

Togi and his sons looked where Blue was pointing, and Kobe dropped his spear and started sprinting towards the village. Togi picked up Keanu, who was still holding onto his spear, and ran as fast as he could right behind his oldest boy.

Blue also started to run. He felt bad that he didn't have time to warn the others that were in the lagoon. But he was somewhat relieved when he saw a person or two running from the corners of his eyes.

The village was still reeling from the shock of the earthquake. When Blue arrived from the beach, he saw people sitting by their damaged homes with their hands on their heads, feeling overwhelmed and remorseful. Blue knew there was no time for the villagers to feel sorry for themselves. The wave was coming, and it was coming fast.

"Tsunami!" Blue yelled in English. He quickly thought they would better understand what was coming if said in Samoan. "Wave! Giant wave!! Get to high ground!"

Running near the trading store, Blue saw Savea and Vaveao with their four children carrying clothes and other sundries from the store.

"Vaveao! A wave is coming! Get your children to high ground!!" Blue shouted. "Savea! Grabbed that case of water and get to the forest!"

The family began running towards the forest.

"Vaveao, have you seen Aumua?" Blue frantically asked.

"She was at the community center this morning."

As Blue made his way to the community center on the grounds of St. Cecilia's, he could hear Togi screaming for villagers to run to the forest and higher ground. Blue saw dozens of villagers running as fast as they could across the grassy field and, perhaps, to the safety of the hills.

At the community center, Blue saw Aumua and a couple of other villagers helping a woman who had a gash on her forehead. A few children, including Mele, were trying to help, but seemed to be more in the way.

"Aumua! We have to go! There's a wave coming!"

The church bells began to ring as if it was a warning signal for the village. By now, the entire village knew that something threatening was heading their way.

Aumua helped the injured lady to her feet. The others who were helping had already started running for the church, where Father Edgar was standing by the side door and telling people to go upstairs to the balcony. Blue wasn't sure that this was the best place to go, but he followed Aumua and Mele inside and towards the spiral staircase. The balcony was already crowded with people, and Blue wondered if it would be able to hold more.

Aumua and Mele pushed their way up the stairs, but Blue stopped at the bottom. He questioned if he had time to run back to his *fale* to grab his computer. It contained his novel, his life's work thus far, and to lose it would mean many years wasted. He couldn't bear the thought of losing his work, as it was, he believed, the only thing that validated his existence. Without hesitation, he moved towards the front doors of the church.

"Ronin! Come up here!" Aumua shouted from the balcony.

"I'll be right back. Stay safe!"

Outside the church, Blue could hear the roar of the wave, which he believed by now was approaching the beach. As he ran against the traffic of villagers and chickens to his *fale*, he tried to guess what key the wave's rumble was in. Once he got to his place, he knew that he would only have a few seconds to grab his computer, then run for his life towards the forest. He endeavored to remember exactly where his computer was because he knew that he had little time for error. He had to be precise—a stumble or hesitation would mean certain drowning.

Blue ran into the *fale* and went straight to his bed. The computer was where he thought it was on the mat, and he only had to brush aside the mosquito net to grab it. He left through the side and was quickly on the grassy field running desperately with the last of the fleeing villagers as if he was part of a stampede. He could hear the wave's growl, but he dared not turn around to see how close it was, which would waste a precious second or two.

On the grassy field. Blue didn't notice who was running next to him until he heard a familiar voice.

"It's huge, Papa," screamed Mele.

"Mele- what the hell you doin'?" Blue asked in English with a strain. He could envision her squeezing underneath people in the church to get out and help her father.

Blue didn't break stride. He knew Mele would keep up.

Although Mele didn't understand what her father was saying, she answered her father anyway. "I wanted to make sure you were all right!"

"Mele, head for the chestnut tree and climb it!"

The tsunami struck the village as a series of swift, powerful floods of water. It was the second or third wave that was the largest, perhaps fifteen feet high, that hit structures like a wrecking ball. Some of the houses were flattened, and everything in them was swept away towards the grassy field. But the waves didn't discriminate or became picky as to what to steal and took everything like an overconfident thief in the daylight. Furniture, cars, boats, canoes, trees, fences, animals, and pieces of housing became easy pickings. Sadly, even the famous Vaimasina purple-and-black bus was easily compromised and rudely placed in the wave's pocket.

At the edge of the grassy field, Blue and Mele arrived at the chestnut tree. Blue looked up the giant, solid tree that had probably seen its fair share of floods over the past hundred years and saw dozens of other villagers already ensconced on branches and bracing themselves for the waves to strike.

"Climb Mele, climb!" Blue ordered in Samoan. The girl complied and quickly scampered up the trunk as she had done a myriad of times while playing with friends.

The roar of the wave got louder, angrier. Swallowing a human being would only add to its collection of items. Blue looked back and saw that the wave was only about fifty yards from him. He started to climb, but he wasn't as coordinated as his daughter, and he stumbled and misplaced his feet often. Blue felt another villager climbing right behind him, and he felt that this person would climb over him if he didn't speed his climb.

"Hurry!" the villager bellowed.

After handing his laptop to another villager higher in the tree, Blue was able to climb a little quicker and got to a large branch. He looked down to see that it was Lance Lafau that was behind him. It was at this time that the first wave struck the tree, shaking the branches. Blue instinctively reached out his hand for Lance to grab, which he gladly did, and helped pull his nemesis up. Lance continued to climb pass Blue. Other villagers in the tree began screaming and praying.

Another wave hit. The water level rapidly rose, and Blue felt as if he was in danger again.

"*Tamā*, get higher!" Mele yelled.

Blue started to climb. The water was licking his feet.

"Faster, *tamā*! Faster!"

Blue tried to climb higher, but it was like the water was holding him still and waiting for the right moment to peel him off the tree. Blue desperately reached out his hand above him, hoping someone would grab it. The volunteer felt a sense of relief when someone, indeed, grabbed his hand. He looked up to see that it was Lance, and for a moment, Blue thought that perhaps this monster actually contained an ounce of compassion. But then, Lance devilishly smirked while another wave struck, and Blue knew that it was too good to be true.

Lance let go of Blue's hand.

Damn me.

The water effortlessly tore Blue from the tree.

"No!" Mele screamed. She crawled along a long branch over the water to find her father. "*Tamā! Tamā!*"

Blue twirled and whirled under the murky water. He held his breath as long as he could before trying to lift himself to the surface. The current was pulling him in all kinds of directions as if he was tied to a rope that he couldn't free himself from. He was constantly bobbing above and under the water. When he reached the surface, he could see the serene blue sky and wished he were sitting upon the clouds. He had lost all sense of direction. He had no idea where he was, or where the water was forcing him to go. Sharp objects such as tree branches or pieces of metal bit at his legs and arms like a piranha fish. The water forced Blue against a stationary wooden pole, most likely, a *fale*. The collision smashed the right side of his face, and he could feel his skin tingle, his lips fatten, his nose bleed, and a couple of his ribs crack. Something metal then stabbed him in the back near his left shoulder. He could feel blood spurting from the wound, but he couldn't do anything about it because he could only fight the current to keep his head above water.

Because he was in such great pain, he thought about giving up and allow himself to succumb to drowning. Although he had read that drowning was a peaceful way to go, he was still quite scared to go through the process of letting his lungs fill up with water. He thought about Scarlett on that fateful day at Sabatini's Beach, and he couldn't believe that he was also trapped in a deadly current, fighting for his life. He questioned how much fight Scarlett truly put up.

Seconds later, Blue saw the tops of coconut palm trees in a line, and in the distance, he could've sworn that he saw the bell tower of St. Cecilia. A horrifying and sickening feeling came over him that he was in the lagoon and being dragged out to sea. If he didn't get crushed on the reef, the open ocean would surely drown him. Blue knew that his position was dire and that it was just a matter of time before he perished in the sea.

Debris from the village was streaming all around him, and he tried to hold on to items such as tree trunks or tin roofing, which would eventually sink, taking him underwater. After resurfacing, Blue tried again to climb on top of a wooden table, but it too sank under his weight. Descending under the water, he became distraught, and the pain that shot throughout his body was intense and demoralizing. Exhaustion began to set in, and he could feel his bruised legs begin to cramp. Although he held his breath, he let his limbs dangle loosely. It helped ease the pain. Soon, he'll have to make the decision if he was going to free his held breath and give himself to the water's welcoming world.

Tumbling in the current, preparing to meet his end, Blue

thought about Mele. He pictured the last time he saw her, supposedly safe on the tree branch, watching him with terror as the wave grabbed him and pulled him from the tree. He tried to remember her at a time when she was smiling. He always loved her smile. The thought that his last memory of her would be a horror-stricken glower upon her face couldn't be more painful to him.

Blue opened his eyes for a brief second.

Mele won't be in this watery grave. Ever. She doesn't belong in this kind of world. Blue couldn't bear the thought that he'd never see his daughter again, and it was this reason that he decided to try one last time to save his life.

As he raised himself to the surface, his lungs burned. They wanted to let the water in and cool them down. But Blue fought the urge, and at the surface, he let the air pacify the needs of his lungs.

Remarkably, a small boat brushed against his head. At first, Blue thought that he was going to be crushed. However, he looked up and became aware that it was just a small boat that was simply floating on the current. He grabbed the gunwale and tried to lift himself inside the boat, but the pain from his cracked ribs was too great, and he collapsed back in the water. He tried again and again. On the fourth try, he was able to get both of his hands on the gunwale and, with all his might, he pulled himself up out of the water. It was painful. But he didn't stop. He was determined to get in the boat. His perseverance paid off, as he lifted himself above the side of the boat and plopped on its floor. Blue winced in pain. He coughed up seawater and blood. The right side of his face was severely swollen, and he could barely see out of his right eye.

It would be a day or two before Blue realized that the boat he was in was, indeed, *Calypso*, the same boat that he swore he would never get back into after the shark incident many years ago. Nevertheless, he floated upon a current that took him over the reef and well out to sea, where other ocean streams waited to carry him helplessly through many horizons.

For the moment, he was grateful to breathe only air.

For the moment, he cursed his dumb luck.

For the moment, he lived in severe pain.

For the moment, he felt vulnerable.

For the moment ... there was nothing better than being alive.

8

As the house lights of the Stern Auditorium at Carnegie Hall brightened for intermission, people began to file out of their seats. All the movement and shuffling snapped Blue out of a glum funk. His ghostly companion, Scarlett, had faded away, but he could still detect the lingering scent of seawater. He was surprised that he had experienced another Scarlett encounter after not seeing or feeling her for a long while. He felt that, perhaps, he overreacted to the initial touch of Scarlett when she leaned her seawater, salty head on his shoulder. He knew she was not there to haunt him. Rather, she was there like everyone else, to listen and watch Mele.

"Extraordinary," the old woman sitting to Blue's left said. "How'd you like that?" she asked her husband.

"So advanced for one so young," he said. It was his usual response after waking from the audience's applause.

The three young women sitting to Blue's right wasted no time crawling over Blue and the old couple to get to the aisle. Blue thought that they couldn't wait to hit the bar in the lobby. There was no doubt that the concert was just the beginning of their night. As they passed Blue, he smiled at the one who was sitting next to him. She smiled back. Although the women were close to in age to Blue, he felt awkward and worlds apart. These were beautiful city girls who were used to getting what they wanted. When the three hit the aisle, the woman that Blue smiled at leaned into her friends and told them that he had smiled at her. They all giggled, and Blue could even hear one say, "Oh my God," as they paraded up the aisle.

Blue sunk in his seat. He had just remembered that he probably looked like Quasimodo with his eye puffing out. His wounds once again became uncomfortable.

"I have to drain the lizard," the old man said to his wife. Blue looked queerly at him.

Who says that anymore?

"You're always draining that thing," the old lady stated. "I'm surprised you made it through the first act."

The old man pretended he didn't hear his wife and left.

"He's got a urinary problem," the old lady said to Blue. "I keep telling him to see the doctor, but does he listen to me? No."

It was too much information for Blue, and he wished he were still on *Calypso,* floating aimlessly in the open ocean. He thought about that for a second and decided that he wouldn't wish that on anyone. His suffering was severe, and although he survived the tsunami, his ordeal would be just as severe in an open boat lost at sea.

———

Blue had been going in and out of consciousness while

coasting in *Calypso* after the tsunami. His body ached, his throat thirsted, and his mind dreamt. During the day, the sun burned him, and at night, the air chilled him. On the second day at sea, he awoke long enough to understand his surroundings and quickly comprehended the dire situation he was in. This was also when he knew he was in Togi's boat, and he saw that a couple of Fiji water bottles were inside. He quickly grabbed one and slaked his thirst before realizing that he should probably ration his water. He then searched the boat for an oar, but he didn't see one.

Damn it, Togi.

The constant undulation of the boat made Blue queasy, and he couldn't help vomiting. Wiping his mouth, he fell back in the bow of the stern and fell unconscious once again.

It was the sound of the tongue twisting lyrics of the song, "I Am the Very Model of a Modern Major-General," from the Gilbert and Sullivan play, The Pirates of Penzance, that awoke Blue. He immediately recognized the voices to be those of his mother and aunt. From each side of the bow of the boat, the two women climbed aboard. They took turns singing the verses:

"I am the Very Model of a Modern Major-General,

I've information vegetable, animal, and mineral," Juliet sang.

"I know the kings of England, and I quote the fights historical,

From Marathon to Waterloo, in order categorical," Ophelia sang.

. . .

"I'm very well acquainted, too, with matters mathematical,
    I understand equations, both the simple and quadratical," Juliet sang.

"About binomial theorem, I'm teeming with a lot o' news,
    With many cheerful facts about the square of the hypotenuse," Ophelia sang.

The two women were now sitting in the boat in front of Blue. They were both as dry as a desert tortoise. Blue strained his eyes trying to get a better look at the women, which was a struggle due to a possible concussion that blurred his vision.

"Holy shit," Blue incredulously exclaimed.

The women continued the song:

"I'm very good at integral and differential calculus," Juliet sang.

"I know the scientific names of beings animalculous," Ophelia sang.

They finished the verse by singing in unison with vim and vigor.

"In short, in matters vegetable, animal, and mineral,
    I am the Very Model of a Modern Major-General!"

. . .

The women laughed when they finished the verse and hugged each other.

"Come on, love, take the next verse," Juliet instructed Blue. He stared at them in disbelief. "Surely you remember how it goes."

"You drove us crazy when you were five and used to prance around the house singing that annoying song," Ophelia added.

"Tush. It's a lovely, whimsical song," Juliet retorted, then turned her attention to her son. "Give it a go, love. Come on."

Blue stared at the two with skepticism.

"The boy looks affright," Ophelia said.

"Now don't make him nervous, Ophy."

"You always mollycoddled the boy. It's good for him to be nervous. Nervousness brings out the wonder in a person."

"Stop. You're going to give him a complex. Then he'll never leave the house and will never get a girl."

"Nah. He's an explorer like his aunty. Girls love explorers."

"They do?"

"Of course. Indiana Jones, Jack Aubrey, Tintin, Bilbo Baggins, and Dora."

"Wasn't Dora a girl?"

"Was she? I couldn't tell." Ophelia leaned toward Blue. "Look at that face. You've seen some adventure already, haven't you, boy?"

"Why... why are you here?" Blue suddenly asked.

The women stared at him for a second or two, then laughed. They answered Blue at the same time.

"To hear the whale song," Juliet said.

"To take the bite out of the ocean," Ophelia said.

The three of them looked at each other, and then they all laughed. For Blue, it really hurt to laugh. But he couldn't remember the last time he had a good laugh, and despite the pain it caused in his cracked ribs, it was well worth it.

"I really miss you two," Blue lamented.

"You need a hug, don't you, love?" Juliet asked. Blue nodded. "Come here."

Blue positioned his body to lean back in Juliet's waiting arms. She could see how bruised his legs and arms were. His open wounds trickled blood.

"You took a beating, my dear boy. Poor thing. Does this feel better?"

Blue answered the question by snuggling closer to his mother.

"That's a lot of ocean out there," Ophelia commented. "I'm glad I'm not in the middle of it."

"Now don't you scare the boy," Juliet scolded her sister. "He's in enough pain."

"I don't want to sugarcoat the situation, but he's screwed."

"Ophy."

"Just saying, Jules. It looks grave."

"Don't say grave."

"Looks grave, but that doesn't mean it is grave," Ophelia said, augmenting her tone to a more positive attitude. "How often has a Blue been in this kind of predicament?"

"What predicament?"

"Lost at sea. We've all been there."

"The boy's fine where he is now."

"I was afraid of that," Ophelia said with a sigh.

A sober moment ensued. Blue shuffled his body and tried a different position in his mother's arms, hoping it would be more comfortable. Juliet and Ophelia stared at the sea, swaying back and forth as the waves kicked and kissed the boat.

As if he couldn't help it from being in the presence of his mother and aunt, Blue melodiously mumbled the last the verse of the song, "I Am the Very Model of a Modern Major-General":

"For my military knowledge, though I'm plucky and adventury,

Has only been brought down to the beginning of the century," Blue sang.

Juliet and Ophelia's spirits rose, and they became quite proud that their boy would continue the song despite being in such pain. With much verve, the three of them finished the song together:

"But still, in matters vegetable, animal, and mineral,

"I am the Very Model of a Modern Major-General!"

The women cheered. Blue forced a smile and then closed his eyes. The singing zapped all his strength. His body became numb, lifeless, and he was soon snoozing in his mother's embrace.

———

"Did you even hear me?" the old lady asked Blue, and it seemed to echo in the auditorium.

"I'm sorry," Blue answered.

"You must've gone somewhere dark."

"It's been an emotional night."

The murmur at intermission reached a crescendo among the audience and seemed to get louder as more people exited the lobby.

"I don't think there's anything to worry about. Your daughter is a natural on stage."

Blue liked the word, "natural," to describe his daughter. He had always admired how pure Mele remained since she came to the States. Blue wondered how much his daughter understood how she was able to stay "natural," especially in such an unnatural world. Mele came from an organic place where nothing was manmade or synthetic. Her attitude and expression on stage suggested that she could've played those pieces anywhere in the world. Tonight, she could have as easily performed in a subway, a village, a park, a farm, or wherever. The music would've been just as beautiful as it was on stage in Carnegie Hall.

The smell of gardenias got stronger, and Blue knew that Mele's private teacher, Donna Ledante, was standing in the aisle behind him. When he turned around to greet her, he noticed that she had two leis wrapped around her neck, and that it was the handy-dandy work of his daughter.

"Hello, Donna," Blue said.

"Ta- talo—how did you say it in Samoan?"

"*Talofa*," Blue answered.

"Yes." Donna looked peculiarly at him and could feel that Blue's right side of his face throbbed in pain. "You doin' all right? You look like you ran into a couple of street toughs."

"Yeah, I'm fine."

"Take a moment. It's all about Samoa tonight, isn't it?

She played the Bruch piece beautifully and impeccably, but what will be remembered is her bringin' Samoa to us."

Blue thought that was a very "Donna" thing to say. She had always had a more profound examination of what music means to the world. To her, music enlightens one's culture, and it helps people connect with their deepest passions and understanding of themselves.

"It's a shame that more of her family couldn't make it tonight," she added.

"New York's a little far."

"Yes. True. That's what I love about music. It'll find a way to travel to them."

Blue liked how she talked about music as if it was a tangible object, a living organism that breathes and is mobile.

"As long as it doesn't get lost at sea," Blue said awkwardly. He didn't really know what he was saying, but he was trying to keep up with the metaphors.

"Oh, no. Let's hope not. Yes? All music has a purpose. If it dies, a piece of cultural identity dies with it."

An uncomfortable pause ensued. The two never became good friends over the past year or so. They were from completely different worlds, and Donna felt that Blue was a little aloof and odd. In fact, she often asked Mele if her father was hiding something. Mele usually laughed and would simply say that he lived on his own planet. Nevertheless, Donna respected Blue for permitting Mele to study with her, which she felt would allow the prodigy the opportunity to flourish and share her gift. And, of course, Donna could never disregard a person who can play an instrument the way he can. She had always felt that he had much to say through music if only he would l release it.

"You're probably aware that promoters are here evaluatin' Mele," Donna said.

"I didn't know."

"Yes. There's no doubt she possesses a unique passion and artistry that would complement any orchestra throughout the country. Take a moment and just think of the many ghostly composers who would look down from their heavenly perch and smile upon her."

Blue didn't want to think about the possibility of Mele going on some kind of tour. It sounded daunting and exhausting.

"Let's just get through the second act tonight, then we'll see."

Donna smiled, and another awkward pause followed. The smell of the gardenias was very overpowering, and Blue felt a sneeze coming on. He knew that a sneeze was going to hurt, and thus, he tried to muffle it, which made a strange squeaking noise.

"I love the flowers," the old lady said to Donna. Blue welcomed the interruption. "Gardenias are my favorite."

"The young violinist on stage made these," Donna confirmed.

"Unbelievable. So talented in so many ways," the old lady said.

A man dressed in a suit and tie and looking like a dean of a school, or at least someone of importance, approached Donna and said hello. He asked her if he could have a quick word with her.

"Yes. Enjoy the rest of the engagement," Donna said

with a smile to both Blue and the old lady. Blue nodded, and Donna left with the man.

"You look like a prize fighter with that eye," the old lady said to Blue. "Are you sure you're going to be able to see the rest of the show?"

Blue wanted to say to her that the performance "was only meant to be heard," but then he quickly questioned himself what Donna would've thought about that. For sure, Donna would have disagreed with him. Music was meant to be experienced. Blue could hear her say that music should be heard, seen, felt, adored, and suffered. She would even make a case that music should be tasted, too.

Blue looked to the stage and saw that some of the musicians had returned to their seats. They were still wearing their leis that Mele made for them. The vivid colors of the leis blended together and made Blue to reminisce again.

———

He awoke again in *Calypso* with his head leaning against the gunwale. Squinting, he saw a lei bobbing in the water and questioned himself if he was close to land. He lifted his head, looked around, and saw nothing but water. He then quickly remembered that his mother and aunt were with him. He looked for them but quickly realized that they were gone. He became downtrodden at the thought that he was alone. He took a deep breath. The pain shot from his ribs down to his toes and up to his neck.

Damn me.

Blue repositioned himself in the bow of the boat. He grabbed another water bottle and took a swig. He looked in the water at the lei that seemed to be floating along with the boat and wondered if it came from Vaimasina. He thought about Aumua and Mele and hoped that they were safe. He was comforted by remembering that when he was being dragged within the lagoon, he saw the bell tower of St. Cecilia, which meant that the old church withstood the series of pounding waves. He knew firsthand that the receding waves were just as strong as the initial, forthcoming waves, and he hoped the church's foundation was able to withstand such pressure.

The late afternoon sun slowly began to sink under the clouds towards the sea as if it was getting ready to take a dip in the cool water. A soothing, warm breeze blew through Blue's hair. It felt good against his salt-encrusted face, and it wasn't long before he fell asleep again.

It was nighttime when Blue groggily awoke. A full moon played hide-and-seek with the clouds, but when it was found, it shone brightly upon Blue and the ocean. The warm wind of the day turned cooler at night and chilled Blue's bruises.

Unexpectedly, a cello and bow were hurled from the sea and into the stern of the boat from the ocean just as the moon disappeared behind a cloud. Blue shifted and pulled his legs towards his body. Blue narrowed eyes with uncertainty as a female climbed out of the water and into the boat. She picked up the bow and positioned her cello between her legs. The moon moved out of the clouds and became a spotlight for the young woman as she tuned her instrument.

"Scarlett?" Blue asked.

"Try to guess this piece," Scarlett said and began to beautifully play Beethoven's, "Moonlight Sonata." Scarlett always played superbly, even when she joked around, which was rare.

"Why are you here?"

"Pretty appropriate for a night like tonight, don't you think?"

"Sure... why not?"

"You think Beethoven wrote it while drifting on a boat during a full moon?" Scarlett asked with a slight giggle and kept playing.

"I don't think the piece was coined the 'Moonlight Sonata ' until after Beethoven's death," Blue stated.

"Yeah, I doubt Beethoven ever saw an ocean or a boat."

The shine of the moon silhouetted Scarlett, and Blue was relieved that he couldn't see her disfigured face.

"So where are the rest of your ghoul friends?" Blue asked about the rest of the *Teine Sa* that typically accompanied her. He wanted to laugh, but he knew that it would hurt.

"Oh, they're waiting for me."

"You know, I don't appreciate you terrorizing me since I arrived in Samoa."

"Terrorizing?"

"Yeah."

Scarlett stopped playing.

"I only came to you when I thought you were lonely."

"I'm not lonely."

"You were a lonely kid, and you're a lonely adult."

"I was a normal kid, and I'm a normal adult."

"Artists are never normal."

"And you, Scar?" Blue asked.

"What about me?"

"Were you normal?"

"I was abnormally normal."

"Okay, but I'm not lonely. I've got a woman and a child and an entire village."

Scarlett began playing again.

"But they don't entertain you."

"I don't need to be entertained, Scar."

"Everyone needs to be entertained. That's why people like you and me are so important."

"Why don't you go haunt your parents or something?"

"You think my grandmother would allow me to haunt our house?"

Blue tried to laugh, but it hurt too much. However, he knew she was right because her grandmother was a tough old bird that bullied him over the years.

Scarlett continued to play, and Blue listened. He tried to remember if the two of them ever performed the piece together. Regardless, she always played pieces impeccably and perfectly, even if she wasn't trying to do so. She was simply exceptional. Blue was often jealous of her talent. Although he knew that she had an abnormal childhood, she had a future in music and a career doing something she loved. Fame and prestige would have been inevitable if she would've lived. Perhaps more importantly, people would've wanted to work with her. She would've never gone a day without work.

"The more enjoyment you get out of your work, the more money you will make," Blue quoted. "Uh, Mark Twain."

"Huh?"

"I, uh, I still feel sorry for you, Scar."

"Why?"

"You know, your—your future could've been awesome."

Scarlett stopped playing.

"I'm sorry. Did I disappoint you, too, Ronin?" Scarlett asked and poked him in the chest with her bow.

"Too? No. I wished I had your work ethics."

"Really?"

"Yeah, man. You were worked your ass off to get where you were. I was a nose-sniffling fuck-up."

Scarlett laughed and began to play again.

"I like this talk. I feel like we're at Sabatini's Beach," Scarlett said.

"Yeah... I wish."

"I always thought you thought that I was a dull doll."

"Well..."

"A dull doll that disappointed."

"Come on. You... you've never disappointed anyone in your life."

"Well, guess what? I'm finally at peace, Ronin," Scarlett stated. She stopped playing.

"What are you talking about?"

"I'm free to swim with the fishes."

"Free? You call what you've been doing free?"

"Yeah."

"You've been scratching on my roof the past four years, Scar," Blue exclaimed with some venom. "You've been trying to frighten me. You call that free?"

"Did you know, Ronin, that when I play now, I can't hear it?"

"Hear what?"

"I can hear a note anymore. I swear."

"Yeah, right. You play as beautifully as you ever did."

"I wish I could believe you."

Blue scoffed.

"Perhaps I don't care because I'm free. I don't need the cello anymore like I used to," Scarlett declared. "There was a time when playing the cello was just an extension of me, my personality, my frailties, my strengths. Now, I'm as deaf as Beethoven and can barely feel the vibrations."

Scarlett then picked up her cello and tossed it in the sea.

"Scar, what are you doing?!"

"Why play if I can't hear it? You know, it's not so much the cello that I miss, it's music in general. I hear nothing. I might be free from responsibility, but I don't want to be free of music."

Scarlett stood in the boat.

"Scar, what are you doing?"

"I'm going now, Ronin."

"Please, sit down."

"The sea has a voice. Maybe I can hear it sing."

"Come on, sit down."

The boat turned, and the moonlight lit Scarlett's ghastly and decaying face.

"I can sit, or I can swim in the sea. I have options."

"Scar, come on. Sit. You don't have to leave now."

"I don't?" Scarlett asked with a smile.

"Keep me company."

"You know how many times I used to say that to you? Good luck, Ronin."

"Scar!"

And Scarlett jumped into the sea.

"Scar!"

Blue awoke, still screaming Scarlett's name. The night

had given way to day. He searched for Scarlett and rapidly lunged from one side of the boat to the other. The sudden movements hurt his ribs. Nevertheless, he didn't see any sign of his friend and fell defeated in the boat.

"Freud just called, and he wants to buy my dream," Blue said. "I must be losing my goddamn mind."

The daylight sun threw flamed daggers at him, and the heat of the day seemed to intensify with each passing second. Blue wanted to fling himself overboard into the refreshing water, but he knew better than to separate himself from the boat. He had nowhere to go to protect himself from the streaming, steaming rays of the sun.

Blue crouched further in the boat. Staring along the bottom of the boat, he noticed something that looked like a fishing pole. He reached out and grabbed it and held it up.

It was undoubtedly a bow for a cello.

"What the hell?" Blue asked himself. "No way. No fuckin' way..." He threw the bow on the floor of the boat. "No way."

For the rest of the day, Blue tried not to look at the bow. When he did peek at it, he tried to rationalize how it got there. It baffled him like an unsolvable puzzle. He recalled that nobody played the cello in the village. In fact, how many people played the cello in Samoa? Blue addled his brain that took his mind off the perilous position he was in. He became somewhat relieved when day turned to night, and he couldn't see the bow on the floor of the boat.

Before daybreak on the next day, Blue awoke to severe pains in his stomach. He wasn't sure if his discomfort was getting bashed around by the wave, or if he was hungry. He tried to think how many days he had been drifting at sea.

Was it three or four days? He looked around the floor of the boat, including underneath the boarded seats. Besides the water bottles that he found a few days ago, he also picked up some rags, candy wrappers, and cigarette butts. He also jabbed his fingers on a couple of fishhooks that made him shout an expletive.

He leaned back against the bow of the boat. He stared at the items he found and thought how futile they all were. Then the boat hit a swell and forced the cello bow to move from one side of the boat to the other. Blue observed the bow moving back and forth. And then it hit him, and he wondered if Togi acquired the bow thinking that it was some kind of fishing pole.

Blue grabbed the bow and held it up and stared at how it was composed. He felt the bow's hair and examined the strength of the wood. He looked at the fishhooks and then at the blue of the ocean.

"Do the math," Blue said to himself, although he was never good at math.

Blue had seen villagers making string out of pandanus and coconut tree leaves on many occasions. He believed that the hair of a cello bow was no different. Blue quickly pulled off the hair of the bow and tied chunks of it together, creating a long line. After this, he took one of the rags and tore a small piece off, which he used to tie the hair on the end of the bow. Blue then connected a hook at the end of the line and pierced it through the shiniest part of a candy wrapper. He was pleased with his makeshift fishing pole.

"I wonder if Yo-Yo Ma would've thought of this."

The line was dropped over the side of the boat.

Blue waited and waited. Nothing happened. An hour passed, and no fish seemed interested in his bait.

"Fishing is so damn boring."

Damn it, Togi.

Finally, after two hours, Blue felt a tug on the bow. He pulled the bow, but whatever was on the other end seemed heavy. Because the bow almost broke, Blue grabbed the line and began to pull it up. Although the wet line was slicing his hand as he was pulling it up, he was determined to bring his catch out of the water. As he got the line halfway out of the water, it went limp. Blue couldn't feel anything on the other end. He finished pulling up the line to see that his catch had swum away with the hook and bait.

Damn me.

Without hesitating, Blue grabbed the remaining hook, pierced another piece of the candy wrapper through it, and dropped it in the water. He held onto to the bow and waited. The boredom, however, was unbearable, and after an hour, he fell into restless slumber full of bizarre dreams that included fish dancing around cellos and cellos catching fish.

It was the tug of the bow that awoke Blue. In fact, the bow flung out of his hands and was pulled towards the side of the boat. Because it was dusk, he could barely see the bow, but he knew he had to react. Blue quickly pitched forward and sprung for the bow, catching it just before it went over the side. He held on to it, trying to think how he could manage it without losing the fish on the other end of the line. Blue decided to wedge the bow between his legs and steadily pull the bow hair up with both of his hands. Within seconds, he saw the outline of a fish dangling on the line. He brought it into the boat and ravenously began eating it despite the fact that it was still flopping about between his teeth. Blue had had his fair share of eating raw fish, but this just seemed different. The fish was straight from the sea—salty and scaly. Although it tasted nasty and made Blue gag, it was nourishing, and it was much better than starving to death. Ironically, the feast only made Blue hungrier. After feasting, it wouldn't be long until he fell asleep again.

By dawn's early light, the sea got rougher, which aroused Blue from his sleep. The large swells were unkind to not only his bruised body parts, but more seriously, the up and down motion of the boat was too much for his ribs, and even the slightest movement made him wince in pain.

As *Calypso* was lugged up to the top of the swell, it fell over the hill of water like a small rollercoaster at a church carnival. Blue placed his hands down on the bottom of the boat to brace himself, only to realize that he had put his hands in about two inches of water. Blue quickly looked around himself and the bottom of the boat and saw that the boat was, indeed, taking on water. A sobering inquiry about whether or not the boat was sinking came over him, which was confirmed by the fact that his swim trunks were wet. He even noticed that the bones of the fish that he ate were floating in the boat. Blue desperately looked around the boat to find something that could help him bail the water, but there was nothing that he could see that could be used for such a purpose. He wondered if the leak was coming from the same hole that compromised the boat during the ordeal he had with the shark in the lagoon many years ago.

"Damn it, Togi."

Blue tried to cup his hands and splash the water out of

the boat. The saltwater stung the slit on his hand from when he tried to pull the fish out of the water. His ribs also didn't enjoy the rapid movements. Plus, he didn't have the strength or stamina to continuously bail water. After a minute or so, he sunk back in the bow and road the boat over another crest of a wave.

Dark clouds began to overlap with one another making morning feel like it was late arising. Blue looked skyward and sensed that the clouds were eventually going to unload their bellies full of water. In fact, as he told himself that it was going to rain, he could already feel the pattering of raindrops on his unprotected head. He hoped that the rain gods would postpone any deluge, which he knew would only hasten the sinking of *Calypso*.

About an hour later, the rainstorm did come, and the shower was steady and cold. The swells became a little stronger, which made Blue seasick. Instinctively, he leaned over the side of the bow to vomit. However, not having much in his stomach, he was mostly dry heaving into the sea.

When his boat hit the top of a swell, he thought that he noticed a dark mass through the slanting curtain of rain in the horizon. He wiped his mouth with his arm and spat the salt away from his lips. Before he could officially determine if it was land or not, the boat had already fallen into the trough. He had to wait until the next swell to get another look.

As the boat reached the summit of the wave once again, he strained his eyes at the mass in the mist and determined that it was, in fact, land.

Blue didn't know how the ocean currents worked, and

thus, he didn't really know what land he was seeing. Was it still Samoa? Fiji, perhaps? He didn't care. It was land, and that's all that mattered. He convinced himself that it wasn't an oasis, and that he wasn't dreaming, although he had to slap himself on the good side of his face just to make sure. He knew that if he were going to survive, he had to find a way to get to that land. The land was too far to swim, and besides, he was way too weak and in pain to even dive into the water. He also couldn't rely on the current to carry him closer to land. Thinking of his luck, it would take him further away. Therefore, his only means to get to land was to do it in *Calypso*.

Blue sunk back into the bow of the boat and tried to think how he could get it to land. The rain began to fall heavier, and another inch of water quickly accumulated in the bottom, which made him think faster. If the storm got worse, he knew that there wasn't much he could do to stop the water from rising in the boat, and he would surely sink.

Staring across the boat toward the stern, he noticed the bench seat that went from one side of the boat to the other side. He wondered if he could make an oar out of it and row the boat towards the land. The bench was made of laminated wood that was fastened to each side of the boat by a hinge with two screws. A narrow beam came from the floor and supported the seat in the middle. Blue crawled towards the bench and shook it. One side was a little loose, and he tried to shake it sturdily with both of his hands, hoping that it would become loose. It didn't work. He tried to kick it with his feet, but that only hurt his feet and his ribs. Confounded, Blue scratched his head, which hurt as well.

Blue leaned closer to the hinge on one side of the boat to get a better look. He noticed that only two small screws fastened it. He tugged at it the hinge again and cursed himself for not having a screwdriver. He looked around the boat to see if he could use anything as a screwdriver, then remembered the fishhook that he used to catch the fish. It must be still in the fish's mouth. He didn't recall throwing the fish head overboard, and he frantically started to look for it under the water that was steadily rising in the boat.

Blue picked up the cello bow and used it to poke around under the water, hoping that it would stir the fish head to the surface. After about thirty seconds, it worked, and Blue grabbed the fish head. He pried the mouth open and tugged at the hook. It didn't come out as easy as he had hoped, and he had to apply more strength. The more recent endeavor tore the flesh of the fish, but the hook came out.

Examining the hook, Blue straightened it as much as he could to make it more useful. He was impressed that Togi's son, Keanu, learned how to make such a practical yet functional tool. No doubt that he caught countless fish with it.

With the boat bobbing up and down, Blue struggled to place the hook in one of the screws. He had to wait until there was calm, then he got the hook just right and began turning. After he got one side of the seat loose, he looked through the rain to ensure that the land mass was still there. Once that was confirmed, he shifted over to the other side of the boat and began loosening the other screw.

The rain drove down harder, helping the water in the boat to rise. Although the seat was loose, it seemed that it was still connected in the middle. Blue tried to push it free, but it felt stuck. Also, he really didn't have the strength to unfasten it with his hands. He then used his feet to kick at it and jar it free, which it did after several lunges from his legs. Blue grabbed the seat and clambered to the bow of the boat.

Paddling the boat was strenuous and exhausting work. He could feel the weight of the boat, and each stroke shot excruciating pain from his ribs to his legs and up to his neck. Nevertheless, he was determined to keep rowing towards the land.

As he got closer to the beach, he realized that there was one obstacle in his path: the reef. However, he didn't have time to look for an opening, as his boat was gaining more water, and he was losing stamina. Blue figured he had nothing to lose by going over the reef. Either he would slowly die floating at sea, or he would be swiftly crushed to death by the pounding waves. He preferred the latter. Besides, the villagers of Vaimasina probably already thought that he was dead. The storm didn't help him, as it made the waves even bigger, scarier, and louder as he got closer to the reef.

Blue squinted and could now see through the lashing rain a line of coconut palm trees along the shoreline and wished he were lazily sitting underneath them. The reef posed as a giant and wet face of death, and he began to build his courage to confront it. The nearer he got to the reef, the stronger the current would push *Calypso*, and he could stop rowing. Before he knew it, he was sitting on top of the wave, and the palm trees seemed so close to. Then, as *Calypso* dropped into the reef, it was the ultimate rollercoaster ride, and Blue hung on. Eventually, he would abandon ship. The next thing he knew, he was tossing and turning underwater, which reminded him of being dragged about by the tsunami.

As *Calypso* was crushed by the pounding surf, the coral that was as sharp as razors was ripping through Blue's body. He felt the coral slashing deep along his leg and across his arm. But the cut was the least of his problems. He had to get up for air. He reached the surface and took a breath just in time for another wave to pummel him back underwater. The force of the water was violent and powerful enough to give him a concussion. He felt another rib crack.

Helpless under the water, Blue believed that he saw Scarlett sitting on a clump of sea rock with her cello between her legs. He considered that this was the end and that he would be joining her in a watery grave. He thought he would never see Aumua and Mele again. He thought that he would never hear his Aunt Ophelia's voice, and he would never feel the imaginary touch of his mother. He would never again smell the bad breath of his hounds.

As luck would have it, the ocean gods did not want to claim another mortal on this day. They had felt that he had endured enough punishment. A wave pushed and carried the volunteer forward to shallow water. He rolled a few times like a pair of dice on the sandy floor and ended up staring at the grey sky. Quick surges of water bowled over his body. Blood protruded through the wounds from the coral. His torso shivered in shock, but he was alive.

He wasn't sure how long he was lying paralyzed in the water before a couple of men grabbed his arms and pulled him to the safety of the beach. He could've sworn they were encouraging and speaking to him in Samoan. He thought that, perhaps, he was dreaming. Regardless, he was relieved that he was possibly still in Samoa.

Lying on the beach, he realized he still gripped the cello bow.

———

The scar on Blue's hand was a constant reminder of the harrowing moments and days that followed the earthquake and tsunami. As Blue stared at his hand, the scar seemed to glow under the lights of Carnegie Hall. In fact, his entire body still showed the signs of survival, which he was never proud of because they seemed to be more of a nuisance than anything else. Years later, the wounds remained prominent, and sometimes even ached. He often wondered if his mind was scarred from the ordeal. In the aftermath, he didn't experience any epiphanies. He didn't turn to religion. He didn't join or create a volunteer group for preparing for natural disasters. He didn't even feel guilty for surviving while other villagers along the tsunami-affected coastline were killed or swept out to sea, never to be seen again. Blue simply tried to repress the watery nightmare and never really told anyone about it. He often thought that no one would believe him anyway.

The houselights flickered, indicating that everyone should return to their seats, as the musicians made their way back to their appointed chairs.

It wasn't long until the old lady's husband returned, got settled into his seat, and anticipated a pleasant slumber during the second half of the show.

"You were in the bathroom a long time," the old lady observed.

"The line was long."

"Long? Did you use the women's room by mistake?"

The old man pretended not to hear her. Instead, he shifted in his seat to better maximize his comfort level.

Blue wasn't paying much attention to the old couple. He was lost in thought and wondered how much Mele remembered about the earthquake and the subsequent tsunami, as she was only four when it happened. But then he thought how she had a photographic memory and probably could recall every second of the tragedy. Thinking about Mele, however, eventually brought him back to the present, and he couldn't believe that his daughter was halfway done with her performance. After a year of rehearsing and planning, it had finally come down to the last forty-five minutes or so.

The three young ladies seated next to Blue returned to their seats. He stood up to allow them to pass. As they shuffled by him, they were still giggling. The first woman to pass Blue accidentally stepped on his foot. Her high heel felt like a spear went through his foot, but he managed to stifle the pain.

"Sorry," she said with a laugh. Her friend behind her gave her a push to her seat.

Blue wondered how they could sit comfortably in such tight dresses.

"Your daughter plays good," the young woman sitting next to Blue said. "Does she get nervous?" Her two friends laughed at the question.

"Oh, she acquired a gene at birth that doesn't make her nervous," Blue quipped.

"Really? That's so cool," the young woman stated. "If I were up there, I'd get so nervous I'd puke on the conductor."

Her friends laughed and argued how she never got nervous. They even provided examples, like the other night at a bar.

The book of dumb blonde jokes just called and it, uh, it found its subjects for its, uh, next edition.

Blue raised his eyebrows and thought how bad that joke was.

In fact, raising his eyebrows reminded him of the pain on the right side of his face. He felt his face and thought that he probably looked like the Hunchback of Notre Dame. He had no doubt that the girls sitting next to him would ask each other what was wrong with his face when they met for drinks after show. Although he never opened up about his fight with Death in Samoa, he felt compelled to defend his current looks and tell the young woman next to him about his encounter with the tormenting tsunami. Perhaps, she would be impressed. Perhaps, she wouldn't think he was a chump. Perhaps she would invite him for drinks.

Blue turned to her, and she looked at him.

The lights of the auditorium went dark. The musicians began to tune their instruments. A door opened on stage. The audience applauded.

And Blue didn't say anything.

———

A couple of rapid slaps on Blue's face forced him to open his eyes. He saw white sheets rippling from a breeze and heard a cacophony of voices coming in all directions. Although he was lying on a cot, he felt as if he was still rocking at sea. He grabbed hold of the sides to steady himself. He then saw a Samoan man's face lean over him.

"There you are," the man said in English. "I'm Doctor Alfred. Who are you?"

"Ro- Ronin Blue."

"Well, Mr. Blue, you are one lucky son of a bitch."

"Where am I?" Blue asked in Samoan, which surprised the doctor.

"You speak Samoan."

"I've been here for five years."

"You're in a Red Cross field hospital for earthquake victims," the doctor answered in Samoan.

Blue tried to rise in the cot.

"I have to get back to Vaimasina," Blue continued in Samoan, then felt woozy. He quickly realized that he wouldn't be able to stand and fell back in the cot.

"I'm afraid you won't be going anywhere for a while. You really got battered."

Blue noticed that his cuts, gashes, and bruises were treated. Some of them were covered with bandages of various sizes. He also felt that his head was wrapped with a dressing, and his ribs were swathed with a binding made of cotton, which helped keep his torso tight. Despite all this first aid, his body ached. Each time he coughed, sneezed, or moved, a jolt of pain shot erratically through his body like a pinball.

"We need to get you to the hospital in Apia," the doctor continued. "We need X-rays to make sure you don't have anything else broken besides your ribs."

"I don't feel as if I have anything else is broken."

"Well, we want to make sure. But they're inundated with patients right now. You'll be watched here until we can get you there."

"I have to get back to Vaimasina."

"That's impossible," the doctor said while getting a

syringe ready. He then stuck it in Blue's arm.

"Am I not in Samoa?"

"You're in Samoa, but Vaimasina isn't."

"What?"

"The village was wiped off the map by the tsunami just like the other villages in the area," the doctor stated firmly. "Now, relax. The shot will help you rest."

Before Blue could ask any more questions, he was out.

After a few days in the field hospital, Blue slowly regained his strength. He was able to get out of his cot and walk to an area where food was being prepared and served. Each time he went there, he tried to get reports regarding Vaimasina, only to receive conflicting information. It was frustrating for him. Whenever he pushed for more news, he would only get more confusing accounts and hearsay.

Lying in his cot, Blue thought about nothing except the fate of Vaimasina and its villagers. He felt helpless, thinking that everyone probably believed he was dead. He wished there was a way to let the villagers know, especially Aumua, that he was still alive. Of course, the contradictory report that Vaimasina was washed away only added to his fears and worries. Blue's only consolation was that he recalled seeing the church tower as he was being carried out to sea. If the church stood, so did Aumua on the balcony. He also was encouraged that Mele remained safe in the chestnut tree until the water receded. He would never forget seeing Mele's face with a horrified expression as he fell out of the tree and into the rushing water. It was this thought, more than any other, that haunted Blue and kept him awake all night. He was determined to return to Vaimasina.

During the next night, Blue nonchalantly got out of his

bed, picked up the cello bow, and went to the portable toilets. He wore a T-shirt, shorts, and a pair of flip-flops that were given to him from a box of international donations for the earthquake victims. It didn't occur to him that these clothes were the only ones he would own, as his wardrobe in his *fale* was most likely washed out to sea. Clothes now, however, were the furthest problem from his mind. He was only obsessed with finding a way back to the village. If he had to, he'd walk back in the nude.

After using the toilet, Blue didn't return to the tent where his cot was. Instead, he made his way towards the Main South Coast Road and tried to flag down any car that was heading east. The cars were sparse in the evening, and a few that did drive by didn't stop for him. Finally, a car stopped for him, and Blue hopped in the front seat. He told the driver that he needed a lift to Vaimasina. The driver didn't know where that village was, but would drive Blue as far as he was heading. The drive was slow, and with each passing mile, Blue became more anxious and impatient.

The driver took Blue about halfway to Vaimasina. Blue got out of the car, thanked the driver, and waited for another ride. It wasn't until dawn that a truck with a group of volunteers heading to a village that was close to Vaimasina stopped and let Blue jump in the back. The ride was rough on Blue's body. He felt each bump around his ribs, and he tried to brace himself for the next thump in the road, which inevitably took him by surprise. The ride, however, didn't dissuade him from asking his companions if they had heard anything about his village, but he only received the same answers. Half said it was gone, the other half said that they weren't sure if it was still there or not.

When the truck got to the tsunami-affected areas, it had to slow down and use alternative dirt roads because the main road was washed away in parts. This was when Blue saw the destruction firsthand. Everything was a mere shadow of its former self. Villages were, indeed, wiped off the face of the earth. Blue could see where houses and *fales* once stood and had been reduced to rubble. In many cases, only the foundation or *paepae* were left. Survivors would try to gather around the slow-moving cars, hoping to acquire aid such as food, clothing, toiletries, and any donation they could get their hands on. Blue got anxious. He wished he had something to give to the people, but he, too, probably lost everything as well.

The truck stopped about two miles short of Blue's destination. It was, perhaps, for the best, as the road going further was completely washed out. Blue bid his farewell to his travel mates in the back of the truck and had no other choice but to walk the rest of the way. His route led him along dirt roads, surrounded by deep, thick foliage. The journey was even more difficult because he wore flip-flops. At times, he used the cello bow to push back branches and leaves. With each passing minute, the heat of the morning began to rise, forcing him to stop and rest. He sweated profusely. This had an adverse effect on some of his bandages, which peeled off under the strain of the heat and sweat.

Eventually, Blue made it to the coconut plantation. He was pleased to see that it was unscathed, as it was protected by the hills. He noticed that another harvest of cocoa pods should take place soon. But he understood that this was probably not going to happen as there would be more pressing issues to deal with in the village... if it were still there.

After climbing a hill, Blue was in the forest that would lead him to Vaimasina. He started to see the debris that the tsunami had left in its wake. It was like the waves left behind the items they didn't want to take back to sea with them. The forest was littered with materials. He observed articles of clothing, mats, pieces of boats and canoes, blinds, metal scraps, a pew of the church, and pots and pans. Some of it was hanging in trees and bushes. He tried to guess why the villagers hadn't come to try to salvage any of it. Maybe they didn't know that any of it was here, or maybe there weren't enough villagers left.

Blue quickened his pace.

Arriving at the edge of Vaimasina's grassy field, the debris was even greater than in the forest. It was a real mess. There was even a large yacht wedged by sand, coral, and mud in the middle of the field. Quickly surveying the village, Blue noticed that many of the *fales* were left standing. Most of the Western-style houses, however, were gone, and only their foundations remained. He was pleased that the church, indeed, still stood. The community center and school were also spared, with the exception of windows and doors. No doubt the contents inside were washed away.

The village seemed deserted, which depressed Blue. There wasn't a soul moving about, and the area felt eerily quiet. He made his way to the church. If anything, it was to get out of the hot sun. He would use the church's shade to rest, and he would take a moment to try to piece together what happened to everyone.

The church was dark when he entered from the

brightness of the day. He could see that there was about a foot of mud and sand that covered the entire church. The altar table and pews were askew. Some pews were, of course, missing. Blue also observed how high the waterline got to on the coral and stone walls. It was at least eight feet high—almost as high as the stained glass windows, which seemed illuminated by the sun and enthusiastically told the story of St. Cecilia despite not having an audience.

He was relieved to see that the balcony was still intact. He quickly ran up the spiral staircase and noticed that the floor was strewn with water bottles, mats, sandals, clothes, and food wrappers. Blue thought that the area suggested that people survived the waves, and he couldn't help but smile. He then saw the piano and went to it.

After wiping off trash on the piano bench, he sat down. He stared at the black-and-white keys and took a deep breath. Scarlett appeared behind him, and he could feel her presence. Blue placed his hands on the keys. It had been years since he positioned his hands to play. He hesitated for a second or two and then began to play Frédéric Chopin's "Fantasie Impromptu in C Sharp minor, Op. 66." As he played the piece as beautifully as he once did, Scarlett placed her hand on his shoulder, closed her eyes, and smiled peacefully and restfully. Could she hear the music?

At the beach, the Vaimasina villagers were working together, fishing in the lagoon, climbing coconut trees to gather coconuts, piling bananas and other fruits, and making mats, baskets, and other sundries needed for everyday living. It was Blue's hounds that heard the piano first. They raised and cocked their ears before darting towards the church. They knew who had returned and barked as if saying, "Welcome Back," to their best friend. One by one, the villagers stopped what they were doing to listen to the music. They had never heard anything like it before. They wondered who had come to the village. They wondered who was playing so beautifully and pondered how something so exquisite could happen in a place of destruction. Everyone except Mele.

"*Tamā's* home," Mele said with a smile to her mother.

9

On the day Blue incredibly returned to Vaimasina, the villagers waited another week to see if any of the missing would astonishingly come back before having a funeral. Traditionally, the deceased would be buried the day after death. However, it was more common these days to delay the funeral until overseas family members arrived, or in this case, to give an appropriate amount of time for the perceived dead to return. Indeed, the majority of the missing were elderly and were not very mobile to begin with. Nevertheless, during this period of waiting, the new priest, Father Edgar, couldn't help but use Blue as an example of how God's mercy and love was instrumental to the volunteer's survival. Blue, naturally, disagreed, saying it was a rowboat, a cello bow, and Keanu's fishhook that kept him alive. Most of the villagers laughed at him, thinking that he was joking. But Blue's ordeal would go down in Vaimasina's lore, and he would become the man who tamed the giant wave and survived.

Although everyone was glad to see that Blue had survived, many of the villagers were cautious and suspicious whenever he was in their presence. It took some time to ensure that he wasn't a ghost that had come back to haunt the village. Out of the fourteen villagers that were swept away from the tsunami, only Blue returned after he was given up for dead. Blue knew the fourteen villagers that didn't make it. He often felt guilty that he somehow miraculously survived, and they didn't. But he also knew that the village would honor their valor against the waves and their exemplary lives for generations to come.

When Blue returned from the dead, Aumua and Mele immediately moved back in with him in his *fale*. Although the *fale* was left standing, they made the best of the space with the very few furniture pieces that the waves didn't carry away. Aumua was concerned at how skinny and in pain Blue had become, and she made it her mission to nurse him back to health. As Blue would later learn, she saw him fall from the tree from the church window on the balcony and thought that she would never see him again. Now, she was constantly out foraging fruits and vegetables from the forest, and eels and shrimp from the pool, then bringing them back to the village to feed him. She would share leftovers with the rest of the village.

For several weeks, Mele took it upon herself to entertain Blue to keep his spirits up. She would sing and dance in different costumes that she would make with her mother or aunties. Although the wave stole her ukulele, she had her uncle Togi make her a new one. He then taught her how to play a few songs, which she would then immediately perform for her father. Togi also made his niece a flute-like instrument that, when she played it for Blue, his hounds couldn't help but sing along as if they were a choir. It was all amusing to Blue until he wanted nothing more than to rest with peace and quiet. On a few occasions, he would send Mele away, much to her disappointment. However, he would quickly regret sending away his daughter when he heard the distant hum of the waves clattering against the reef. This made him paranoid that another giant wave was barreling down on the village. It was a sound that he would hear in his head and never trusted for the rest of his life.

When the right time came, the village decided to have a funeral for all the deceased over a two-day ceremony. On the first day, each family of the departed had a member who acted as the *tulafale*, or orator chief. This person was the designated storyteller and funeral leader and would conduct a special ceremony called a *saofa'i*, where the family recounted the late victim's passing and shared stories. Despite the scarce resources, *umus* were made, and the villagers came together with a feast.

On the second day of the ceremony, a funeral service was held at St. Cecilia. It took many days prior to the Mass to clean the church. Because the church was a symbol of stability, it was one of the first buildings that the villagers restored as close as it was originally before the earthquake. Mud, sand, debris, and decaying fish were removed, and the walls and floors were cleaned. Pews were straightened, and the ones that were somehow flushed outside were retrieved and placed in their proper spot. The altar was tidied and readied for Father Edgar to conduct his services.

Blue attended the funeral Mass and sat in front of the pews on a mat. Mele sat in his lap, and he didn't let go of her throughout most of the service. The Mass was packed, and people even stood and sat outside the church. Even Ben Krimple attended, and it seemed that everyone wanted to sit next to him. It was a solemn occasion with much crying and head bowing that was paused only when the choir sung. Just before Communion, Blue and Mele went upstairs on the balcony where they met Aumua. She hugged him, and he went to the piano, sat down on the bench, and began to play the song, "Amazing Grace," which Aumua joined him in singing. Mele sat in his lap and watched how his fingers effortlessly stroked the keys. A choir eventually harmonized with Aumua. If there was a person who wasn't crying before the song, he or she was sobbing now. At the end of Mass, the choir sung a traditional funeral song called, *Mo'omo'oga Samoan,* and Blue played along on the piano. As the song progressed, the entire congregation couldn't help but sing along and give a final farewell to their loved ones.

After the Mass, the village had another feast around the community center, which had mostly been cleaned from debris. Relatives and friends that lived in Apia, overseas, or from other areas unaffected by the disaster, brought most of the food. The mood was much merrier, and it became more of a celebration of life. The families of the deceased lived the *Fa'a Samoa* way, in which they never treated the dead as though they were gone forever. Instead, the dead were believed to be still with them, and their spirit would stay with the family for the rest of time.

During the celebration, Blue saw Joseph sitting on a mat in the community center, eating from a couple of plates of food. He didn't attend the funeral Mass, but instead he waited at the center until the Mass was finished. After

Father Edgar blessed the food of feast, the chief said a few words about his comrades and acquaintances (some of whom he had known since childhood) that were lost at sea. It was short, but poignant. Fiame also spoke, which took longer, as she talked about each person and how they contributed to the village over the years. Nevertheless, once the speeches were finished, the feasting began.

Blue walked up to Joseph and sat next to him on the floor. Blue hadn't had the chance to talk to him since his return. The *matai* smiled and grunted, happy to see the volunteer. It wasn't long after Blue sat down that Aumua hurried over to him with a plate of food.

"The sea has a way of sometimes being forgiving," Joseph stated. "And sometimes it spits out what it doesn't want."

"Maybe we *palagis* taste bad."

"Mmm." The chief thought about what Blue said and shook his head as if to agree.

"How did you survive the earthquake and tsunami?" Blue asked. "I mean, I never saw you that day."

"I was already at the plantation having a conversation with some relatives who had passed."

Blue thought that was probably one of the best places to be, as the plantation was protected by hills.

No tsunami would be able to budge this man mountain.

He also didn't think twice about what the chief said. People were always talking to their dead relatives, especially when advice was needed.

"I really can't believe I'm sitting here with you," Blue expressed. "I guess I was pretty lucky."

"It is good to be lucky," the chief declared. "I only got

lost at sea once in my lifetime. I was fishing and had a bad day. Nothing was biting, and I couldn't return to the village empty-handed. I never returned empty-handed. So I went further out to sea. A gale that turned unexpectedly into a squall drove me even further out to sea. But I did not care. I never returned empty-handed."

"How long were out there?"

"A month."

"A month?! Did you have food or water?"

"No."

"How did you survive?"

"I drank from the sky and ate from the earth."

"Earth? You mean your bait?"

"Mmm," the chief implied but didn't confirm. "The sea played a game with me. It likes to play with man."

"It's not a fun game. I can attest to that."

"Not always, no. For a few days, I did not know it was playing with me. I was still fishing because I never returned empty-handed."

"What kind of game were you playing?"

"The sea sent a serpent to track me, to taunt me, to eat me. There were times when its tentacles wrapped around my boat and tried to squeeze it until it shattered to pieces. And so I fished it. That's what the sea wanted me to do. It loved to watch a man fight with a monster."

"I take it by this time you weren't really lost at sea, were you?"

"No. I can navigate by stars. I only stayed at sea longer to fight with the serpent. I never returned empty-handed."

"Well, if I was a betting man right now, I'd bet the farm that you won."

"It took ten days. I finally jumped in the sea and wrestled with it. It was big. The biggest monster I had ever seen. Its fangs were as large as my head. But I killed it with my wit, strength, and knife. The sea laughed. It really enjoyed the game."

"What did you do with it?"

"I tried to haul it into the boat, but it was too big. So I hooked some of its tentacles to the stern and towed it back to the village. I never returned empty-handed."

"Unbelievable."

Blue would later verify this story with other villagers, who all agreed that the chief's encounter with a serpent happened the way it was told. It was another legend that was retold from time to time. Blue surmised that the *matai* was probably at sea for a couple of days and caught a larger than normal octopus or squid that nobody had ever seen or caught before. It was an anomaly, a once-in-a-lifetime catch, and the village never wanted to forget it.

The two men paused for a moment to eat. Blue stared out at the grassy field and watched Mele play with other children on and near the large sailboat that the waves deposited. Blue thought about Joseph's statement on the things the ocean spat out and wondered if the ocean did the same with the sailboat out of rejection. He then zoomed in on Mele who was dancing with friends on the bow of the boat. Blue stared at her, and for the first time, questioned her potential to become more than another devoted and loyal villager. Like most parents, Blue wanted only the best for his daughter and the opportunity for her to showcase her talents on a larger stage. He wasn't exactly sure what the talent would be, but he could see that Mele was gifted. Most of the villagers never thought about a career or even life beyond the village. Some might work in Apia, and a very few may leave abroad. Both were admired and respected by other villagers. Misi, for example, was one of the few who was brazen enough to leave, develop, nurture, and boast a talent that reached an international audience.

"I believe I need to return home," Blue said. "I feel I have run my course here."

"Mmm." The chief had heard this before, about four years ago. Back then, he knew that it wasn't the right time for Blue to leave. This time, however, the *matai* would have to agree.

"I want to take Aumua and Mele with me. I think they'd do well in the States. They could share their culture in appropriate places."

"I will miss them."

"Doesn't one of your sons live in Oceanside?"

"Yes. It has been years since I have seen him and his family. They do not come to Samoa often. Too expensive."

"Well, Oceanside's close to where I live. So family will be nearby."

"The stars will follow Mele to your country. When they dance and shimmer for her just as they did the night she was born, I will watch, too, and know that she lives brightly and contently."

Blue left it at that. He knew that Mele would find the move exciting and adventurous. Aumua, on the other hand, might need more convincing. Blue definitely labeled her as one of those who had never dreamt of leaving the village. But Blue believed that if Mele left, the odds on Aumua following would be greater.

The funeral feast continued well into the evening. Blue decided that it was time for him to return to his *fale* to rest. He bid farewell to several people, and Aumua told him that she was going to help clean and then come home. Mele jumped on Blue's back. Although the exertion hurt his ribs, he couldn't resist giving her a piggyback ride. Everyone laughed when they saw her ride her father like a pony.

Blue's hounds followed the two back home. They were replete from a good day of acquiring scraps of food. When they got tired of waiting for a handout, they simply took food off people's plates, particularly those from inattentive children who had better things to do than waste their time eating. Mele even hopped off Blue's back, which was much to his relief, and tried to play with the hounds. But they were more interested in hurrying to the *fale* to find a cozy spot to sleep off their bloated stomachs and dream of better eating days to come.

Blue noticed that there was a group of people hanging out in the *fale tele*. He told Mele to take the dogs home, and he'd be along shortly. He then made his way to the *fale tele* and saw that it was Togi, Misi, and Ben Krimple, sitting on the ground and smoking weed. Togi's wife, Iris, was also there holding a baby (her and Togi's fourth son). She surprisingly sucked a puff when a joint was passed to her.

"Go on. There's the Wave Tamer!" Krimple exclaimed when he saw Blue approaching.

"I heard you danced on the wave like Fred Astaire," Misi said, and added a little flare by shimmying her shoulders and swaying her arms. Blue thought the statement was odd. *Who knows who Fred Astaire was in this part of the world?* Only Misi would.

"Do I look like someone who tamed anything? That wave tossed me around as if I was a cricket ball," Blue stated, and everyone laughed.

Blue sat next to Togi, who gave him a joint. Blue took a puff and didn't give it back.

"Sorry about *Calypso*, Togs," Blue sincerely said. "It did save my life."

"It was a good boat," Togi declared fondly.

"I heard you caught a fifty-pound *masimasi*," Iris said.

"Oooh, those are delicious," Misi added.

Blue wondered where this information came from. The fish he caught was barely a pound, yet he knew that this wasn't how his story would be told. The villagers believed it was a fifty-pound *masimasi* that he caught. Who knows? Ten years from now, the fish will change to an eighty-pound shark, and Blue had to stand on the back of a sea turtle to fight and kill the maneater.

He figured he had nothing to lose by adding to drama, "It took me an entire day to pull it into the boat. It was so heavy that the boat took on water, but I could've eaten for a week. And to think I caught it with a little hook that Keanu made."

Togi perked up. He loved the idea that his son was part of Blue's legend.

"Father Edgar has been telling us that the disaster was a warning sign from God," Iris said. "He asked us if we were prepared to enter heaven."

"He's always been a kind of a doom and gloom fellow," Krimple added.

"I like the way he made the earthquake and flood the villagers' fault," Misi sarcastically stated.

"Would you have used the disaster to remind us to fear the Lord, Father K?" Iris asked.

"Go on. I'm not a priest anymore. You can just call me, Mr. K from now on."

"You'll always be this village's priest!" Misi emphatically pronounced. The others cheered.

"Thank you, but my priesting days are over."

"And Father Edgar hasn't acknowledged your presence since you arrived," Iris said. She loved to goad others into gossiping.

"I guess I'm a bit of a priestly pariah in the diocese's eyes. I have a reputation I'm not proud of now across the island."

"You can always come sing with me. I like singing with the bad boys," Misi said with a wink.

Blue took another long drag of the joint. The marijuana eased the pain throughout his body. He kept quiet for a while, listening and enjoying the banter among the rest of the group. He thought how much he would miss them when he left.

It was, perhaps, getting stoned that made Blue have many thoughts flash through his mind. Eventually, one of them compelled him to speak.

"So what'd we do with the yacht that's in the middle of our yard?" Blue asked, referring to the sailboat that the tsunami deposited on the grassy field.

Everyone stopped talking and stared at the volunteer.

"Burn it," Iris uttered.

"Turn it into a playground for the children," Mr. K added.

"Togi will drag it to the lagoon," Togi exclaimed,

standing up. "Togi will repair it and sail it to where no man has gone before to fish. Togi will be legend."

Everyone laughed. Everyone was high. Everyone felt alive.

It wasn't very long afterward that the pot made Blue sleepy. He bid goodnight to the group and made his way to his *fale*.

Along the way, he stopped momentarily and looked up at the stars. They twinkled vigorously, reminding Blue that he should be living a life full of vitality. He appreciated looking at them much more on land rather than at sea. In fact, he couldn't recall even seeing a single star at sea.

"You mind if I join you..." a voice said in the darkness in English. Blue turned around to see his old friend, Mr. K, approaching. "...at least to your home?"

"Please do. I'm so stoned, you might have to carry me," Blue responded in English. The two would continue to speak in their native tongue.

"Go on. I'm glad we're not far from your *fale* then."

"I have to admit it, though; the stars can really tease a person when he's high."

Mr. K looked at the stars and was impressed with their intense luster.

"They light the path to heaven, don't they?"

The two stared at the sky until their necks became sore.

"I'm so glad you survived, Ronin," the fallen priest said. "When I heard you were one of the ones missing, I was dumbfounded. I couldn't believe it. I said to myself, 'No, not Ronin Blue. He didn't travel halfway around the world to die in a tsunami.' I prayed for you. Day after day, I prayed for you...for your return."

"I appreciate that."

"I heard the rumors from other villagers about how you ended up in the wave."

"Yeah, I relied on the wrong person at the wrong time."

The past few nights, Blue had had nightmares of that fateful moment in the tree when Lance let go of his hand. Aumua was quick to wake him when he started moaning. He didn't know it at the time, but this nightmare of falling in the wave and being lost at sea would haunt him in his sleep periodically for the rest of his life. Blue wished that Lance was around to have words with and ask him why he was such an asshole. But the despicable disrepute left the village the day after the disaster, particularly because he knew that there were others who witnessed his wanton act. If Blue wanted to confront Lance, he would have to go to Apia and find him. But this didn't seem prudent. Instead, he hoped to never see the malicious, bald man again.

"I'm so sorry," Mr. K said in a tone as if it was his fault.

The two started to walk to Blue's *fale*, which was more like a saunter.

"You have nothing to be sorry about."

"I believe the same hoodlum was the one who ratted me out to the diocese."

"Maybe someday he'll get his comeuppance."

"I'm just really happy you're here to be with your family. I can't believe how much Mele has grown since I last saw her. Sorry to say this, but she looks more like her mother than you, and she is as smart and creative like her."

"She's extraordinary. They're both extraordinary."

"Go on. You're a lucky man, Ronin."

"That's what I kept thinking to myself out at sea."

"And I had never seen Aumua cry like she did when you were missing. I mean, I've known her since she was a little girl, and she was always as tough as nails."

"She'll surprise you. One thing I've learned from her over the years is that I can never take an unpredictable person like her for granted."

Mr. Krimple chuckled. The two had reached the *fale*. Blue looked inside and saw Mele lying down on her mat. She was wearing headphones and listening to music via Blue's computer. The hounds were passed out all around her, and every so often, their legs incongruously twitched, depending on the kind of dream their minds were engaged with.

Blue sat on a step that led up to his *fale*.

"I miss the peacefulness of the village," Mr. K stated, lost in nostalgia.

"What have you been doing since you left?"

"I'm working with the SVSG in Apia."

"What's that?"

"The Samoa Victim Support Group. We support victims of domestic violence and sexual abuse. Our mission is to protect and promote the rights of women, children, and other vulnerable people. We want them to be safe and retake control of their lives."

"Sounds like you found your second calling in life."

"It's hard and trying work, but the organization is so important in Samoa. I handle cases by requests, or police referrals, and then I evaluate the best way to respond. I get to work in all the villages of Samoa."

"I can see you working twenty-four-seven in this job."

"I'm used to it."

There was a slight pause as Blue looked skyward again.

"Maria and the children moved in with me in Apia," Mr. Krimple disclosed.

"What about Lemanu?"

"The woman he had an affair with dumped him. So he's been coming around trying to win Maria back."

"Did the two ever get a divorce?"

"Yes, but I think she wants to go back to him."

"And get beat again."

"It's common."

"It's sad."

"I asked Maria to marry me, but she has yet to answer."

"Oh."

"It's been a couple of weeks."

"Oh... shit."

"I think she's unsure she wants to marry a fallen priest. She's afraid of what others will say, particularly her family. Plus, she may still love Lemanu."

"Love will find a way through paths where wolves fear to prey," Blue quoted. "Uh... by, um... I forget who said it."

"Go on. It's the pot. I'm sure it'll come to you. But I pray every day for God to give her strength and me patience. I truly love her."

There was a momentary pause as the two men looked away from each other. Blue felt sorry for Mr. K because he knew that the former priest was most likely in a lose-lose situation. Although Blue knew that his friend was deep in this relationship, he hoped that when the end comes, it comes peacefully without getting physically hurt. Blue could also understand why Mr. K was back in Vaimasina. Besides lending his hands to help with the cleanup and rebuilding of the village, he was also taking a much-needed respite from the love triangle drama he was enduring in Apia.

Aumua, who was returning from the feast, then walked up to the men. She was concerned that Blue wasn't lying down in the *fale*.

"They're starting to dance," Aumua said in Samoan, and then she recognized the prominent figure standing near the *fale*. "Oh, *Talofa*, Father Krimple." The men would continue to speak to her in English, and she would respond in their language.

"Mr. Krimp... no. Please call me Ben."

"You're not dancing?" Blue asked Aumua. "When have you ever turned down dancing?"

"No. I came home to make sure you rest, but you are not."

"It's strange there's dancing at a funeral anyway," Blue added.

"It's a celebration of life," Mr. K declared as if making an excuse for the dancers.

"I think some are drunk," Aumua added and sat down next to Blue.

"Yes, for sure. Well, I think I'm up for some dancing. Perhaps, I'll head back and check it out," Mr. K said. "Good night." Then to Aumua, he said, "*Manuia le po.*"

"*Manuia le po.*"

As Mr. K walked away, he stopped as if was reminded of something. "Oh, Ronin. You played unbelievably well at the Mass. The moment I first met you, I knew you played the piano. I just knew it."

"How?" Blue asked.

"I could see that you craved playing like a fever craves a

sweat. After so many years of denying yourself the gift you were given, why all of a sudden do you play now?"

"I made a deal with the demons of the sea that if they spared me, I would play again."

"The demons of the sea?"

"I was in no condition to bargain."

The former priest chuckled. Aumua haplessly slapped Blue on his shoulder, which was a feeble attempt to tell Blue to stop fibbing, especially about demons.

"Are you sure it was demons?" Mr. K asked, a bit amused.

"It's been demons for a long time."

"Go on. You're just high."

Mr. K walked away towards the grassy field. He chortled and shook his head back and forth as if he had just heard the most absurd anecdote he had ever heard in his lifetime.

Aumua rested her head on Blue's shoulder, and the two watched Mr. K walk away. The darkness quickly greeted the former priest and gently wrapped its arms around him. Within seconds, he was gone, and it would be the last time Blue would ever see him.

Ben Krimple hung around the village for a few more days, but then he left without saying his goodbyes to anyone. Villagers asked where he was and why he had left so suddenly. Blue had a feeling that Mr. K had made up his mind to leave because it was time for him to return to Apia and face his own demons.

10

———

Several more months passed, and the village of Vaimasina began to look like its former self. Fiame was instrumental in arranging the organization, Habitat for Humanity, to come with building materials and help restore homes and some of the public buildings. Chief Joseph's house was the first one to be rebuilt. Most people lived in their *fales*, or they established a section of the community center until their homes were constructed. Gardens were replanted, fruit trees were bought at markets or brought from other villages that weren't affected by the twin disasters, then planted around the village. Savea reopened his trading store after many trips back and forth to Apia. The Internet Café, however, would take several more months before a couple of computers could be found and internet connection reestablished. Blue would eventually have to go to Apia to use an Internet Café to let his Aunt Ophelia know that he was safe and healthy. He would spare her the details of his harrowing ordeal with the tsunami and the subsequent solitary suffering in an open boat lost at sea.

Even Ringo, the supposed cocoa expert and salesman, would return to the village under the pretense of lending a helping hand. He would give advice on how to properly salvage and maintain the cocoa plantation despite the fact that the dual disaster hardly damaged the area. In fact, there was only one cocoa tree uprooted by the earthquake, but it was quickly replanted. Other than that, work at the plantation carried on as usual. Aumua would thank Ringo for his ideas, but that was as far as she would go. She had decades of practical and traditional knowledge caring for the plantation in her DNA, so she was already one step ahead of the salesman's ideas.

The distinctive and prominent Vaimasina bus was pulled from the muck and mire, and several villagers would work on it day and night to restore it to its former glory. The entire bus was dried and cleaned, and the driver, with his brother, got the engine humming again, which also meant the reggae-infused pop songs began to pump from the speakers. In fact, the first song that blasted through its open windows was an energetic island version of Bob Marley's "Three Little Birds." Once the road leading to the village was fixed, or more likely, was temporarily patched, the purple bus was able to make its daily run to the capital. This was a significant moment as it allowed the villagers to be reconnected with life outside their village.

Blue was amused watching Togi plan and scheme many different ideas on how to move the yacht to the lagoon. He first tried to recruit as many villagers as he could and lug the boat with rope that was tied around railings of the bow.

They heaved it like a group of ancient Egyptians moving slabs of stone to build a pyramid. After an hour of backbreaking work, they managed to drag it about twenty yards before they all gave up, complaining that it was too heavy. They got to a point where they couldn't budge it because it got stuck in the soft earth. But Togi was determined to get it to the lagoon. He used the same rope to tie it to the bumper of a car. When the car drove away, its bumper fell off, and the boat didn't budge an inch.

Many of the villagers sat in the shade of the trees and became engrossed and entertained while watching Togi try to move the yacht. They couldn't help but laugh after each failed attempt. Although many people provided Togi with their ideas and suggestions as to how to move it, not one villager would jump up and put their recommendation to the test. Thus, the yacht sat on the grassy field for a couple more weeks until Togi finally figured out a way to move it. In fact, it wasn't until the Vaimasina bus was fixed, and Togi thought that the bus was sturdy enough to pull the boat. Indeed, it did, but it also seemed to cause more damage, particularly to the bottom of the boat. Nevertheless, after Togi managed to get the yacht to the lagoon, he and his sons immediately started to repair it.

After several months of working on the yacht, Togi and his sons looked forward to the day that they would take it out to sea. They discussed about going further than they have ever been to catch large fish, and the brothers would bicker over who would catch the bigger fish. They also talked about the adventures they could take, like traveling to the larger, less populated island of Savai'i. Unfortunately, a day or two before they would go on their maiden voyage,

Fiame approached them with an elder Australian couple who claimed that the yacht was theirs. They had lost it during the tsunami, and they produced the necessary paperwork and photos of the boat to reclaim it. Togi was somewhat devasted, but he handed over the yacht to them for only a handshake of gratitude. Although the yacht owners tried to give Togi money for his efforts, he wouldn't accept it. To Togi, simply having the opportunity to work on such a fine vessel was priceless. A couple of days later, he and his boys watched as the elderly couple had the boat towed through the break of the reef. As storm clouds filled the horizon, they stood on the shore and watched until the yacht disappeared under an arching rainbow.

As the days turned to weeks, Blue became more eager and impatient to leave Vaimasina and take his family to his home in San Diego County. He would ask Mele if she would like to live in America, and she enthusiastically would say yes. She would follow up with questions about what people eat, drink, and wear there. She would also ask insightful questions like, what songs Americans sing and dance to, or what kinds of mats do they make, or how big are the trees there. Whenever Blue walked to the pool or plantation, Mele bounced around by his side, inquiring about the size of the *fale* they would live in, how many friends she would have, and if he knew Mickey Mouse. There were times when Blue wished he hadn't mentioned moving away to her.

It wasn't long before everyone in the village heard the rumor of Blue's eventual departure. It seemed as if each person would ask the volunteer the basic questions of when, where, why, and for how long. Some wanted to take advantage of Blue moving back to America and tried to think of ways it would benefit them. Fiame, for example, wanted Blue to create a Non-Government Organization (NGO) that would raise funds for Vaimasina. She wanted to see some kind of partnership where Samoans would receive scholarships and opportunities to live and work in the United States for a period, then bring back this knowledge and apply it in Samoa. Blue quickly grew tired of answering the same questions, and he wished he could've produced a memo or email that would satisfy them. Eventually, after a couple of weeks of interrogation, everyone in the village had obtained the information they needed about Blue's leaving, except Aumua.

Blue didn't really know how to broach the subject of leaving the village to Aumua. He knew that she was happy with her family and church life, and she enjoyed managing the cocoa plantation. She was becoming a village leader in the traditional arts of dancing, singing, and *siapo* making, and she was proud representing the village and showcasing these skills at festivals and competitions. Blue also noticed that Aumua's father was confiding more and more in the politics of the village with her. In fact, the two would stay up late into the night discussing issues like a couple of clandestine ancient Roman senators. Be that is it may, there was no doubt that Aumua had already heard the rumors of Blue's desire to leave through other villagers, and especially from Mele. Sooner or later, he would have to confront her.

It was a sticky, hot day, and dark clouds crudely covered the bright morning sun. Blue was sitting in the shade of a breadfruit tree, staring at the cocoa plantation. A light rain began to fall and drops filtered its way through the leaves onto the unresponsive volunteer.

Aumua approached him carrying a basket of freshly picked cocoa pods and sat down next to him. "Your body is here, but I feel your mind is far away," she said in English, trying to stare in the same direction as Blue.

Blue snapped out of his trance, smiled, and put his arm around Aumua.

"My thoughts are across the sea."

"You want to return home."

"I'm sure Mele has told you."

"The entire village told me. I am the last to know. Why do you not tell me first?

"I guess I was afraid what you might say about it."

Aumua slapped Blue on the top of his head. "I should have been the first person to tell."

"I know. I'm sorry."

"Why do you want to go back there?" Aumua asked. Everything you need is here."

"I want to return for Mele and you."

"Everything I need is here."

"Yeah...uh, think of it as an adventure."

"How long would we have to stay?"

Blue wasn't sure how to answer the question. He would want to stay indefinitely, but he knew Aumua being away from her village would only last, perhaps, a few years. "I don't know... as long as we can?"

"Where would we live?"

"At my house. It's a big *fale* with lots of space...and air conditioning."

Aumua slapped him on the head again. "That's no reason," she said.

"Look, I just think you'll find the place fascinating. It's different. You'll have many choices for everything."

"Where would Mele go to school?"

"That won't be a problem. There's lots of schools."

Aumua thought about it for a second. "It seems so distant and cold."

"Well, yeah, the warmth doesn't exactly wrap you like the flames from hell do here," Blue said facetiously.

"There's no hell here," Aumua responded with her own flippancy and slapped him again. "This is my home, Ronin."

"No, your home is me and Mele."

"Here."

"Anywhere."

Although Aumua was now a young woman in her early twenties, she sometimes still possessed the tomboy, island-girl instincts. She managed to climb the breadfruit tree to the lowest hanging branch just as she did a thousand times in her younger days. Sitting above Blue, she plucked a breadfruit and threw at him.

"Hey! What are you doing up there?"

"Climb up to me."

"Come back down, Aumua," Blue ordered. But Aumua only giggled.

"No. Come up. You have never sat in a tree with me before."

Damn me.

The branch that Aumua was sitting on was about ten feet high, and Blue was hoping to shimmy up it as quickly as possible. But he only managed to get about a quarter of the way up the trunk before jumping off and landing on his feet. Aumua laughed.

"Shit. What are you? Part panther?" Blue asked. Aumua laughed.

"Come on, lover. You want me to go to America? Come and get me," Aumua teasingly said and laid her body straight along the branch.

"Look at you. You're like Bagheera from The Jungle Book," Blue stated.

"Climb, lover. Don't be afraid."

Blue tried climbing the tree again. He shimmied and shanked on his way up, and he almost fell off a couple of times. Indeed, it was a difficult and uncomfortable climb. Blue used muscles that he didn't even know he had. Nevertheless, a few minutes later, he got to the branch that Aumua was sitting on.

"I know. That wasn't pretty," Blue said and took a deep breath.

"You climb like pregnant pig."

"Pigs climb trees?"

"No," Aumua answered and laughed.

"I scraped my leg. Am I bleeding?"

Blue tried to look at his injured leg. Aumua leaned towards him and kissed him on his temple. She then grabbed both of his cheeks and pulled him closer to kiss him on his lips. "Will you kiss me in a tree at your home?" she asked.

"I will kiss you so long and so hard that the birds will blush."

"Then I will go with you," Aumua said with a giggle.

The rain began to fall harder, but the two remained on the branch of the tree despite the thicker raindrops that became too heavy for the leaves to hold and drizzled down upon them. Aumua snuggled next to Blue, and he held onto her, mostly to keep his balance. As the wind became stronger, the two watched the leaves of the cocoa trees flap and flail. However, they stared through trees to an uncertain, yet exciting future just beyond. Aumua only knew the island life, and Blue couldn't remember the suburban existence.

"So, how are we to get down?" Blue asked, looking down at the ground.

"We jump."

"What? You can't just…" and before Blue could finish his sentence, Aumua was already on the ground. "Oh shit. The Olympics just called. They're making tree-climbing and jumping a sport, and they want you to represent Sa…Okay, that's just bad."

"Jump," Aumua said. "You can do it."

"Yeah, right…when pigs climb trees."

Blue went down the same way he went up, and it took him just as long.

Blue was relieved that Aumua agreed to travel with him and Mele back home. He knew his Aunt Ophelia would love them, and on the following day, he hurried over to the Internet Café to send her an email telling her the exciting news of his return with Aumua and Mele. As a world traveler, Blue's aunt always seemed more comfortable interacting with people from a different country. She knew how to speak several languages, or at least, she knew how to communicate to a point to get what she needed. The world was, indeed, her work office. Blue wondered if she had spent any time in Samoa and wouldn't be surprised if she were able to chat with Aumua and Mele in their language.

For the next few weeks, Blue spent time getting ready to move his family to the States. He traveled to Apia to get the necessary paperwork for Mele, as well as purchasing airfare from Fiji Airways with the last of the money he brought with him. He obtained a copy of Mele's birth certificate that showed he was her father from St. Cecilia's records. Aumua already possessed a Samoan passport from the times she danced at festivals throughout the Pacific Islands region. Despite getting everything in order, Blue knew that US Immigration would still give him a hard time, particularly since Aumua and he were not officially married. Thus, Blue would have to spend time figuring out the intricacies of applying for green card or visa, status. But the first important business was to get his family settled at his house in San Diego County.

The family's last week in Samoa was quite emotional and tiring. Blue and Mele packed with enthusiastic excitement, though most of their belongings were washed away in the tsunami. Blue had to acquire a couple of suitcases through Savea, which to Blue was like pulling teeth. Eventually, they came in, or didn't, according to Savea, but then they did. Blue also felt thankful and blessed that his computer was saved, although he couldn't use it because the battery life had run out. Since his charger got swept away, he had to wait until he returned home to replace it. Fortunately, for the past several months, he was never in the mood to work on his novel, as he was too absorbed in helping the village and himself heal. But he knew that once he got home, his attitude would change. He and Mele, however, did miss listening to the diverse playlists that Blue had saved in his iTunes library.

Perhaps what made the last week entirely moving and exhausting was that everyone wanted to send the family off to their new home with a feast. Every night, Blue's family would have dinner at someone's house. It was a way for the families of the village to say goodbye and wish them well. Gifts of mats, headwear, and necklaces were made and given to the family, and one family even tried to give Blue a pig, which he had to respectfully turn down. Blue thought about what US Customs would say about these handmade items, and he anticipated that it was going to take hours for him and his family to get out of LAX.

Blue was concerned about the way Aumua was acting during their last week in the village. At the different dinners throughout the week, she acted as if only Blue and Mele were leaving. When questions about their new life in America arose, Aumua would be disinterested, and she would often leave the room to get involved with the cooking, cleaning, or any other kind of distraction. On a couple of occasions, she would simply leave and return to the house later. Even more worrying to Blue was the fact that she hadn't started packing. If Blue asked her when she was going to start getting ready, she would laugh and playfully change the subject, or she would say that there was still a lot of time to pack. In the late evenings throughout the week, however, Blue noticed that she displayed the oddest behavior. Aumua would send Mele to her family's house to sleep, then would take her time seducing and making love to Blue. It was as if she was trying to procrastinate packing or talking about moving, which naturally, Blue didn't mind until their last night in Vaimasina.

The last night was, indeed, a strange one for Blue. As Aumua used Blue's chest as a pillow and snored away, the volunteer had a hard time falling asleep. When he dozed off from time to time, he had many thoughts running through his mind, and he couldn't stay asleep for more than thirty minutes. Blue worried about Aumua and Mele assimilating in a vast and impatient country, and he fretted about how he would be able to conform to what was expected as a provider. He had no career or job prospects waiting for him upon his return. Typically, the village night was quiet and quiescent unless rain was relentlessly racing down the tin roof. But this wasn't the case on Blue's last night, as it seemed especially still and silent. He didn't even hear the rhythmic sounds of the insects creating their nocturnal symphony from the forest. He tried to remember what the nights were like back home and couldn't remember. He wondered if he was actually deaf before coming to Samoa.

It wasn't until five in the morning when Blue finally fell into a deeper sleep. He didn't have time to dream, however, as Mele awoke him in the brightness of morning. He quickly sat up, and a sense of excitement that he was going home came over him. Mele, too, was bouncing around, ready to travel. Even though the flight wasn't until four in the afternoon, she was already dressed in a new flower print skirt of different shades of blue with a pink blouse, and a new pair of white sandals. A fake pink hibiscus flower was placed behind her ear. All of these items Blue had bought her at the market during one of his trips to the capital. Blue had to warn her not to get her clothes dirty before they left, and Mele was careful to heed the warning even after a few of her friends came calling, wanting to get one last play in with her. Before she leapt out of the *fale*, Blue also reminded her that they had to catch the morning bus to Apia, which was leaving in about two hours.

After Mele scampered out of the *fale*, the first thing Blue noticed was that Aumua was gone. He hoped that she was at her family's house, packing for the trip. He wanted to check on her, but he had become busy with last-minute preparations. Besides, he knew that she understood the plan was to catch the morning bus. Once they got to Apia, they would have to take a taxi or another bus to the airport.

The two hours went quickly, and Blue found himself hurrying to the bus, struggling with the luggage and calling out Mele's name, even though he had no idea where she was. At the bus, Blue threw the luggage in the back and looked for Aumua and Mele. He saw his daughter running with her friends towards the bus. Other villagers were there to say their final farewells and put *'ulas* made of coconut shells and seashells around Blue and Mele's necks. They were also adorned with elaborate and colorful leis and head wreaths made with flowers and leaves.

Fiame gave Blue a hug and had a tear in her eye. She had made a special trip from Apia the day before to say goodbye to Blue and his family. Blue, however, wondered if her hasty return was to question who would oversee the cocoa plantation. Blue and Aumua agreed that Lupesina and her family would harvest the cocoa pods and sell them in the various markets.

"You'll stay in touch with the village, Mr. Ronin?" Fiame asked.

"I'll try."

"We can make this village sustainable and profitable once we finish rebuilding."

"I have no doubt," Blue said, impatiently looking to see if Aumua was arriving.

Fiame smiled. "We will stay in touch," she said. "*Tofa.*" Fiame then gave Mele a kiss on the cheek. "*Tofa,*"

"*Tofa,*" Mele responded.

The bus started its engine, and the music began to play a Samoan cover of the Frank Sinatra song, "Somethin' Stupid.".

Blue told Mele to hop on the bus. She leaned out a window, waving to her friends who tried to jump up and high-five her.

Blue then took a step on the bus only to be tapped on the shoulder. When he turned around, he was surprised to see Saitele. Blue noticed that the piano tuner had gained some weight since the last time he saw him.

"Saitele. When did you get here?" Blue asked.

"This morning. I ran into Fiame in Apia, and she told me how well you play the piano, so I came to hear for myself."

"I only played twice in church: the day I came back from the dead, and the day that others officially didn't return from the dead."

"The playing sounded beautiful," Fiame said.

"It should. I tuned the piano," Saitele stated with a bit of self-assured hubris.

"Sorry, but I'm leaving for the US."

"That's a shame," Saitele said with a tone of disappointment. "When will you return?"

"It's indefinite."

"That's a shame."

"Your trip here will not be in vain," Blue encouraged. If you find Lupesina, she will make you some *Koko Samoa*." The piano tuner's mood quickly brightened. "And, of course, Fiame will fill your belly with her tasty *sapasui*."

"Wonderful. Yes, you're correct. My trip was not in vain."

Fiame shot Blue a look that said, *you bastard*. Blue smiled mischievously.

"You can come for dinner tonight. But only tonight," Fiame affirmed.

"I'm sure it will be a night that I will remember forever," Saitele said to Fiame as they walked away. Blue went back up the steps of the bus.

"Hey, can you give me ten minutes?" Blue asked the driver. "I have to find Aumua."

"Only ten minutes," the driver replied.

Blue hopped off the bus and tried to decide which place to look for Aumua. He knew she wasn't in his *fale*. He decided to try the church first, and if she wasn't there, he would go to her family's house. Blue took off running towards the church.

"*Tamā*! Where are you going?" Mele asked.

"To find your mother!"

Blue entered the church partially to see if Aumua was inside and partially to take a shortcut to the community center. The story of St. Cecilia was in full motion, and Blue paused his rushing to watch the show in the stained glass windows. He wondered if there was a way for Fiame to make money off this show. However, he didn't have time to dwell on this, as time was against him. He took one last look at the ancient way of telling a story through light and color. His last image of the narrative before exiting the church at the door near the altar was St. Cecilia's excruciating and vivid execution.

As Blue approached an open door of the community center, a Samoan song was softly playing from a radio. The brightness of the day made it hard for him to see inside the room. But once Blue got to the doorway, he abruptly stopped and peered in. He choked on held-back tears when he saw Aumua sitting on the ground, adding color to a large *siapo* with Lupesina, Maeva, and Iris. Aumua looked up at Blue, smiled, then returned her attention back to the tapa cloth. Blue's self-questioning the past week on whether or not Aumua was preparing for a move was now confirmed. The mother of his child would not be joining them on their journey.

Damn me.

For a quick second, Blue thought about postponing the return home. Perhaps this would bide him some time to convince Aumua that the adventure would be good for her. Unfortunately, seeing her sitting there completely indifferent to his presence turned him off, and the thought that he would probably never see her again entered his thoughts. To Blue, she looked like a village girl devoid of dreams—a girl who was incapable of looking beyond the borders of her village and accept anyone and anything that wasn't Samoan-made. The sight saddened him. He felt lonely, like a shipwrecked sailor on a desolate island who counted the days, making hash marks in the trunk of a tree.

Blue turned to leave but stopped. However, his

melancholy quickly turned to rage, and he couldn't help himself but to turn back to Aumua.

"Aumua, what the fuck?!" Blue questioned in English, exasperation in his tone. He felt bad for using the "F" word.

Although Aumua looked at Blue with concern, it was Maeva who spoke with venom, protecting her friend. "This is a church!" she reminded him in Samoan.

"Sorry. Aumua, what the hell?" Blue asked again in English.

"Watch your tongue," Maeva demanded.

"Shit, you've been the one who's been hissing at me for years," Blue snapped back at Maeva in English. He then added in Samoan, "Why don't you shut up before I pull your forked tongue out of your mouth and tie it around fuckin' papaya tree!" Blue wasn't sure if he said that correctly in Samoan.

"How dare you!" Maeva exclaimed and stood up.

Blue said it correctly in Samoan and was quite pleased with himself.

"The only good thing you've done around here was to father Mele!" Maeva added.

"I'm here to talk to Aumua," Blue said in English.

Aumua stood and moved between the two. Lupesina and Iris kept their heads down and continued working on the *siapo*. They were a little embarrassed at being caught in this unexpected unpleasantness.

"Please, you two. Stop with the yelling!" Aumua commanded in Samoan.

Maeva sulkily sat back down on the ground, watching Aumua approach Blue.

"The bus leaves in a few minutes, Aumua."

"Ronin, I can't go with you and Mele right now."

"Why?"

"Because I'm needed here for the Teuila Festival."

They stared at each other for an uncomfortable moment.

"I will come to you and Mele after the festival," Aumua added before turning her attention back to her project.

Blue wasn't shocked by what she said. It was kind of obvious to him over the past week that she wasn't going to California with him and Mele. There was no reason to try to persuade her to change her obstinate mind. Watching her work on the *siapo,* Blue understood that her destiny was to stay in Vaimasina and bring honor to the village through cultural and traditional arts that she had practiced since she was very young. This made him feel disenchanted and disillusioned, especially after she had told him that she would go to California with him weeks prior. Now he wondered if she had any intentions to go. Angrily, he aggressively pulled her away from her work. The other ladies quickly stood ready to protect Aumua if they had to. Blue immediately felt bad for using force. It was unlike him. He eased his grip of Aumua's arm.

"Sorry, Aumua. But we need to talk."

"You should go to the bus, Ronin," Aumua commanded in an adamant tone, that there was nothing else to talk about.

"Mele will be upset if you don't come with us," Blue stated. He knew that it was a feeble attempt to change her mind when he said it.

"She's too excited right now to be upset," Aumua calmly responded.

"Don't you think she'll need her mother in a strange country?"

"She will always have me, Ronin. *Moana* will connect us."

"But, you'll come, right? As soon as the festival's over."

"You should go to the bus."

"You will come?"

"As soon as I can."

Blue stared at Aumua, somewhat lost for words. A piece of hair dangled over her forehead and left eye. He wanted to gently push it back up on her head. He always loved running his hands through her black, thick hair. Instead, he pulled her close to him and hugged her.

"It won't be the same without you," Blue said.

"You will live and thrive in your new world."

Blue thought that the words "new world" sounded funny to him, as if he was traveling on *The Mayflower*.

Fiji Airways just called, and they're looking for pioneers to settle Los Angeles.

Blue didn't have time to think much about the bad joke that dashed through his mind.

"I will think of Mele every day," Aumua added. "And she will know that she will always be in my heart and my thoughts and prayers." The bus driver laid on the horn. "You should go to the bus."

These were the kinds of words that made Blue wonder if she would come to California at all. He thought that something else important would arise after the festival that would delay her joining Mele and him.

"Promise you'll come the day after the festival ends," Blue demanded.

"You should go to the bus."

Aumua smiled and gave Blue a kiss on the lips. She then turned around and went back the *siapo* that she was working on.

Although it was hard for Blue to accept Aumua's restrained rejection, he left the community center. He questioned himself if Mele and him should remain in the village a few more months. But he decided to be stubborn and resolute with his plan. A couple of years later, however, Blue would be somewhat vindicated when he learned that the next day, after he left with Mele Aumua, went to cry in Blue's empty *fale*. She would do this regularly throughout the first weeks they were gone.

Blue didn't run or even rush back to the bus. He didn't care if the bus left without him, as long as Mele had enough sense to hop off. But it was still there, and he jumped on. An odd Samoan version of Willie Nelson's song, *Always on My Mind*, was playing. He slunk in the seat next to Mele hating every word of the song.

"Where's *mother*?" Mele asked in Samoan.

"She's not com- she's, uh, going to come after you and I get settled."

Blue stared forward, wondering if Aumua was being profound or just cold. He watched the bus driver chatting with a friend in the seat right behind him. The heat was starting to rise, and it felt like sitting in an oven. Although the windows were down, all the seats were full, and it seemed as if all the bodies were blocking any breeze that might provide a little relief. As sweat started to trickle down from Blue's forehead, he wished the bus driver would start to drive.

A man started to yell outside the bus. Blue was too lost in thought, or he was simply too much in a heat-induced torpor to pay attention to someone yelling. It wasn't until Mele tugged on his shirt that Blue snapped out of his stupor.

"It's Uncle Togi," Mele said.

Blue leaned towards the window to get a better look. He saw Togi at the edge of the village wearing only a *lavalava* and thought that the man had grown even bigger since the last time he saw him. In fact, Blue hadn't seen Togi the past ten days and wondered why his friend didn't want to see him. Aumua told him that her brother was too distraught to come around, knowing that Blue was leaving. Togi couldn't bear the thought that he would never see Blue again.

"I am Togi, the greatest of all fishermen! Son of the man who drowned sharks!" Togi exclaimed, flexing his muscles that looked like rolling dunes in the desert.

"I have come to say goodbye to my friend, Mr. Blue, and my darling niece, Mele! *Soifua Manaia! Ou te alofa ia te oe!*"

The bus closed its doors and revved its engine. As it drove away, the engine muffled the words of Togi. Mele stuck her head out the window and waved to her friends.

Blue sat back in the seat until he heard his hounds barking. He leaned towards the window once again and saw that all three of his dogs were running by the side of the bus, yapping their farewells and yowling at each other. He thought how well they said goodbye. A chicken then had the audacity to scamper out of their path, and the dogs turned their attention to it, chasing it back along the grassy field. Blue didn't feel insulted—it was a chicken after all. He leaned back in the seat. He knew his hounds would be all right. They were never really his dogs. He believed that the hounds belonged to the village, and the village took care of its own.

As he looked at Mele, who was beaming with excitement, he thought about that for a second and smiled...

The village takes care of its own.

—————

Blue barely remembered the layout of the Faleolo International Airport. When he arrived in Samoa all those years ago, he brushed through the airport and didn't bother to take any notice of its interior. Blue and Mele found the check-in line for their first leg of the long trip to the US, which was a flight to Nadi, Fiji. Waiting in line, he could feel Mele's enthusiasm as she anticipated flying on an airplane for the first time. Blue tried to pass the time in line by watching a group of five Australian children from ages two to seven run amok just outside the door that led to the departure lounge. A mother eventually gathered the children together and made them sit in a row of waiting seats. After she got them settled, she looked up towards Blue, and he thought she looked familiar. The woman stared at Blue for a moment and then made her way towards him. It wasn't long before he recognized that it was Lola, the often-pregnant administrator from the Helping Hands Volunteer Organization, heading towards him. Blue looked away, hoping that she wasn't coming to him. He felt trapped in the line.

"Ronin Blue," Lola stated.

"Yeah."

"You look different, but I still knew it was you."

"Great."

"I'm taking my kids on holiday back to Melbourne. Let 'em see a little civilization, eh?"

"Okay."

"You remember who I am, don't ya? I'm Lola… from Helping Hands."

"Of course. The one who fired me."

"Right. That was unhappy business, wasn't it? But you deserved it because you breached your contract. You didn't teach the children. You went native. And you…" She looked at Mele. "You inappropriately fathered a child out of wedlock."

Blue didn't like the sound of her tone. "There's nothing inappropriate about my daughter," he said. I'm taking her to the States." Blue put his arm around Mele.

Lola stared at Mele for a few seconds. She wasn't embarrassed for her statement in front of Mele.

"We're going on an adventure," Mele said in Samoan.

"Good luck; you'll need it," Lola answered in Samoan with a smirk.

Blue wasn't pleased with Lola's snarky tone with Mele. "What do you want, Lola?" he asked.

"Right. I didn't come over to start an argument, Ronin," Lola stated. "I really wanted to ask you how Vaimasina is, you know, after the tsunami."

"It's still recovering."

"We heard it was completely wiped off the island."

"You heard… but you didn't bother to come and see?"

"We preferred to stay away and not interfere with the relief and recovery personnel."

"Yeah. Well, you heard wrong. The village is still there, and the villagers are stronger and closer than ever before."

"I believe it."

"They could still use help," Blue added.

"As you probably reckoned, Helping Hands decided not to send another volunteer to the village after you. It was felt that the village was too cursed."

"Cursed?" Blue thought that was a strange word to use. "Are you kidding me?" He could see the villagers using that word, but not a Caucasian living and working for a modern, international company.

"It's just that we felt that the Vaimasina wasn't the right village for us."

Blue sarcastically choked. "You'd think that would be one of the main reasons your organization would send a volunteer."

The two stared at each other for a second.

"Right. Maybe," Lola said.

The line moved. He then took Mele's hand and moved with the line, leaving Lola standing where she was.

"You know what, Lola? You should stay away from Vaimasina. The volunteers you send there just suck."

Lola watched Blue and Mele move along in the line for a moment before returning to her children. She then gathered them together and hustled them through the departure lounge door.

———

The flight back to the US on Fiji Airways was uneventful. The realization that they were leaving Samoa became sobering to them. Blue and Mele were reserved as they made their way to Fiji and then the long haul to Los Angeles. Mele's enthusiasm returned when she boarded the plane bound for LAX and saw that her seat contained a television screen in front of her. She immediately began pushing buttons on her remote until Blue helped her choose an appropriate children's movie. She watched television in the village on a few occasions, especially at the village community center, where they would show Samoan rugby matches and other national events. Blue wondered how she'd react when she reached the land of a thousand channels. Mele was able to view a couple of movies until she crashed with her headphones on, sleeping either against the window or Blue's shoulder. Blue covered her with a blanket and took off her headphones.

He had a tough time falling asleep. He kept questioning whether he was doing the right thing, uprooting and moving Mele, especially without Aumua. He tried to take his mind off the nagging topic by watching movies on his seat's screen. He hadn't seen very many movies since he arrived in Samoa. In fact, he was only able to watch a film when he was visiting someone's house that had a DVD player. Looking at the list of movies on the screen, he felt that he had much catching up to do. Eventually, all the emotions of the day exhausted and drained his senses, and he finally fell asleep. Even the battle scenes of a wizardry war from the movie, *Harry Potter and the Deathly Hallows Part 2,* couldn't keep him awake.

It was the bump of the landing gear approaching LAX that awoke Blue. He reached over Mele and opened the window shade where he could see tops of houses and businesses in barren and brownish neighborhoods. Mountains protruded mightily within the summertime haze and looked as dry as the valley below. The traffic along the roads and freeways reminded Blue that he was a world away from the tranquil and verdant village of Vaimasina.

Blue gave Mele a light shove on her shoulder to wake her. She sleepily rubbed her eyes and leaned forward, stretching her arms.

"Mele, we're here," Blue stated in English.

Mele looked at her father, who pointed towards the window. Mele quickly leaned towards the window to look at her new home. She wasn't as impressed as she thought she would be at the landscape below. "It looks like death," she said to Blue.

Blue thought the word "death" seemed a bit morbid, particularly coming from Mele. He was kind of glad she spoke in Samoan, so that no one sitting around them would understand her.

"What do you mean?" Blue asked.

"There are no trees."

"Well, it's a desert," Blue said. He didn't know the Samoan word for desert and had to say it in English.

"What's a desert?"

"It's a dry, sandy place with not much water and hardly any trees."

"There are no breadfruit, coconut, or mango trees?"

"I'm afraid not."

"Then there's no life?"

"There's life," Blue responded in English. "Lots of it. It's diverse, adaptable, and, uh, avaricious." He used English for the last word.

Mele returned to look out the window. Blue thought how different the environment was going to be for Mele. He remembered an Albert Wendt quote, which made him produce a wry smile: *It is difficult to die in Samoa, for Samoa in all its greenness invites you to live.* Indeed, the tropical island was full of life, but so was the desert. Blue had no doubts that Mele would find her new home fascinating, and she would easily assimilate.

After the plane landed, Blue and Mele made the long trek through the Tom Bradley International Terminal to Customs and Immigration. Because of the long flight, it was a tiring walk. However, at times, Mele was completely intrigued with her new surroundings that she would stray away from Blue like an untethered boat in a dock. At one point, she stopped to examine a colorful Disneyland advertisement of Dumbo flying above Minnie and Mickey Mouse, who are greeting two young girls dressed as princesses. The slogan read, "Don't just fly, *soar!*" It was several seconds before Blue realized Mele wasn't walking next to him. He stopped and stepped out of the way from hurrying passengers and saw Mele staring at the amusement park's promotion. He then swiftly went to his daughter and grabbed her hand.

"What does that say?" Mele asked.

"Don't just fly, soar," Blue answered and then tried to translate it in Samoan. She had a hard time understanding the word, "soar," until he tried to visually show her by spreading his arms out wide and pretended to fly vigorously. This made Mele laugh before he pulled her away. "Come on, let's go."

As Mele was being led away, she kept an eye on the vibrant poster and repeated to herself in English, "Don't just fly, soar."

Despite having all the necessary paperwork for Mele,

Blue was still nervous getting through Immigration. When the immigration officer looked at the two, they were still adorned with their leis and *'ulas*. Blue and Mele were eventually sent to another booth where Mele's paperwork was examined even more closely. It took so long that Blue started worry about missing their connecting flight to San Diego. He thought about mentioning the flight to the officer and how they were pressed for time, but he got the impression that the office would care less about their impending flight. Blue didn't say a word. After about forty minutes, Blue and Mele were cleared to proceed.

"*Faafetai,*" Mele said, and left one of her leis on the officer's counter as a gift.

Rushing to their United Airlines gate, they were fortunate to learn that their flight to San Diego was delayed. Blue sat down in one of the last remaining seats, and Mele sat in his lap. They people watched, and Mele was captivated by how others were dressed, particularly the different kinds of shoes that everyone wore. She never wore shoes even to church, and she questioned why everyone was covering their feet. She wondered if Americans had toes. She felt a little better when she saw a couple of women wearing fancy high heels or sandals that showed their toes.

Watching other children was what captivated Mele the most. In fact, there were two sisters that were not much older than Mele who obviously spent time at the Disneyland Resort. They were dressed as Disney princesses. One was wearing the blue costume of Cinderella while the younger girl was donned in the distinctive Snow White dress, just as in the Disneyland advertisement that Mele saw earlier.

Mele hopped off Blue's lap and hesitantly made her way

towards the girls. Blue watched as his daughter approached the sisters and gave them a quick bow of the head. Mele then delivered a quick *siva* using her hands in a peaceful and reverential way that Aumua must've taught her. Blue stood up and locked eyes with the sisters' mother. The girls looked bewilderedly at Mele and then at each other. After the dance, Mele gave the older girl her flower-adorned headdress, and then she gave the younger girl one of her *'ulas*. The sisters didn't know how to react and looked at their mother, who told them to say, "thank you." Mele then rushed back to Blue and jumped in his lap just as he was sitting down.

Blue held onto Mele and squeezed her with a proud grip. He watched the sisters play with their gifts by exchanging them with each other. Although Blue believed that it was a considerate and friendly gesture on Mele's part, he couldn't help but think about the two customs clashing for a moment. He came to the realization that Mele was moving from an obsequious culture of *Fa'a Samoa* and traditional values to an obsessive culture of pop, self-indulgence, and the dream of success of owning a white picket fence. The two couldn't be more different. He wondered how Mele would react to this. He vowed that, despite whatever dream she tries to pursue, he will do his best to help his daughter keep to her traditional Samoa values, although knowing Mele, she would most likely do this on her own. The American dream could be frustrating, unpredictable, and full of people who have and have not, but it could potentially be a lot of fun to achieve.

Blue and Mele were one of the last people to board. Their spirits swelled, as they knew they were on the last leg of their journey. As they walked down the jetway, they didn't notice the flower head wreath on the ground that Mele gave to one of the girls. It had been trampled and kicked to the side.

"Don't just fly, soar," Mele said in English. And she couldn't have said anything more American than that.

ACKNOWLEDGMENTS

I'm very grateful to have the support in creating a project of this magnitude. I can't express my deepest gratitude and appreciation enough for publisher, Frank Eastland, and the team at Publish Authority for their genuine dedication and hard work bringing the written words to book format. Not to sound cliché, but it truly takes "a village" to produce a publication. I also must add a very heartfelt and profound recognition to Janie Mills for her diligent and constructive editing work on the book. Her professional scrutiny helped the story be told even better. A special thanks has to be given to Melissa Fisher and Reaghan Rebstock, respectively. They devote many hours throughout the year promoting and making my books accessible to the public. Additionally, I would be remiss if I didn't acknowledge my friend and colleague Simi Tanielu in Samoa. I cherished our time talking about the Samoan culture over a cup of *Koko Samoa* that Simi's mother prepared for us from the coco trees in her backyard. Another individual that I'd like to call out is Jared Chou for his passionate research on Ragtime piano players. A sincere appreciation definitely needs to be given to my wife, Shannon, for her patience and love of me for taking over the kitchen table and working late into the evening on occasion. I also have to recognize my daughter, Devin, whose continued, enthusiastic exploration of violin performance has been an inspiration to the story. I also must convey an honest acknowledgement for the time I spent writing the novel in the many lonely motel and hotel rooms in Fiji, Kiribati, Samoa, and Thailand, as well as American cities from California to New York. And, finally, I have to give a barky thanks to my biggest fans- my dogs: Daphne, Dutch, and Finny. When I worked outside, they sat devotedly by my side, eagerly wondering what was going to happen on the next page... okay, more likely, they were just wondering when suppertime would roll around.

ABOUT THE AUTHOR

Brandon Oswald is a native Southern Californian who has never lived far from the ocean; he became fascinated with stories of adventure in the South Seas at an early age. His interest in the culture and history of the Pacific Islands was heightened by a volunteer trip to Rarotonga, Cook Islands in 2002. There, he had the privilege of organizing and cataloging the material of several different kinds of libraries throughout the island, including facilities at a college, a primary school, and a public library. Brandon obtained his Master's degree in Archives and Records Management at the University of Dundee, Scotland, where he developed skills in preserving records of enduring value. His experiences inspired him to create the nonprofit organization, Island Culture Archival Support (ICAS), where he currently serves as the Executive Director and Archivist. ICAS provides voluntary archival assistance to cultural heritage organizations in the Pacific Islands. Brandon has volunteered at various archives, libraries, and museums in the Pacific Islands, helping these organizations preserve their records, heritage and history. He has served all over the region, including Kiribati and Palau in Micronesia, Fiji, Solomon Islands, and Vanuatu in Melanesia, and the Cook Islands and Samoa in Polynesia.

Additionally, Brandon is the author of the books *Mr. Moonlight of the South Seas: The Extraordinary Life of Robert Dean Frisbie,* and *The Darkland: A Melanesian Experience.* He has had several articles published in archival newsletters and has had the honor of publishing several papers regarding cultural preservation in the Pacific Islands for major international conferences. These papers include *Partnership in Paradise: The Importance of Collaboration for Handling Traditional Cultural Expression Material in the Pacific Islands, Keeping the Canoe Afloat: Project Sustainability in Pacific Islands Cultural Heritage Organizations* and *The "Aloha" Archives: A Nonprofit Organization's View of Collaboration, Peace and Harmony in Cultural Heritage Organizations in the Pacific Islands.*

GLOSSARY

aiga: family
aitu: ghost
ali'i: high chief
alofa: love
'ava: beverage made from the Piper methysticum plant
Fa'a Samoa: the Samoan way of doing things
fa'afafine: in the manner of a woman, a third gender
fa'apapa: sweet coconut bread
faafetai (lava): thank you (very much)
fale: house
fale tele: meeting house or big house
ioe: yes
lavalava: a sarong-like garment, a wrap
leai: no
malie: shark
malu: traditional female tattoo
matai: chief
moana: ocean
Ou te alofa ia te oe: I love you
oka i'a: raw fish marinated in lemon juice and coconut milk
paepae: stone foundation of a fale
palusami: coconut milk baked in taro leaves
panikeke: Samoan pancake
palagi: European, white man
puletasi: traditional item of clothing worn by Samoan women and girls
sa: daily curfew at dusk for 30 minutes for prayer
sapasui- Samoan chop suey
sau loa: Come on
siapo: traditional fabric, art
siva: Samoan dance
soifua manaia: Good luck

tala: Western Samoa's currency
talo: taro
talofa (lava): hello
tamá: father
tanoa: wooden bowl used for mixing 'ava
tatau: tattoo
Teine Sa: spirit women
tina: mother
toe feiloai: see you again
tofa: goodbye
toonai: Sunday morning meal, brunch
tulafale: orator chief
'ula: necklace
ulu: breadfruit
umu: earth oven

THANK YOU FOR READING

If you enjoyed *The Wave Tamer*, Book 2 of *The Barefoot Serenade* trilogy, we invite you to share your thoughts and reactions online and with friends and family.

www.ingramcontent.com/pod-product-compliance
Lightning Source LLC
Chambersburg PA
CBHW051502030726
47592CB00006B/2052